HARD TARGET

A COBRA ELITE NOVEL

PAMELA CLARE

WWW.PAMELACLARE.COM

HARD TARGET

PAMELA
USA TODAY BESTSELLING AUTHOR
CLARE

Hard Target
A Cobra Elite novel

Published by Pamela Clare, 2019
Cover Design by © Jaycee DeLorenzo/Sweet 'N Spicy Designs
Cover photo: Drazen Vukelic

This is a work of fiction. Names, characters, places, and incidents are products of the author's imagination or are used fictitiously, and any resemblance to actual persons, living or dead, business establishments, events, or locales is entirely coincidental.

ISBN-13: 978-1-7335251-2-1

ISBN-10: 1-7335251-2-2

This book is dedicated to midwife Jennifer Braun and International Midwife Assistance, whose work on behalf of mothers and babies has saved lives in Afghanistan, Uganda, and Haiti. Jennifer, your courage and compassion are an inspiration.

Please consider donating to International Midwife Assistance at https://www.midwifeassist.org. Your dollars, pounds, and Euros in any amount will help train skilled birth attendants and save the lives of women and babies.

ACKNLOWLEDGEMENTS

A world of thanks to Jennifer Braun, not only for her work in Afghanistan, Uganda, and Haiti, but for sharing her experiences with me. Without that, this book could not have happened.

Thanks, too, to Lisa Farhana, one of my Muslim readers, who read this manuscript to check for mistakes about Islam and offensive representations. I am so grateful.

Special thanks to Christopher Wu and Reid Miller for sharing their military and EMS expertise, respectively, with me. You guys rock.

Much gratitude to New York Times bestselling authors Kaylea Cross and Katie Reus for their support in getting this series off the ground. I am so grateful to the two of you. If the three of us are ever together, I'm buying the first round. You can visit their websites at:

http://kayleacross.com/v2/
https://katiereus.com

Thanks as always to Michelle White, Benjamin Alexander, Jackie Turner, Shell Ryan, and Pat Egan Fordyce for their support during the writing of this book. Special thanks to Shell Ryan for a last-minute proofread.

My acknowledgements would not be complete without a big thank you to my readers, who lift me up and support me all year round, whether I'm writing or not. You are the best!

AUTHOR'S NOTE

It's tricky these days to write about real subject matter. The moment you delve into any substantive topic as an author, you risk offending someone. This book is not a political statement. It's a story drawn from the real world about one woman's attempt to ameliorate the suffering of other women half a world away.

I was in the middle of the story when a man with evil in his heart gunned down Muslims at prayer in New Zealand. Like all decent people around the world, I was horrified by this. I attended an interfaith prayer service at our local mosque together with Muslims, Jews, Hindus, and other Christians. The prayer room was packed with people who had come to tell our Muslim neighbors that they are welcome here and that we sympathize with their terrible loss.

It was an amazing experience—more than a thousand people of all faiths praying to God for forgiveness and mercy and vowing to support one another and protect one another from violence and bigotry. Ministers and rabbis shared the microphone with an imam and other Muslim speakers. I was moved to tears as a nephew of one of the men slain in New Zealand spoke of his uncle's final heroic moments, trying to save others.

One Muslim man spoke eloquently to the tendency of human beings to conflate the actions of extremists with the groups to which they claim to belong.

I have tried not to do that in this story. I've made a sincere effort to differentiate between Islam as a world religion and the violent extremism of the Taliban and Daesh/IS. It is not my intention to vilify or misrepresent any group of people or to offend my Muslim readers. I wanted to share just a tiny bit of the tragedy of Afghanistan, a once-thriving nation that has been hurled backward by four decades of brutality and warfare, by focusing on the desperate plight of Afghan women.

Back in 2004 when Jennifer Braun, who inspired this story, began her effort to set up a midwifery school and hospital in Bamyan, Afghanistan had a stillbirth/neonatal mortality rate of roughly one in six. That's almost unfathomable. Imagine coming from catching babies in the U.S., where stillbirths are rare, to Afghanistan, where they're a daily occurrence, even at a small rural clinic. I saw a photo of four newly stillborn babies, lying in a row with little handmade string-and-paper tags on their tiny ankles.

It broke my heart.

Though things have improved and Afghanistan is making heroic efforts to improve women's access to healthcare, most Afghan women still give birth without skilled attendants outside a hospital. Many never receive prenatal care. As a result, Afghan women currently face a one-in-eight lifetime risk of dying from pregnancy- and childbirth-related causes.

One in eight.

That's the same risk women in the U.S. face when it comes to breast cancer.

But this isn't a National Geographic article. It's a love story about a man who has been a part of the war there for most of his adult life and a woman desperate to make change. I hope you enjoy their story.

Peace,

Pamela Clare

April 14, 2019

1

November 10

Derek Tower strode down the hallway toward Conference Room One, a mug of black coffee in hand, his reflection moving with him along walls of burnished steel. A woman's silky laughter told him that Holly and Nick Andris were already there. A husband-and-wife team—and two of Cobra's best operatives—they had just returned from a covert job in Colombia and were here for a debriefing.

This needed to be quick. Derek had a flight to catch.

He was due in Istanbul tomorrow morning. A Cobra operative had infiltrated a ring of IS recruiters, and tomorrow they were going to take that ring down. It was the kind of covert work Cobra did well, the kind that involved perfect coordination, flawless execution, and complete secrecy.

Derek entered the conference room, its glass walls soundproof and equipped with built-in blinds that were already closed. "Morning."

Andris dragged his gaze off his wife. "Morning."

"Hey, Derek." Holly's lips curved in a smile that turned men into idiots.

Naturally platinum blond with big brown eyes and lethal curves, she could have been a movie star. Instead, she'd put her brains and good looks to work for the CIA, gathering intel through intimate contact with men—and occasionally women—who were deemed a danger to the United States. When she'd been exposed and almost killed, Derek and Javier Corbray, Derek's business partner, had offered her a job. They'd also taken on Andris, a former Delta Force operator who'd worked as muscle for the CIA.

As far as Derek was concerned, Holly was Cobra's most valuable asset. Anyone could be trained to point a gun and shoot, but not many could gather intel while being groped by a drug kingpin, terrorist organizer, or foreign assassin.

"You got him. Good work. How was your flight?" Derek sat and punched a button on the control panel that would turn on the view screen and bring Corbray into their meeting from Washington, D.C.

Andris shared a look with his wife. "We slept most of the way."

Right.

The two of them were crazy in love. They'd once been caught on camera fucking on the table in Conference Room Two. Derek didn't understand love, but he understood lust. He would bet his ass they hadn't *slept* at all. "Corbray, you there?"

"Great job." Javier Corbray's grinning face appeared on the screen.

Corbray, a former Navy SEAL, had worked with Derek to put this company together, lifting Derek from the ashes of his private security firm—Tower Global Security, which had been forced into bankruptcy. Corbray spent a lot of time in D.C., where his wife, Laura Nilsson, worked as a television journalist.

That was fine with Derek. He didn't miss dealing with the suits in Congress.

Derek glanced at his watch. "I need to get to the airport, so let's do this."

Corbray went first. "I had a message from the Attorney General in my inbox this morning. She is elated to have this asshole in custody."

The asshole in this instance was Christopher David Hansen, a former Coast Guard officer who'd been using his position to help a Colombian cartel run cocaine into San Diego. When he'd realized the DEA was onto him, he'd fled to Colombia and tried to hide in the jungle. The DEA hadn't been able to get near him. There were too many leaks, too many eyes along the roads, too many people ready to tip off the cartel bosses the moment any gringo asked about him.

But the DEA's intel had revealed that Hansen liked to beat up hookers and left his lair a few times a month in search of prey. That's when they had given Cobra a call.

Andris slid his written report across the table. "Based on the intel we received, we set up our operation outside Characa. There's a little cantina in town where he likes to drink and pick up working girls."

Holly told them how she'd driven to the outskirts of town, alone but wearing a mic, while Andris and his team had placed themselves strategically out of sight. She'd walked into the cantina pretending to be a tourist whose boyfriend had ditched her and whose car had broken down.

"When no one spoke English, I started crying and asked for a drink and then another. I pretended to get wasted. He sat in the corner with one of the girls, watching. I did a little drunk dancing, and eventually, he took the bait."

"Of course, he did," Derek said.

Helpless, drunk, and drop-dead gorgeous—an irresistible combination for a predator like Hansen.

Holly told them how she'd tagged Hansen with a micro GPS transmitter during a hug just in case he didn't try to pick her up. But then the bastard had offered to let her stay at his place and send a tow truck for her car. She had feigned gratitude, let him buy her another drink, and left the cantina with him—and his two armed *sicarios*.

Derek had worried about this part of the plan. It had been risky as hell for her to be alone with that fucker and his trained killers.

Then again, Holly was a pro, and managing risk was part of the job.

"He stopped a few miles down the road and had his men take away my phone and passport—for safekeeping, he said."

"Safekeeping." Corbray's tone was sharp with sarcasm. "What a hero."

If Holly *had* been an ordinary tourist, her life would have ended that day. Hansen would have destroyed the phone, taken his time raping and beating her, and then blown her head off and tossed her body in a marsh.

Holly finished her part of the story. "He told his guys to get out of the vehicle because he and I were going to have some fun. I waited till his pants were down and then threw up on him. He slapped me, but he lost his erection."

Andris' jaw tightened, his expression hard. "The target stepped out of the vehicle to clean himself up and still had his pants around his ankles when we moved on him. We eliminated the two bodyguards, bagged Hansen, shoved him into the back of our vehicle, and headed straight for the airport. It took less than two minutes. I might or might not have punched him square in the face."

Hansen was lucky Andris hadn't gelded him on the spot.

"Did you run into any—" Derek was cut off by the persistent buzzing of his cell phone. He glanced at the display. *Fuck*. "I need to take this."

"Istanbul?" Corbray asked.

Derek shook his head, got to his feet. "Senator Hamilton."

Corbray grimaced. "What the fuck does he want?"

"I'm about to find out."

DEREK BIT back a burst of laughter. "You want me to fly into Afghanistan with a team and abduct your daughter? I can't do that, sir. It's illegal."

What a crazy son of a bitch.

"I don't give a goddamn what's legal!" Hamilton shouted into his ear. "Jenna won't listen to reason. She has no business being there. The Taliban *kill* midwives."

It was the truth. Talibs deliberately targeted midwives. When they'd attacked the town of Ghazni last summer, they'd made their way to a midwifery school in the city and put a round through a midwife's head while the student midwives hid in a safe room. They claimed that midwives were violating the rules of Islam by giving women contraception, even though Islam permitted the use of contraception.

The truth was more straightforward than that. Nothing frightened Talibs more than an educated woman. But that wasn't the issue here.

"Cobra cannot use force to bring a U.S. citizen back to the country without a warrant and the orders of DOJ."

"Don't forget what you owe my family." Hamilton's voice turned cold. "My son died for you. He—"

Derek knew what Jimmy had done for him, but *no way* was he putting up with this guilt trip. "Nothing changes the fact that I cannot kidnap a U.S. citizen. Once she's here, what happens then? After she sues Cobra and wins, she's free to fly back to Afghanistan—unless you're willing to lock her up."

"I would do no such thing."

Derek wasn't so sure.

Before Jimmy had joined the Army, his old man had tried to control every aspect of his life—how he wore his hair, where he went to college, the classes he took, the girls he dated, his choice of career, even his diet. If Jenna had gotten the same treatment as her brother, she'd no doubt left the country to get away from her asshole father.

For a moment, Senator Hamilton was silent. When he spoke again, there was an oily tone to his voice. "Jenna is my only living child. Grab your gear, get on a fucking plane, and talk her into coming home."

"You want me to act as her bodyguard?"

"Jenna is wasting her potential over there. I didn't raise her and send her to the best schools so that she could help poor people overpopulate the world with kids they can't feed. She needs to come home, find a husband, and stop trying to fix that place."

Could the man be any more of an asshole?

Derek knew what it was to be poor. The orphan son of a teen mom who'd overdosed on heroin, he'd been found in an alley and had grown up with nothing, moving from foster home to foster home, being raised by drunks and losers who liked the extra money from the state but didn't give a damn about him.

"Where is she?"

"At a clinic in a rural area outside of Mazar-e-Sharif."

Balkh Province.

It was one of the safer parts of Afghanistan. The Taliban controlled about forty-five percent of the country at the moment, but Balkh Province was under the protection of a wealthy warlord-turned-politician who hated Talibs even more than he hated the U.S. As the attack on Ghazni had proven, however, no city was truly safe.

But there were other forces at work in Afghanistan besides the Taliban. There were also militias, uncontrolled bands of armed men who roamed the rural parts of the country and thought nothing of inflicting suffering on the civilian population. IS fighters were there, too, hiding out, smuggling supplies, and killing and raping at will.

"Doesn't she have local muscle guarding the hospital?"

"Yes, yes. She's got Afghan guards with American weapons, but I don't trust them. How much do you think it would take for someone to bribe them? What if one of them tells his Talib cousin about the American midwife?"

Okay, so the senator had a point. Still, it wasn't a simple thing to fly into Afghanistan with weapons and ammo and set up a babysitting operation.

"My presence there could provoke an attack on the hospital." Did Hamilton not understand this? "By sending me, you could bring about the crisis you hope to avert."

The local militias and likely the Taliban, too, would know that some American military guy was hanging out around the hospital before Derek's boots hit the dirt, and that might prove irresistible to someone looking to put another notch in his AK-47.

"I thought you special operators were the best. I thought you could go anywhere unseen, change how you look, disappear into the local population."

Derek was about to explain that there was a world of difference between a covert military operation and driving up to a hospital in an armored vehicle and standing guard in broad daylight, but Hamilton cut him off.

"If you don't get your ass on a plane tonight and do your best to bring Jenna home, I will ruin Cobra. I'll make sure the company is never tasked with a government assignment again."

It wasn't an idle threat. Hamilton sat on the Armed Services Committee. Cobra could probably survive without his support, but he could make life rough for a while, especially given the demise of Derek's company.

Derek's reputation in the private military field had been rock solid—until the day al-Qaeda had used a new kind of cell phone hack to get the jump on his men, killing his team and kidnapping Laura Nilsson, Corbray's wife. The attack had happened live during one of Laura's news broadcasts. Millions had watched terrorists gun down his men and carry Laura, screaming, from the room. The resulting backlash had driven his company into bankruptcy.

Derek didn't want to bring controversy down on Cobra.

"Don't threaten me." He tried to meet Hamilton halfway. "I'll get in touch with our assets in Mazar and get men I trust—"

"I want *you* there. I know you would do anything to keep James' little sister safe."

Stick the dagger in and twist it, why don't you?

Fuck.

Jimmy had been Derek's best bud in the Green Berets. He had died saving Derek's life, and Derek truly didn't want his little sister to get hurt or killed. Derek could fly to Afghanistan and explain the dangers to her. If she refused to come home, at least he would know that he'd tried.

You're going to regret this.

"Okay, I'll take the job, but I won't abduct her. That's not even open to discussion. Expect an invoice this afternoon."

"That's fine. I don't care about the cost. Just get on that plane, and talk her into coming home."

That was the other thing.

"I won't be able to head to Afghanistan for a few days because of a priority operation that has the president's signature on it. I'm due in Istanbul tomorrow."

"Just bring Jenna home."

Derek ended the call and walked back to the conference room, where the debriefing was all but completed. His fury must have shown on his face because the discussion stopped when he walked in.

"What's wrong?" Holly asked.

Derek looked up at Corbray's image on the screen. "I need to catch my ride to the airport, so I'll fill you in on the way. In the meantime, start pulling assets together for Balkh Province. After Istanbul, I head to Afghanistan."

JENNA HAMILTON SAT on the floor, surrounded by village women and doing her best to keep the conversation on the subject of prenatal warning signs. This village was the last stop on her three-day education and outreach tour of the countryside. Almost forty women of all ages had come and now packed the small space, their burqas cast off or pulled back like veils, smiles on their beautiful faces.

Their enthusiasm and their welcome were heartening. Their lack of knowledge about their bodies was not.

It was a tragedy. Afghanistan had once been a developed country where women walked the streets without veils, went to college, and worked as professors and doctors and artists. Now, thanks to religious extremism and decades of fruitless war, those days were gone. A generation of women had been deprived of education, forced to stay indoors, isolated from the world, their lives controlled entirely by men.

"Swollen ankles—who has seen a pregnant woman with swollen ankles?" Jenna spoke in Dari, using words that everyone would understand and not clinical terminology.

Faces old and young lit up, and the women spoke all at once.

"My daughter's ankles were fat with her first child."

"Swollen ankles are part of being pregnant, aren't they?"

"I had swollen ankles with all eight of my children, but I am well."

Jenna waited until the talk died down to go on. "When a pregnant woman has swollen ankles, it is a warning sign. Her relatives should bring her to the hospital so that we can check her and make sure she isn't getting sick. Swollen ankles can be a sign of a serious problem like high blood pressure, and that can kill both the mother and the baby."

She wasn't sure the women understood what blood pressure was, but that didn't matter. As long as they knew what to watch for, lives could be saved.

Jenna knew what it was to grow up without a mother. Her mother had committed suicide when Jenna had been tiny. She barely remembered her mom—but the hole that her death had left in Jenna's life was too real. If Jenna could save even one mother, this entire trip would be worth it.

Then a woman named Afarin spoke. "My daughter-in-law's ankles were swollen for weeks. One day she fell to the ground and started to shake. We asked my husband to take her to the hospital, but he refused. She died that night with the baby still inside her."

It was one of the harsh realities of life here. Men controlled women's access to healthcare, and too many of them refused to let their wives, daughters, and daughters-in-law leave home for medical treatment, even when it meant days of needless pain—and preventable deaths.

Delara, one of the Afghan midwives at the hospital, had said it best.

"It is better to be a goat in Afghanistan than a woman."

Afarin took in the words of comfort offered by the other women. This exchange of sympathy had become a social ritual in the lives of Afghan women—a response to oppression and suffering beyond anything Jenna could comprehend.

It was their suffering that had brought her to Afghanistan. She'd read the statistics about the one-in-eight lifetime risk Afghan women faced of dying from pregnancy-related causes. As a midwife, she'd felt she *had* to do something, so she had signed up to teach and work at a hospital that also served as a midwifery school. Training a generation of Afghan women to become skilled birth attendants was the key to improving maternal and infant mortality in the short term—and enabling Afghanistan in the long term to meet its own healthcare needs.

Jenna waited for a lull in the conversation to make her point. "If your husband had brought your daughter-in-law to the hospital, we could have given her medicine and done surgery to take the baby out. We might have been able to save both her and her baby."

The women fell silent again.

Jenna let that sink in. "Bleeding is another warning sign that you should come to the hospital. Sometimes early in pregnancy, it's normal to bleed a little, but lots of blood means you should come to the hospital right away."

"We soak cotton in whiskey to stop bleeding," said an older woman, her face wrinkled like an old apple. "We put that inside a woman if she bleeds too much after giving birth."

Heads turned to see what Jenna would say about this.

"Bleeding happens when the womb won't contract hard enough after a baby is born—or when a piece of the after-birth is stuck inside. At the clinic, we can give a mother medicine to make her womb contract. We can also put her to sleep so she won't feel pain and take out the part of the afterbirth that's stuck. If she has lost a lot of blood, we can give her a blood transfusion. All of this can save her life so that her child will have a mother."

"Won't you hurt her liver if you reach inside her?"

Jenna turned and pointed to the side-view cut-away diagram of the pregnant woman behind her. "The womb is closed at the top. See? You can't reach a woman's liver through her womb. The liver is here."

The conversation went on for another two hours over sugared almonds and cups of sweet *kahwah*, a kind of green tea spiced with cardamom and cinnamon bark, prepared by Sayah, their hostess and the wife of the village headman.

Jenna had just finished telling them that fever was also a warning sign when she heard the rumble of big engines and a shout outside the door.

The room fell silent, and the women donned their burqas. None of them had known an Afghanistan that wasn't at war.

Jenna drew her gray headscarf over her hair, stood, and closed the anatomy chart just in case. "I'm sure all is well."

"*Inshallah*," Sayah whispered. *God willing*.

Farzad and two of his men stood guard, together with men loyal to Sayah's husband, against any incursions by the militias or local Talibs. Farzad had her paperwork—the letter from the region's governor, Abdul Jawad Kazi, that gave her permission to work in Balkh Province. But written words meant nothing to men who couldn't read and wouldn't help her at all in the case of the Taliban.

She heard Farzad telling someone that it was the will of both God and The Lion of the North—the name Kazi had earned during his days fighting Soviets as a Mujahedeen—that the women of this village should meet today.

Someone shouted something in a dialect Jenna didn't understand.

Farzad spoke again in Dari. "It is a meeting of only married women discussing childbirth. It's of no consequence. If you have questions, you should call The Lion."

Then Sayah's husband spoke. "Friends, we have no disputes between us. Come. Let us drink tea together."

The silence stretched on, Jenna's pulse ratcheting.

Men's laughter.

The rumble of engines as the intruders drove away.

Jenna exhaled, smiled. "All is well."

A moment later, Farzad knocked on the door. "Miss Jenna, it is time to go!"

Farzad, an Afghan of Tajik heritage who had trained and worked with U.S. forces, had been head of the clinic's security unit for the six months that she'd been here. She trusted him with her life. If he said it was time to go...

Jenna embraced Sayah, thanked her for her hospitality and kindness, and urged the women to share what she'd taught them today. Then she gathered up her anatomy chart and other materials and wished the women farewell. "*Khoda hafiz.*"

May God protect you.

A chorus of good wishes followed her out the door, putting a knot in her chest. In the six months she'd been here, she'd come to love Afghan women. She'd never met people who were more welcoming than they were. In six months, they had taught her so much about generosity, hospitality, and resilience.

Had she taught them anything today?

She had no way of knowing.

Jenna hurried with Farzad through the cold to their vehicle. "Who were they?"

"Militia." Farzad opened the rear passenger door for her, rifle slung over his shoulder. "I've seen their leader before. He's Uyghur, a foreigner. I don't trust him. Never trust the motives of a man who won't share a cup of tea."

If Farzad didn't trust him, neither did Jenna. "Let's get back to the hospital."

2

They drove through the gate at Kazi Women's Hospital just after sunset, Jenna breathing a sigh of relief as the heavy panel of steel closed behind them. Snow was beginning to fall and—

What the hell?

An armored Land Cruiser sat in the courtyard.

"That's not Afghan Security Forces," Farzad called back to her before she could ask, shouting so that she could hear him through the Plexiglas that separated the men in the front seats from any women who might ride in the back.

"Is it militia or Coalition?" Jenna called back.

She had yet to run into the Polish troops that patrolled the province.

"I don't think so. Stop the vehicle."

The driver stopped just as a man stepped out of the Land Cruiser. Tall and dressed in khaki pants and a parka, he looked military to Jenna. She'd bet her life he was armed.

"Stay here, miss." Farzad climbed out, weapon in hand, and closed the door behind him. "*Salaam aalaikum.*" *Peace be upon you.*

"Wa'alaikum salaam." Peace be upon you, as well.

The man returned the Arabic greeting, then broke into flawless Dari. But there was no way he was Afghan. He had no beard, his jaw square and clean-shaven. His short hair gleamed blond in the headlights, and he stood at least a head taller than Farzad, who was taller than most Afghan men.

"I've just been to pay my respects to The Lion of the North," he told Farzad. "Abdul Jawad Kazi sends his wishes for peace and health to you all."

As Jenna listened, she found herself wondering where she'd seen him before. He looked familiar somehow. Had he told Farzad his name? No, she didn't think so.

Farzad seemed to relax. "Health and peace be upon him as well. I am Farzad Mazari, head of security here."

"I'm Derek Tower, Jenna Hamilton's half-brother. I've been sent by her father to bring her home."

Stunned, Jenna gaped at him through the closed window.

Derek Tower.

She recognized that name, but he wasn't her half-brother. He'd been her brother James' best friend, the fellow Green Beret whose life her brother had saved at the cost of his own. But Derek's lie wasn't what made her blood boil.

Her father had sent Derek to bring her back to the United States.

To hell with that!

Jenna threw open the door and jumped to the snowy ground. "You can turn your fancy Land Cruiser around and get out of here. I'm *not* going back to the U.S."

She knew she had probably startled Farzad with her lack of hospitality, but this wasn't any of his concern.

She'd spoken to Derek in English, but he kept speaking

Dari, a smile on his face as if he were happy to see her. "Hey, sister. I've missed you."

"This man is your relative?" Farzad asked in Dari.

Jenna had no choice but to go along with the lie—unless she wanted Farzad and his men to beat the hell out of Derek and drag him away. "Yes."

Farzad seemed satisfied. "He says he has come at your father's request to take you home to America."

"That's too bad." Jenna turned and reached inside the Land Cruiser for her anatomy chart and other things. "I'm not going anywhere."

Farzad seemed surprised. "But your father sent him."

Jenna took the venom out of her voice. None of this was Farzad's fault. It wasn't Derek's fault either. "In the United States, a grown daughter can do as she chooses without her father's approval."

Farzad turned to Derek as if to confirm this.

"She tells the truth," Derek said. "She can go wherever she wants—even if it is unsafe and gets her killed."

"I came here to save women's lives and train student midwives, not to be safe. I'm sorry you made the trip for nothing, *brother*." Jenna shut the vehicle's door and stomped off through the snow to the dormitory, leaving Farzad and Derek in the cold.

She keyed herself in and walked back to her small dorm room, where she dropped the chart and other materials on her bed.

Oh, the *gall!*

It was just like her father to do something like this. He always claimed he was acting in her interests, but it was really about control. She was thirty years old, for God's sake, not seventeen. The man had no say in any aspect of her life. It wasn't really about her anyway. Her father was a toxic narcissist who viewed his children, his staff, and everyone around him as nothing more than extensions of himself. The more she tried to block him out of her life, the more he tried to interfere.

"We need to talk."

Jenna whirled to find Derek behind her. "You can't be here. It's a women's dorm. You'll get all of us in trouble."

"I won't stay." He was so tall that his head almost touched the top of the door frame, his body filling the space. He stood there, arms crossed over his chest, watching her through hard blue eyes, his skin tanned from the sun, his face rugged—and irritatingly handsome. "Your father is worried about you."

She ignored the punch of attraction—or tried to. "He told you that?"

Derek nodded. "You're his only surviving child, and he wants you out of the line of fire. He paid me a fortune to fly here just to ask you to come home."

"Well, you've got your answer. Hopefully, he paid for your return flight as well."

The room went dark—another power outage. Then the generator kicked in, and the lights came back on.

"He did—but I'm not leaving yet."

Delara buzzed her on the old intercom system. "If you're back, Jenna, I need your help. We have six women in labor, and one is in distress."

"I'll be right there." Jenna hung up her coat and adjusted her headscarf. "I need to go. You know the way out."

Derek moved just enough to let her through. "We'll finish this conversation later."

"There's nothing to talk about." She caught the clean, masculine scent of his skin as she passed, the warmth of it curling inside her.

Ignore it. You're probably just ovulating.

She didn't look back but made her way through the secured doors into the hospital's labor and delivery wing.

DEREK WATCHED JENNA DISAPPEAR, cries of pain drifting through the doorway. Well, this was going exactly as he'd thought it would. Why had he let Hamilton guilt him into taking this job?

You're a fucking idiot. That's why.

Behind him, someone pounded on the door. "Tower! Come out!"

Women poked their heads out of their rooms to see what was happening. Some gasped when they saw him, disappearing quickly behind closed doors again. Others pulled scarves over their faces, their eyes wide.

Hell.

He couldn't be here. If villagers believed midwives were keeping company with unrelated men, it could put their lives, as well as Derek's, in danger. He headed outside again to find the security guard standing there, fury on his face.

"It is not proper for you to be in there! This is for women only! You will have to speak with your sister outside."

"My apologies." Derek wouldn't pretend that he couldn't read the sign on the door, given that he spoke Dari. "In my impatience, I didn't think."

Farzad seemed to accept this. "Let us get out of this cold and have some tea."

The snow had picked up, icy flakes falling hard and fast as Derek followed the man out of the compound toward the concrete building that was the guards' barracks. Inside, it was warm and well lighted. The hospital compound had been built with UN money and, unlike much of the countryside, had electricity, a backup generator, and running water.

A dozen men in uniforms sat together on the carpeted floor, some wrapped in patoos—traditional woolen shawls—weapons propped against the walls behind them. They fell silent as soon as they saw him.

Farzad introduced Derek, told the men why he'd come. "Like his sister, he speaks our tongue, so watch what you say in front of him."

The last part was mostly meant as a joke—but not entirely.

Derek pushed a grin onto his face, sat beside his host, and accepted a cup of steaming *kahwah*. "*Tašakor.*"

Thanks.

A basket of naan sat on a low table beside a dish of dried dates, empty bowls stacked to one side.

"Dawar, bring our guest a bowl of lamb stew."

Derek wasn't hungry but didn't say so. Hospitality was the cornerstone of Afghan culture. Until he persuaded Jenna to go back to D.C. with him, he was stuck here. He needed to cultivate goodwill among these men, get them to trust him. He also needed to check each one of them against Cobra's database of suspected Talibs, escaped IS fighters, and al-Qaeda sympathizers.

The youngest of the men stood and hurried off toward what must have been the kitchen, returning almost immediately with a bowl.

Derek thanked him, reached for a piece of naan, and used it as a spoon. The stew was hot and savory. He nodded his approval, bringing grins to the men's faces. "Mmm."

"Are you a soldier?" Dawar asked.

"Dawar!" Farzad admonished him. "Let our guest eat."

This was a question Derek wanted to answer. He didn't

want rumors getting out that a U.S. soldier was hanging around the clinic. It might bring the Taliban or one of the provincial militias down on their heads.

"I'm not a soldier," he told Dawar between bites. "I am a security guard like you."

That wasn't exactly true, but it was close enough.

"You came to take Miss Jenna home?" Dawar asked.

"Yes. Her father—my stepfather—wants her to come home. He is afraid for her safety if she stays here. He knows the Talibs have killed midwives."

Dawar and a few of the others looked insulted by this, their protests overlapping.

"We would not let that happen!"

"We watch over her and the others!"

"The Talib scum are no match for The Lion and his men!"

Then Farzad told them that Jenna had refused to go, raising eyebrows.

"Can you not simply command her to go with you?" Dawar asked.

Derek wanted to laugh. He hadn't spent more than a minute with Jenna, but years of covert operations had made him a good judge of people. No one commanded Jenna Hamilton. "Under our laws, women are as free as men to live as they please. My sister must decide for herself."

"What will you do?" asked a guard who said his name was Hamzad.

"I have no choice but to stay here to watch over her and hope I can change her mind." He let the men digest this bit of information while he finished his stew, mopping up the juices with another piece of naan.

That's right. I'm not leaving. Get used to the idea.

"But there is no need," said Farzad. "We are here."

There were murmurs of agreement, and Derek knew he was risking offense to his hosts if he implied that they were incapable of keeping Jenna safe themselves.

"Her father is grateful to you and to The Lion for watching over her, but he is still a father. Is it not a father's nature to worry?"

This earned Derek a few sympathetic smiles.

He went on. "I stay because if I return to my country without her, I will have to admit to her father that I failed."

In truth, he could deal with Hamilton, but he knew his words would strike home for Farzad and his men. Admitting failure was something no Afghan man wanted to do.

The men's smiles faded.

Farzad gestured at the room around them. "Miss Jenna has been good to our women and children. You can sleep here where it's warm. We have a spare bunk."

Derek managed another smile. "*Tašakor.*" *Thanks.*

Staying here in the barracks would put him right where he needed to be—close enough to Jenna to keep her safe and close enough to these men to make sure they were all who they seemed to be.

~

JENNA DRAGGED herself out of bed at six, walked down the chilly hallway to the only shower in the dorm, and turned on the spray, washing quickly because the water was never truly warm. She tried to visualize the water rinsing away her exhaustion and the sadness that had followed her through the night, but it didn't work.

Shima, a girl of only fourteen, had arrived at the clinic late last night after two days of labor with her second baby. Jenna had quickly confirmed that the baby was transverse, which made a vaginal birth impossible. With the girl's mother-in-law acting as the go-between, she and Marie, the clinic's French OB-GYN, had pleaded with Shima's husband, a man in his forties, to allow a C-section, but he had refused. Jenna hadn't been sure the mother-in-law was explaining things to him accurately, but custom forbade Jenna or any of the other women from talking with with Shima's husband.

They had managed to turn the baby—an agonizing ordeal for Shima—but by then it was too late. The little boy had slipped lifeless into Jenna's hands.

It was hardly the first stillbirth Jenna had attended here. Still, the senselessness of it ate at her. Shima was too young to be married, too young to give birth to her *second* child, too young to endure so much suffering and loss.

Stop. Don't do that. Don't dwell on it.

She'd go crazy if she did. Things were what they were. She had known what to expect before she'd come here.

They had at least been able to save Shima's life—and insert an IUD. When her mother-in-law had stepped out of the room, the poor girl had begged Jenna for contraception, something her husband wouldn't discover. Jenna had taken the unusual extra step of trimming the strings to be safe.

That was all she'd been able to do for Shima.

Jenna finished her shower and dried off. She didn't feel more awake, but at least she was clean. She hurried back down the hallway to her room, put her hair into a ponytail, and dressed—long underwear, turtleneck, blue scrubs, a long white coat, and, of course, her headscarf. Though the hospital was heated, it never felt warm.

In the small kitchen, she found Delara making tea for everyone. Though a small all-woman kitchen staff made food for the patients, the midwives and students cooked for themselves.

"Good morning." It had been Delara's turn to take the night shift.

"How was it?"

"Quiet."

"I'm glad to hear it."

A loaf of *roht*, a kind of sweet bread, sat on the table. Together with tea and the occasional egg, that was breakfast.

Delara handed Jenna a cup of tea, then sat and took a piece of *roht*, whispering a prayer before eating. "*Bismillahi wa 'ala baraka-tillah.*" *In the name of God and with God's blessing.*

Jenna sat, too, and drank. The tea was hot and sweet, bringing her back to life.

One by one, the student midwives drifted in, books under their arms—Guli, Nahal, Chehrah, Lailoma, Mahnaz and her sister Mina, Zari, Ruhkshana, and Parwana. They talked about their lessons, asking questions.

Nahal looked down the length of the table to Jenna. "Who was that strange man last night, the one who came into the dormitory?"

The kitchen fell silent.

Oh, God.

Jenna had forgotten about Derek Tower. "I apologize for that. He is my half-brother. My father sent him to talk me into coming home. He didn't know that he couldn't follow me inside."

He almost certainly *did* know, but it hadn't stopped him.

Now all of the women were staring at her.

Delara's eyes had gone wide. "You are leaving us?"

Jenna gave Delara's hand a squeeze. "No, I'm not. He's leaving. I'm staying."

Smiles of relief.

Jenna finished her breakfast and decided it was time to send Derek on his way. She put on her winter coat, adjusted her headscarf, and went out the back entrance. She found him carrying gear from his Land Cruiser to the men's dormitory outside the concrete walls that surrounded the hospital and women's dorm.

Was he moving in?

She called to him in English. "I thought you would be on your way by now."

He stopped, turned toward her, those blue eyes seeming to pierce her. "I'm not leaving without you, sister dear."

Was he crazy?

"Just so you know, I signed on for two years, and I've been here for six months. I hope you like lamb kebabs and naan because you've got a long wait."

"Then I guess the two of us will get to spend some time together." With that, he turned and walked away, giving Jenna a view of his backside.

Oh. My. God.

She'd never actually seen a man's butt fill out a pair of pants like that before, his buttocks shifting with each step. It all but made her mouth water.

3

Derek climbed into the Land Cruiser, shut the door for privacy, and called Corbray on his secure satellite phone. "She won't come back with me."

"No big surprise there. Do you have a plan?"

A plan? *Hell*, no, he didn't have a plan.

"I've told everyone I'm her brother to ensure that I have easy access to her. I'll stay a week and do my best to get her to trust me and change her mind. After that, I'll fly home and tell her old man that she refused to come."

"Hamilton won't like that. He'll make trouble for us in the Armed Services Committee."

Didn't Derek know it? "What the hell can I do? She signed on for two years and is determined to stay the remaining eighteen months. I won't abduct her. If he wants someone here playing bodyguard that entire time, he'll need to find somebody else."

Derek had a business to run.

"You knew her brother, right? Can you play on that relationship and sweet talk her into coming back?"

Derek had already thought about that. "Given that he

died taking bullets meant for me, I'm not sure I'll win her over by bringing her brother into this."

"Think about it. If there's any way to complete this mission..."

"Did you get anything back on those names?" He'd sent Corbray a list of the hospital staff, including Farzad and his security team, earlier today so that Corbray could run them through Cobra's database of known assholes.

"One name popped. Hamzad Shah. As a boy, he attended a madrassa in Punjab that was shut down last year for suspected extremism. That's all we've got on him—no arrests, no known terrorist affiliations."

"Thanks." It wasn't much, but it gave Derek reason to keep a close eye on Hamzad. "Anything else?"

"We got word of some extremists who are posing as local militia in the northern provinces. They've been roving around the countryside, intimidating villagers in rural areas, taking their food and weapons, killing men here and there, and abducting women. So far, they've kept a pretty low profile. Their leader is reportedly Uyghur."

Derek wondered if Kazi knew about this. "I'll find out what I can."

"How did your meeting with Kazi go?"

"I gave him the full ATF treatment—a crate of whiskey, cigarettes, and firearms. He seemed pleased. He lives like a king these days."

"I don't trust him."

"Neither do I. I'll check in at this same time tomorrow."

Derek ended the call, taking a few minutes to think through what he'd learned about Jenna. She was intelligent, educated, and reportedly good at her job. She didn't care for her father. Who could blame her? She'd come to a country with terrible maternal and infant mortality rates to save lives, but he didn't take her for a self-righteous do-gooder. She was direct, truthful, sincere. She believed she could make a difference here, and she was willing to risk her life to do it.

He could only admire her for that.

She knew the dangers, so there was no point in trying to frighten her into coming back to the U.S. She wasn't close to her father—an understatement—so there was no chance she'd head home out of concern for him. She spent long days taking care of others, but what did she do to take care of herself? Was she lonely, homesick?

Maybe if he took a softer approach, showed her sympathy, became her friend, he'd have a better chance of getting her to change her mind.

Shifting tactics was no more complicated for Derek than changing clothes. As a Green Beret, he'd often spent months behind enemy lines, working with local assets, doing whatever he needed to do to get the desired outcome. Assassination, manipulation, intimidation, feigned friendships—it came easily to him.

Hey, whatever works.

As for Jimmy, he had no idea how Jenna felt about her brother's death or the fact that he had saved...

"Sniper!"

Jimmy slammed Derek to the ground just as the Dragunov opened up, the body blow knocking the breath from his lungs, driving his cheek into a rock.

Rat-at-at-at!

Derek's breath froze in his lungs, his body rigid.

One of the other members of their squad had taken the sniper out in a hail of bullets, but it had been too late for Jimmy. That volley had hit him in the helmet.

Blood. Brains. Bits of bone.

Son of a bitch.

Derek squeezed his eyes shut, drew a breath, locked that memory away.

He didn't do weakness.

Jimmy had spoken with his little sister via the Internet or on the phone as often as he could, and it had been clear to Derek that the two were close despite an age difference of almost ten years. He'd noticed it because it was so different from his own experience. He'd grown up with no true siblings, no real mother or father, no sense of family.

The back door of the hospital opened, and Jenna stepped out into the cold wearing only her headscarf, scrubs and white lab coat. She saw him but didn't approach the vehicle. She didn't call for Farzad either. Maybe she just wanted some fresh air.

Derek had only ever seen photos of her—a skinny kid with a big smile, green eyes, and auburn hair. It was clear that she and Jimmy shared DNA. Yeah, she was a hell of a lot prettier than her brother, her features delicate and unmistakably feminine, but the resemblance was there.

Was her hair long or short? Derek had no idea. The layers she wore hid the details of her body but didn't entirely conceal her curves. All those layers did more to provoke his imagination than prevent sexual thoughts, which was their purpose.

Where the hell are you going with this, dumbass?

He hadn't flown all this way to check Jenna out. He was here to protect her.

What was Jimmy's nickname for her?

Punk.

That's right. He'd called her Punk.

And that gave Derek an idea.

He punched in Corbray's number again. "Hey, man,

there's something I need you to ship to Mazar-e-Sharif right away."

He told Corbray where to find what he needed, glancing over at Jenna in time to see her wipe tears from her face with the loose end of her headscarf.

Derek saw his chance. "Got to go."

JENNA DREW another breath of cold air and was about to go back inside when Derek climbed out of his Land Cruiser and walked toward her.

"What's wrong?" he asked.

He must have seen she was crying.

Damn.

"It's nothing."

He touched a hand to her sleeve. "It's not nothing if you're in tears."

Instinctively, she drew away. She hadn't been touched by a male—not even to shake hands—since she'd arrived here. Religious law dictated that she couldn't speak with or be alone with a man who wasn't immediate family. The only exception was Farzad, and that was out of necessity. She had learned to be careful.

Then again, Derek was supposed to be her brother, right?

"We had a rough night last night—just a hazard of the job."

Keeping names confidential, she explained what had happened—how the baby had been turned wrong, and the father had refused to let the mother have a C-section. "So, long, terrible story short, the baby was stillborn, but we saved the mother. It was her second baby, and she's just fourteen."

Derek's brow furrowed, his eyes warm with sympathy. "I'm sorry. That's rough."

"I've been trying to help a new mother—only sixteen, by the way—with breastfeeding, but her mother-in-law refuses to allow it, insisting on giving the baby vegetable oil or melted butter instead. I guess there's some superstition about colostrum—a new mother's first milk—being dangerous for babies or something. It makes me *so* angry. Both the girl and her baby are badly malnourished. Sometimes it just feels hopeless, as if nothing we do..."

Her words faded at the horror on Derek's suddenly pale face. "Don't tell me that a big, bad Green Beret is afraid of obstetrical talk."

His gaze met hers, and she knew she'd hit the nail on the head.

"You are!" She couldn't help but smile. "So, if I say 'uterus' will you faint?"

His brow furrowed. "Of course, not."

"How about 'menstruation'?"

"Not a chance." A grin tugged at his lips.

"Labor pains."

He winced. "I guess that's just part of it, right?"

"Right. Vagina?"

His lips curved into a smile that seemed to draw the oxygen from Jenna's lungs. "Oh, I like that word."

Heat rushed into her cheeks. She'd meant this to be clinical, not sexual.

She tried again. "Episiotomy?"

He shrugged. "I don't even know what that means."

"That's when a midwife or doctor cuts a woman's perineum—"

"Okay, okay!" He held up a hand, palm facing toward her. "That's enough."

Jenna laughed.

He recovered, seeming to study her. "Are you okay?"

She nodded, laughter having smoothed the roughest edges off her mood. "It's hard to see things like this happen and not be able to change them."

He seemed to look past her, his gaze focused on nothing, his smile gone. "I get that. I first came here sixteen years ago to get rid of the bad guys. A lot of good people gave their lives for that cause. They're gone, but the bad guys are still here."

James had died here, far to the south in Kandahar Province.

Jenna shivered.

"You must be freezing."

"I should let you get back to work. Aren't you supposed to be guarding this place or something?"

"I'm supposed to be guarding *you*. If the shit hits the fan, *you* are my sole priority." He drew something out of his pocket. "I've been meaning to give you this."

It looked like a Blackberry with an antenna. There was also a charger cable.

"A cell phone?"

"It's a secure satellite phone with built-in GPS tracking. We can send each other secure text messages and talk to each other. As long as this is on you, I'll be able to find you no matter where you are."

"Why do I need this? You're right here. So am I."

"I can't come inside the hospital, and I need a way to reach you, a way to communicate that can't be hacked or monitored."

"I might not always be able to answer."

"If this thing buzzes, answer it. I won't call if it's not important. I've programmed my number into the phone. Just press the number one."

"Okay."

Derek glanced at his watch. "I'm meeting with Farzad over lunch to talk over his security plan. I want to see if he's got a strategy. Does the hospital have a safe room?"

"Yes. The entrance is behind the refrigerator." Jenna had looked into the cold, dark space with its wooden stairs when she'd gotten her orientation.

"Good to know. Have you ever run drills?"

"Drills? You mean, like, fire drills?"

"No, I mean 'shelter-in-place, bullets-are-flying' kind of drills."

Was he trying to frighten her? "Not while I've been here."

"That needs to change."

"Farzad has been good to me—to all the midwives here. Please don't run roughshod over the poor man."

"Don't worry. I'll be diplomatic."

"Good."

"I haven't told him about my military background, by the way, so don't slip."

"I'll be careful." Jenna turned to go. "Talk to you later."

He caught her fingers, gave them a squeeze. "Hang in there, Jenna. You saved a life last night."

For a moment, Jenna stood there, snared by the sympathy in his gaze. "Thanks."

He released her. "God, your fingers are freezing. Get back inside."

She turned and keyed in her passcode. She stopped on the other side of the door, leaned back against it, the fingers he'd held seeming to tingle.

Oh, knock it off.

She walked down the hallway and went back to work.

~

DEREK LISTENED while Farzad explained the hospital's security protocols, which basically amounted to Farzad and his men standing guard around the compound and checking everyone who arrived seeking medical help for weapons. The bulletproof steel gate remained open during the day but was closed at sunset and remained under guard through the night. Given the situation and the available technology, that was about all Derek could expect of these men.

Derek knew it wasn't his place to take ownership of the security operation from Farzad. Nor could he word any of his observations like criticism. He was an outsider here, welcome only because they thought he was Jenna's brother.

Still, he had a job to do.

He chose his words carefully. "Would it help if I set up security cameras? I could set them up down the road in all directions and here on the building. We could put monitors in the barracks that enable you to see what's happening at any time of the day or night. You would be warned if the militia or the Taliban should come this way."

"You brought such things with you?"

"No, but I know where I can buy them." In truth, he'd left gear and supplies, including security cameras and monitors, in Mazar-e-Sharif. He just needed to get them.

Farzad considered his offer. "Security cameras would give us an advantage."

"Your men would be prepared." Derek moved onto the next thing. "Jenna told me the hospital has a safe room for the women. Have you ever asked them to practice evacuating?"

Farzad's expression told Derek he thought this was a bad idea. "No, no. It would frighten them. Besides, the hospital is rarely empty. The women know what to do. If they hear gunfire, they are to hide."

So, wait for bullets to fly, and then duck and run.

That didn't feel like much of a plan to Derek, but he didn't say so.

"If you approve, I will drive into the city to get the security cameras."

Farzad sipped his tea. "I will send one of my men with you to help."

Derek didn't like that idea, but he couldn't refuse the offer. "How about Hamzad? He seems strong and capable."

Farzad lowered his voice. "Not Hamzad. He is the eyes and ears of The Lion."

Interesting.

"I will send Dawar with you. He is a good boy, and he loves Americans."

"I thank you for your hospitality and your help—and for keeping my sister safe."

Ten minutes later, Derek headed off, driving on snowy, rutted roads toward Mazar-e-Sharif with Dawar in the passenger seat. The kid was thrilled and had lots of questions about the vehicle. He was also an open book, telling Derek all about his life.

He was the only son of a widowed mother and took care of her and his four sisters. His father had been killed by a car bomb set by the Taliban. Dawar was grateful for this job, as it kept him close to home and paid enough for him to keep everyone fed and clothed. He hoped to find a husband for his older sister soon because she was sixteen and old enough now to marry. That would give him one less mouth to feed.

"How many sisters do you have?" Dawar asked.

"Just Jenna."

"Why is she not married?"

Derek could only guess. "It takes many years of training to become a midwife. She is happy working."

"She would rather work than have a husband and children of her own?"

Derek saw the confusion on Dawar's face. "In our country, women choose their husbands. She hasn't yet met a man she wants to marry."

"Does she still live in her father's house?"

"No."

"But who takes care of her?"

"She has her own home and takes care of herself." Derek glanced over at Dawar again. "Is there a reason you ask so many questions about my sister?"

Dawar's face flushed red.

Yeah, that's what Derek thought. Dawar had surely never spoken with her, and he'd never seen her without her headscarf. And yet the kid had a crush on her.

She was a beautiful woman, so that didn't surprise Derek.

What surprised him was the inexplicable urge he felt to tell Dawar to stay the hell away from her.

4

Jenna swaddled the newborn—a little girl—and laid her in the clear plastic bassinet next to her exhausted mother, who pressed her clenched fists against her lower belly, lines of pain on her face. It was Najida's fifth child, so the cramps would be strong. "I'll bring you some medicine for pain."

As she walked back to the pharmacy, she saw Nahal, Lailoma, and Parwana peeking through the kitchen curtains at something that was going on outside, headscarves drawn over their faces.

"What is he doing?"

Jenna filled out the paperwork for two oxycodone and carried them, together with a glass of water and a stool softener, back to the mother's bedside. "Swallow these. They will take some of that pain away."

"Thank you." The woman took the pills and drank.

"You have a beautiful baby daughter. Do you have a name for her?"

Najida glanced over at her new baby. "No. I have three

daughters already. My husband wanted this one to be another son. He will be angry."

The baby gazed around at her new world, sucking on one hand, blissfully unaware that she was a disappointment to her parents simply because she'd been born female.

The thought put an ache in Jenna's chest.

She wanted to explain to the mother that it had been her husband's sperm and not her egg that had determined the sex of their children but stopped herself. "Rest."

Jenna walked back toward the kitchen hoping for some tea and found the three student midwives still staring out the window. "What is it?"

"Your brother is up on the wall."

Jenna walked over, saw Derek standing atop the compound's outer wall, looking to the south, tools in his hand. He pointed, said something she couldn't hear.

"What is he doing?" Nahal asked.

"I don't know."

"Is he married?" Parwana asked.

Jenna was about to say she had no idea but caught herself. She was pretending to be his sister, after all. She guessed. "No, he's not."

With Farzad, Dawar, and a few others looking on, he straddled the wall and adjusted something. Jenna couldn't see what it was from here.

She went to her room, slipped into her parka, and walked out back.

Under normal circumstances, she would never have gone outside in the presence of a group of men, but she had a chaperone now. Derek was her brother, after all.

"What are you doing up there, brother?" she asked in Dari.

He saw her, grinned. "Hey, sister. I'm installing security cameras. Farzad thought it would be a good idea."

Jenna turned to Farzad. "Thank you."

Derek acted like it had been Farzad's idea, but she knew better. Somehow, Derek had talked Farzad into this.

Derek jumped to the snowy ground and walked over to her. "Do you have time to talk? We can sit in the Land Cruiser."

There were three women in labor, but Marie was looking after them. None were close to delivering yet.

"I have a few minutes."

She followed Derek to the Land Cruiser and climbed into the rear passenger seat.

Derek turned on the engine—and the heat. "You could sit up front, you know."

"I suppose I could." Respecting the culture here was her full-time job—if she wanted to help Afghan women. "You bought security cameras?"

He looked back at her, nodded. "I picked them up yesterday afternoon. I installed cameras at the intersections of the roads to the east and west to give Farzad and his men warning if any militia troops or Talibs head this way. There are also cameras on the wall looking to the north and south, on the front gate, and in the waiting area. I still have to set up the monitors and teach Farzad and his crew how to use the system, but I should be done by this evening."

Jenna had to admit, at least to herself, that this made her feel safer. "Thank you."

He turned in his seat so they could speak face to face. "Are you having a better day?"

"Four babies so far, all healthy. Thanks." The concern in his blue eyes made her pulse quicken.

God, you are pathetic!

She'd known being here would mean two years of celibacy, so why did she explode into hormones every time she was around him? First his scent. Then the sight of his butt. Then his touch. Now his eyes.

"I need you to do me a favor. Can you organize emergency drills for the women? Farzad is afraid that running drills will scare everyone, but I think you're all tougher than that. He's willing to wait till bullets fly and trust that you'll manage. I'd rather see you get organized and practice, even in small groups. Keep it low-key, but drill."

"Okay." She wasn't sure how the others would feel about this.

"You'll want to make sure you've got food, water, blankets, whatever medical supplies you might need, and some kind of toilet. The siege at the midwifery school in Ghazni lasted most of a day."

A midwife had been shot in the head during that raid.

"I don't think we have blankets to spare."

"I'll get some. I can get water pouches and halal MREs, too, if that helps."

"The army makes halal MREs?"

Halal was the Islamic equivalent of the Jewish concept of kosher.

Derek grinned, making Jenna's heart skip a beat. "Hey, Uncle Sam thinks of everything."

"I'll do what I can."

"Good. I'll set the MREs and the water outside the back door and text you to let you know it's there."

Then Jenna remembered. "Are you married?"

Derek's expression shifted to amusement. "Why do you ask?"

Heat rushed into her cheeks. "It's not personal. One of

the students asked me, and I wanted to make sure we're not telling different stories."

"Smart. No, I'm not married."

Why this should please Jenna, she couldn't say. "Do you have a girlfriend?"

He shook his head. "I'm not really good at the relationship thing. I'm gone all the time, and I can't talk about my work. That doesn't fly with most women."

Not wanting to pry, Jenna changed the subject. "James told me some things—how grenades work, how helicopters stay in the air, how to load a magazine. He told me stories about the things you two did."

"Did he?" Derek didn't sound altogether pleased.

"Does that mean you have to kill me now?" The moment she said it, she regretted it. He almost certainly *had* killed people, and joking about it was insensitive at best.

His brow furrowed. "God, no."

"Well, that's a relief."

It was his turn to change the subject. "How about you? Why aren't you married?"

"I guess I haven't met the right guy. I had a serious boyfriend, but we broke up when he couldn't change my mind about coming here."

Derek's gaze held hers. "He must have been a loser."

You're staring at him like a teenage fangirl.

"Trenton was a brain surgeon, actually, but, yes, a loser. He loved his job more than he loved me, but when I focused on *my* career, he felt threatened. I'd been ready to end it for a while anyway. I didn't even cry when we said goodbye."

"Do you miss him?"

"Not one bit." Jenna missed sex, but she didn't miss Trenton. She glanced at her watch. "I need to go."

Derek caught one of her hands, held it between his two

bigger ones. "Take those drills seriously, Jenna. I won't be here much longer. You need to be ready."

"I understand. I'll do my best."

DEREK WATCHED HER GO, then climbed out of the vehicle and got back to work. It was late in the day by the time he finished attaching the monitor and booted up the system.

Farzad watched as images of the road, the mountains to the north and south, and the waiting room sprang up on the view screen. "What do you think?"

Farzad grinned. "This is like James Bond."

Derek showed him how to toggle from camera to camera, how to shift to a full-screen view from an individual camera, and how to zoom in. "You can take photographs of license plates on vehicles or get a closer look at faces this way."

"What about nighttime?"

"The cameras are infrared, so you will be able to see what's happening in the dark, too. If the Taliban or a rogue militia group tries to sneak up on you, you will see their vehicles passing by and have time to prepare."

"This is good." Farzad pointed toward the image from the waiting room with a jerk of his chin. "Why did you put a camera there?"

"If someone manages to sneak weapons past the gate or comes here wearing explosives, you might spot it and have a moment to act before they do."

Farzad looked doubtful. "We would have to run from the barracks to the door, and by the time we got there, it might be too late."

That's what Derek had hoped he'd say.

Derek wanted an armed officer in that waiting area at all times. "What if your men took turns sitting in the waiting area as if they, too, awaited the birth of a child? If someone takes out a weapon or is wearing a vest, they will already be there—and they will have weapons hidden inside their clothing."

"Do you think such vigilance is necessary?"

"After the attack on Ghazni, yes."

Farzad rubbed his beard, his gaze back on the screen. "Such a thing could not happen here. *Inshallah*."

"*Inshallah*." Derek repeated the phrase, but, given the shit he'd seen, he put more faith in a loaded M4 than the will or mercy of anyone's god.

He finished teaching Farzad how to operate the surveillance system—how to check each camera to make sure it was live, how to reboot if the system went down, how to capture and save images from the view screen.

Farzad was smart and learned quickly. "It is a great gift you have given us."

"You have given me the gift of your hospitality—and you have protected my beloved sister these many months. I am grateful."

When he had finished, it was time for evening prayer.

The men came together, rolled out their prayer mats, and faced Mecca, Farzad taking the role of imam. Derek stepped outside to give them space, Farzad's singing following him.

"*Allahu akbar*." *God is the greatest*. "In the name of Allah, most gracious, most merciful, all praise is due to Allah."

Derek stood in the cold, his gaze drawn toward the front gate, which Farzad had closed for the night. Jenna was in there, maybe helping a patient, maybe standing as he was, alone, an outsider.

He'd told her he would only call if it was important, so he ignored the impulse to text her to say hello. What kind of stupid idea was that, anyway?

You lonely, man? Tough shit.

He was used to being alone. Yes, he'd had his share of lovers, but nothing that had lasted. He'd never managed to go the distance with a woman. He'd told Jenna that his work was to blame. Truth was, he had trouble getting close to people and dealing with the messy complexity of relationships. The women he'd been with had wanted him to open up, but he didn't know how. Or maybe he just hated being vulnerable.

An image of Jenna's face, her cheeks flushing pink, flashed through his mind.

Damn. Yeah.

She was pretty—clear skin, bright green eyes, long dark lashes. When she'd blushed, he'd felt it down to his balls.

"It's not personal," she'd said.

But the color in her cheeks had said otherwise.

He caught himself, shook his head at his stupidity.

What the hell was wrong with him?

You're attracted to her.

Yeah, okay. So what if he was? He was as human as the next man.

And you wouldn't mind being the next man, would you?

That wasn't going to happen. He left his dick in his pants when he was working. Even if he was willing to break that rule, which he wasn't, Jenna was Jimmy's little sister. He owed the man his life. He couldn't repay that debt by getting Jenna naked. Fucking her would be a serious violation of the Man Code.

Before he could start trying to imagine what she might look like beneath all those layers of loose clothing, he walked to his Land Cruiser, which he had parked near the gate, and started unloading halal MREs. He'd just set the first box on the ground when his satellite phone buzzed. He pulled the phone out of his coat. It was nine in the morning in D.C. Corbray was probably calling to—

Senator Hamilton.

Fuck.

"Tower here."

"I spoke to your partner this morning. He says you haven't yet managed to convince Jenna to come home and that you're planning to leave soon."

Yeah, the man was pissed.

"She refuses to leave before she has completed her contract, and I can't stay here for eighteen months. I can find someone—"

"I thought I made it clear that I want you either to bring her back or to stay and watch over her yourself."

"I never agreed to stay here for eighteen months. I suggest you read the contract."

The bastard spent the next minute yelling into his phone until Derek was tempted to hang up on him. Hadn't he watched Jimmy deal with this same bullshit? Hamilton had tried to procure an honorable discharge for Jimmy while he was in basic training and had spent no small amount of time shouting in Jimmy's ear just like this.

"Senator Hamilton!" Derek put a hard edge on his voice. "You can't intimidate me. If you don't *shut up*, I'm going to end this call."

"You wouldn't—"

"Try me." Derek took advantage of the silence. "I've investigated the security team here. I've also installed cameras in various positions to give hospital security a bit of advanced warning if—"

"It's not 'if,' Tower. It's 'when.' It's only a matter of time, and you know it!"

The man was paranoid. There were NGOs all over the country. Though there were occasional attacks, most of the aid workers who came to Afghanistan went home in one piece. He started to say this, but the senator cut him off.

"I warned James not to join the army. I told him he had a different purpose in life, but he didn't listen. He died over there without ever having lived up to his potential, and now Jenna—"

"Your son died a hero." The words were out before Derek could stop himself. "It's too bad you never knew the warrior James became. As for Jenna, she's an adult. Like James, she can make her own decisions. *You don't own her.*"

"You'd best watch your—"

Derek ended the call, fury slamming through him.

It wasn't often that a person could provoke him like this, but that *son of a bitch* had dared to judge Jimmy's life and death without knowing a damned thing about it. Hamilton had never put on a uniform, never faced live fire, never had to make a split-second decision that meant life for someone —and death for himself.

Fuck Hamilton.

Sniper!

Rat-at-at-at!

Derek shoved the memory away and reached for the next box of MREs.

5

Jenna dragged the refrigerator out of the way to reveal the entrance of the safe room. It was easy to make out the edges of the doorway, but there was no handle on the outside. The idea was to pull the refrigerator back into place to hide the door before closing and locking it from the inside. She pushed the panel, and the door swung open, cold, musty air hitting her in the face.

Mina leaned in to look. "I hope we never have to go down there."

"My brother said we should practice." Jenna turned on a flashlight and stepped through the entrance into the dark.

She found herself on a small landing above a concrete flight of stairs that led down to a small room below. There was no handrail, so she took each step carefully.

Cobwebs stretched through the air in front of her. Or were they spider webs?

God almighty.

She brushed them aside, trying not to look into the cracks and crannies as she made her way down to the safe room. It wasn't a big space, just large enough to hold the hospital's staff and a handful of patients. There was no furniture, but concrete benches had been built into the walls, perhaps so that patients could lie down. Thankfully, there was an electric light.

She pulled the string, glanced around. More webs. Rodent droppings were scattered across the floor, making her wish she'd worn a mask. This was going to be more work than she'd imagined.

She went back upstairs. "We need to clean it. There are rodent droppings. We need to find some way to protect the food so that mice don't get into it."

She and Mina put on masks and gloves and got to work with brooms, mops, and bleach to make the safe room habitable.

"I never thought becoming a midwife would mean cleaning up mouse droppings," Mina said.

Jenna laughed. "Neither did I."

When the room was as clean as they could get it, Jenna washed her hands and then sent Derek a text, explaining that there was a mouse presence and that the food and water, which was in shrink-wrapped boxes, would need some kind of protection.

`I'll see what I can do.`

Twenty minutes later, he buzzed her to tell her he had located some clean and empty fifty-five-gallon steel drums that had once held medical supplies.

She found him carrying one of the drums, his coat off in the sunshine, his biceps visible beneath the fabric of his long-sleeved shirt. "Those will be perfect."

He flashed her a bright smile. "Is three barrels going to be enough?"

"I think so."

He set the barrel down beside her. "Are you able to carry this?"

"Sure." She tried to pick up one of the barrels but found it heavier than she'd imagined. "I could get it inside. The problem is going to be getting it down the stairs."

"I'll talk to Farzad." Derek jogged off, leaving her standing outside the back door.

He returned with Farzad a few minutes later. "If you ask the women to confine themselves to the hospital wing and lock the door behind them, I'll carry these inside and down the stairs for you."

"This meets with the requirements for modesty," Farzad said.

"Thank you, Farzad." Jenna kept her eyes averted so he couldn't see how amusing she found the situation.

Jenna hurried back inside and locked the student midwives together with Delara and Marie inside the hospital wing, then went and opened the door for Derek. "The coast is clear, *brother*."

He picked up the first barrel and followed her to the small kitchen, his body seeming to fill the space. He peered inside the safe room. "It's not big, is it?"

He maneuvered the barrel through the small opening and onto the landing and then bent down and stepped through. There wasn't enough room on the landing for him to stand upright, and he had to keep his head bent as he started down the stairs. "I can see why you thought this might be a problem."

"Don't break your neck." She followed him down, carrying one of the boxes of MREs. She couldn't see her feet this time, so she was extra careful.

Derek set the drum down on its edge and rolled it into a

corner, the ceiling barely tall enough for him to stand upright. He lifted the MREs from her arms as if they weighed nothing and set them down on one of the concrete benches. "I can carry those down. You open the boxes and pack the meals in the drums."

Once again, she caught the scent of his skin, a spicy, masculine smell. She'd become so accustomed to the odor of unwashed bodies that being near him was intoxicating.

Good grief!

He hurried back up the stairs, making four more trips —two for the remaining two drums and two for the rest of the MREs and the water—while she tore off the shrink wrap, opened the boxes, and piled the meals into the barrel. Then she fitted the lids onto the barrels, stepping back as he pounded them firmly into place with the heel of his palm.

"That ought to keep out the mice."

"I'd like to store some medical supplies down here, too, just in case—first aid supplies, IV fluids, pain meds." Her headscarf had come loose, and she instinctively reached up to straighten it.

He caught her hand. "Don't. I want to see your hair."

Jenna forgot to breathe.

What the hell are you doing?

This hadn't been part of Derek's plan. The words had just come out of his mouth, but for some reason, he wasn't taking them back.

A part of him tried to convince himself that he was just doing his job, just trying to win Jenna over. But he knew that was bullshit. He truly *did* want to see her hair.

Jenna stood, frozen in place, looking up at him, green eyes wide, her pupils dilated. "I-I probably shouldn't..."

He took hold of the damned headscarf and pulled it off to reveal thick auburn hair that hung well below her shoulders.

She reached up, ran a hand self-consciously over her hair. "I've gotten used to covering up. I don't spend any time styling it or..."

Her words trailed off when he lifted a handful of silky strands, raised them to his nostrils, and inhaled, the feminine scent sending a dart of arousal to his groin. "You smell like flowers."

"It's ... uh ... my shampoo."

Had he managed to fluster her?

Good.

"I like it." He slid his fingers through the thick tresses, grazing her cheek with his palm, his fingers finding her nape.

Her eyes drifted shut, her lips parting on an exhale.

Lust punched through him, sharp and bright.

Reluctantly, he drew his hand away, fighting an irrational impulse to pull her close and kiss the hell out of her. "You're a beautiful woman, Jenna."

She shook her head, her cheeks flushing pink. "I'm not wearing any makeup."

"You don't need it." He truly meant that.

Her skin was nearly translucent, her eyelashes dark and long, her lips full and...

Hell, he should *not* be thinking about her lips. If anyone caught them kissing, they would both end up very dead. Not that anyone would wander in just now. The women were shut in the hospital wing, and Farzad was likely too afraid to set foot in this place.

Don't take chances.

He wouldn't, not where Jenna was concerned.

Besides, kissing her wasn't his mission.

"I wish you would come with me back to the U.S." He rested his hands on her shoulders. "There are men not far from here who would tear you apart if they could."

"Are you trying to scare me? It won't work."

"No, I'm just telling you the truth. I've seen the aftermath of more than one Taliban massacre—women and girls raped to death or shot in the head, entire families slaughtered."

She took a step backward. "I know it's dangerous to be here, but it's more dangerous for these mothers. If I bail out of my contract and go home because I'm afraid, where does that leave them? Where does it leave Marie, Delara, and the students? The world can't just abandon these women. I know that what I'm doing is a drop in the bucket compared to what's needed, but at least I'm doing something."

Derek could tell she meant every word, and he respected her. That didn't change the fact that he had a job to do. "At least think about it."

"I should get back to work." She reached for her headscarf.

"Let me." He draped it over her hair, tucking it beneath her chin and drawing it around her so that the ends fell over her chest to cover the gentle curves of her breasts. "That should do it. Not a single strand is showing."

She adjusted it, smoothing her hands over her covered head. "Thank you."

He followed her up the stairs, climbed out into the kitchen, closed the door, and pushed the refrigerator back into place. "I'll be on duty in the waiting room tonight."

"Was that Farzad's idea, too, like the security cameras?" The tone of her voice told him she already knew the answer.

"I need his good will."

"Thanks for the help. Have a good day."

"You, too." It took no small amount of effort for Derek to turn and walk away.

He found Farzad waiting outside. "The barrels are in the safe room. I carried the boxes of meals and water down, too. The stairs are steep, and the boxes were too heavy for my sister."

Farzad's expression told Derek that he'd wondered why it had taken him so long. "That is good. It is right to be prepared."

"I tried again to persuade her to come home with me, but she is determined to fulfill her agreement with the hospital."

"Your sister has honor."

"She does." Derek just hoped it wouldn't get her killed.

"THERE IS no way Behar's baby can be born." Jenna spoke to Behar's mother-in-law quietly so the girl wouldn't hear. "She is young, and the opening in her pelvis is smaller than her baby's head. If we can't do surgery, she and the baby will both die."

Behar, who was only twelve, had arrived with her husband and mother-in-law an hour ago after a long day of hard labor. Her cervix was fully dilated, but her contractions weren't bringing the baby down. They'd done everything they could to facilitate delivery—squatting, being on her hands and knees. But after three hours of pushing, the baby was as high in Behar's pelvis as it had been when she'd arrived.

Marie and Jenna had reached the same conclusion—cephalopelvic disproportion. The opening in her pelvis was just too small for her baby's head.

"I will speak to my son." The mother-in-law pulled her burqa over her face and left the room, just as Behar's eyes opened.

Another contraction.

Marie stayed with Behar, held her hand, while Jenna followed the mother-in-law to the door that separated the hospital from the waiting area. She couldn't step into the waiting room, but she wanted to hear what the older woman said to her son so she would know whether she delivered Jenna's message accurately. She waited until the older woman had closed the door then pressed her ear against it.

"They say Behar needs to have surgery to take the baby out or she and the baby might die. They say she is too young to give birth, but I had my first baby at her age."

Damn it!

That wasn't it at all. Yes, she was too young, but more to the point, her pelvis was too small. She and the baby *would* die—there was no question.

Jenna held her breath, listened for the husband's answer.

"*Nachair. Nachair.*" *No. No.* "These surgeries—they leave women unable to bear more children. Many girls give birth while young. It is in God's hands."

Jenna's heart sank.

Back in the delivery area, Behar cried out, sobbing in fear and pain.

To hell with this!

Jenna opened the door just a crack and spoke in Dari,

not to the husband, which was forbidden, but to the mother-in-law. “Grandmother, hear me. If we don’t take the baby out through surgery, it will never come out.”

Shouts of outrage.

Jenna raised her voice to be heard. “Behar’s body is too small, Grandmother. The baby cannot come out. Its head is too big. It is trapped inside her. If we do not operate, she and the baby *will* die but only after many long hours of needless suffering.”

Someone jerked the door shut from the other side, and Jenna turned to find Delara and several of the student midwives staring at her in shock. It wasn’t the custom in this rural area of the province for a woman to speak if she could be overheard by men who were not close relatives.

But Jenna was beyond caring. “I must do all I can to save Behar’s life. Her mother-in-law didn’t tell her son the full truth.”

She could see on their faces that they understood, but they were also afraid for her and for themselves.

In the waiting room, the shouting went on.

Jenna pressed her ear against the door once more.

“What woman speaks like this in our hearing?”

“There is no honor in a woman who speaks immodestly!”

“This is in God’s hands.”

“As you say—it is in God’s hands. But how do you know that God has not brought you here so that this surgery can save your wife and child?”

Derek?

It was his voice.

“This is not your affair, friend.”

Derek wasn’t put off. “In my village, our Imam tells a story of a man who lived near a river. A great rain came, and the river flooded the land. The man was trapped. He prayed to God to save him. An elder came with a boat, but the man would not get in the boat for he was waiting for God to save him."

Barely able to breathe, Jenna listened as Derek shared the proverbial story that would have been familiar to most Americans, placing it in an Afghan context. But how could he pass as an Afghan man? She wanted to peek out but knew she couldn't risk it.

"When the man drowned, he went to paradise and asked God, 'Why didn't you save me from the flood?' God said to him, 'First, I sent a man in a boat, but you turned him away. Then I sent a helicopter, but still, you refused to go.'"

The waiting room was quiet as Derek finished the story.

"I ask again, friend. How do you know that God didn't bring you to this hospital to save your wife and child? Are not all things, even this hospital, in God's hands?"

Silence.

"*Baleh.*" *Yes.* "Tell them they may give Behar this surgery —but not the woman who spoke so rudely. She must be nowhere near my wife."

Relief washed through Jenna, the breath leaving her lungs in a long exhale.

The door opened, almost hitting her as the mother-in-law stepped back inside.

She glared at Jenna, pinched her arm. "You are not a pure woman."

"For shame, Grandmother," Delara hissed. "You should be grateful. Miss Jenna fought for your daughter-in-law's life. Now, you will have a grandchild and not a grave."

The mother-in-law delivered the husband's message to Marie and then went back to wait with her son.

Jenna watched while Marie and Delara moved Behar to

the operating room, the students following so they could observe the surgery. Then she walked to the kitchen, pulled the satellite phone out of her pocket, and sent Derek a text.

`Thank you. Thank you so much.`

He had just saved two lives.

6

Jenna gave Behar's newborn his first bath and put him in a diaper, newborn pajamas, and a knitted hat donated by churches in the United States. Then she gave him a bottle of formula while his exhausted mother slept and her harridan of a mother-in-law went out to make food for herself and her son. Jenna would rather the baby be breastfed, but Behar wasn't yet fully conscious.

Jenna kissed the baby's forehead. "I'm so glad you're here, little one. You had a rough journey, didn't you?"

The baby's head was bruised, and his cranial bones had shifted in response to being pressed into his mother's tight pelvis, giving him quite the conehead. The bones would go back to their normal rounded shape quickly.

Marie walked up to Jenna and pulled off her OR scrubs, anger on her face. She spoke in English, her French accent strong. "What you did was dangerous for all of us. If these men tell others that a midwife here spoke to them, other men might refuse to bring their wives here. Or maybe the Taliban will come to kill us."

Jenna knew this was true, but if she hadn't broken the

rules, Behar would have labored to death, and this innocent baby boy who was so alive in her arms right now would never have taken a breath. "I can't say I'm sorry, because I'm not."

Marie threw her blood-stained scrubs in the laundry basket. "I know you think saving this girl's life and that of her son was the greater good, but is it? If we get shut down or men start refusing to permit their wives to come here, other women and babies will die. What good will you have done then?"

"I have a moral duty to give the best medical care I can to the women who come here for treatment. I can't ignore one woman's suffering for the benefit of others."

Delara, who had assisted during the surgery, pulled off her surgical scrubs. She didn't speak English, but she had clearly understood that Marie was angry. "I wish I'd had the courage to do what you did, Miss Jenna."

Marie closed her eyes, the anger draining from her face. "So do I."

"My brother is the one who changed the father's mind, not I." Jenna told them what Derek had said.

Delara's eyes went wide at the punchline of the parable of the drowning man. "I must remember that story."

"Your brother is a good man," Marie said.

Derek *was* a good man.

Was he still on duty in the waiting area?

He hadn't replied to her text message, but perhaps he couldn't. If he were truly trying to pass as an Afghan man—Jenna couldn't imagine that—he wouldn't be able to whip a satellite phone out of his pocket without arousing suspicion.

"What do I tell Behar's mother-in-law when she finds out I'm the only one working tonight?" It was Jenna's turn to take the night shift, and that meant looking after newborns and mothers alike.

"If that horrid woman gives you trouble, call me," Marie said. "Good night."

"Sleep well."

The baby had a strong suck and finished the bottle quickly, his eyes, which had already been painted with kohl, as was the custom here, drifting shut. Jenna settled him in his bassinette and tucked an extra blanket around him to keep him warm. She watched him sleep, an ache in her chest. At this moment, both mother and baby were safe, but what about tomorrow?

Tomorrow, Marie would have to fight with Behar's family to keep mother and child here for another three days to give Behar time to heal and get past the worst of her post-operative pain. And soon, Behar would be pregnant once more and would face this ordeal again.

Jenna checked on Najida's little girl next. She had finally managed to persuade Najida to breastfeed rather than giving her daughter butter, and the baby was now sound asleep beside her mother. The two would be leaving in the morning, riding in a donkey cart to their village two hours away.

Jenna kept busy through the night, checking on Behar, changing her IV fluids, giving her morphine—and ignoring the dirty looks the mother-in-law cast her way. "You have a beautiful grandson."

"Impure woman," the harridan hissed back.

You have no idea.

Jenna restocked supplies and folded and put away yesterday's laundry, the relative peace of the night giving her time to think, her mind turning to Derek and what had happened in the safe room this afternoon.

I want to see your hair.

Jenna's pulse skipped. No sexy pickup line or attempt at seduction had affected her the way those words had. Derek had taken her completely by surprise, yanking off her headscarf, sliding his fingers into her hair, inhaling her scent, his brow furrowing as if the smell of her shampoo pleased him. After six months of celibacy, separation from men, and hiding under a headscarf and tunics, she had felt exposed.

You smell like flowers.

She could hear Derek's voice, hear the way the words rumbled in his chest.

You're a beautiful woman, Jenna.

For a moment, she'd thought he was going to kiss her. He had stopped himself— which is more than she would have done. Now, she was left to imagine what it would have been like to have all that man and muscle hold her close, his mouth over hers, those big hands fisted in her hair. And so, she *did* imagine it, again and again, until she found herself standing, eyes closed, a half-folded sheet in her arms.

Snap out of it!

On second thought, it was probably for the best that he hadn't kissed her. One kiss would only make her want more, and that couldn't happen, not here, not without putting them both at risk. No kiss was worth that.

Maybe with him it would be.

That was her ovaries. They were getting ahead of her again.

Jenna forced her mind away from Derek and finished folding the sheet.

~

DEREK WANTED TO THROTTLE JENNA. He strode back to the

barracks in search of Farzad, certain things would go better for Jenna if Farzad heard what had happened from him—if the man wasn't already aware.

Derek understood why Jenna had done what she'd done, but she'd come close to landing herself in a world of hurt. The men in that waiting room had been outraged, some of them talking about going to their village mullah. Where things would have gone from there, no one could know. Derek had talked them down, commiserating with them about the ignorance of Westerners and their women, doing his best to make light of the situation. In the end, news of a son had taken the edge off the husband's anger.

Derek found Farzad and his men putting away their prayer rugs. He removed his wool *pakol*—the traditional men's hat—and his patoo, which he'd wrapped around his face to hide his features and lack of beard. "A good morning to you all."

He joined the men for tea and bread, grinning at their jokes about his appearance.

"If you were an Afghan man, you would have a beard," Hamzad teased.

Derek rubbed the stubble on his jaw. "I'm growing one."

When the men had eaten and finished their tea, Derek turned to Farzad. "May I speak with you where we cannot be overheard?"

Farzad's face was expressionless while Derek explained what had happened.

"I would like to deal with my sister myself. I don't believe she understands what she has done. She needs to learn the right way to act."

Farzad's face folded in a thoughtful frown. "Tell me, my friend, when were you a soldier here? You told Dawar you are not a soldier now, but I believe you must once have worn a uniform. You speak our tongue as one born to it, not like your sister, who has an accent. You slip into the clothes of an Afghan man as if you have always worn them. You did not need my help dressing this morning. The way you turned those men away from violence last night... You have been in Afghanistan for a long time."

Derek could have lied, but he wouldn't, not to Farzad. "I was an operator with U.S. special forces for many years. I left the army long ago to work in private security. I did not say this when Dawar asked because I did not know you or your men then, though I did not lie. I said I am not a soldier, and, indeed, I am not—not now."

"Did you kill Talibs and al-Qaeda fighters?" Farzad's face was still expressionless.

"Yes, I did."

Farzad grinned. "Then we are brothers. But I will not tell the others, especially not Hamzad. As I said, he is the eyes and ears of The Lion."

And Derek knew at that moment that Farzad didn't trust Kazi either.

"As for your sister, what she did was kind-hearted but dangerous. The mother and child are well?"

"Yes. A son."

"I'm glad you brought this matter to me. I will do all I can to protect her. Yes, you may speak with her and explain things to her so that she will understand and not bring trouble upon us."

"Thank you, Farzad."

Farzad's expression fell. "My country has not always been like this. When I was a boy, women walked the city streets without burqas. Some went to college, and many held jobs. No woman feared being flogged or shot for speaking with a man. The Taliban ruined that by twisting

Islam. They stole Islam, dragged it through the dung, destroying my country. They are heretics. Once we were a land known for its poetry, music, and food. I grieve for Afghanistan and its people, Mr. Tower."

"The future depends on men like you—and women like these student midwives at this hospital. My sister and I are in your debt."

Derek sent Jenna a text message but didn't hear back until noon, when she told him she had worked the night shift and been asleep. He told her they needed to talk, but she said she was too busy.

Derek took advantage of the time to catch up on sleep himself, crashing on his bunk in the barracks. He fell asleep quickly, but his dreams were haunted by Jenna—her sweet-smelling auburn hair, those kissable lips, those beautiful green eyes. He kissed her, began to peel away the layers that hid her body.

Sniper!

Rat-at-at-at!

Derek jerked awake, heart slamming in his chest.

Fuck.

He glanced at his watch.

It was just after three in the afternoon.

He got up, walked through the frigid wind and sunshine to the Land Cruiser, where he went through his stash of food, reading the options. He chose Menu 4—spaghetti with beef sauce, toaster pastry, peanut butter, multigrain snack bread, infused and dried fruits, fortified cocoa beverage powder, jam, and Accessory Packet B, which turned out to be M&Ms.

After eating, he brushed his teeth from a bottle of water and then went inside for a quick shower. There was no hot water today, the cold a shock to the system that sent his nuts into full retreat.

This is what you deserve for dreaming about getting Jenna naked.

Jenna Hamilton was off limits for many reasons, not the least of which was that getting caught with her could be fatal for them both.

He stepped out of the shower to find Hamzad standing nearby.

The man looked straight at Derek's dick. "If you were a good Afghan man, you would be circumcised."

Derek ignored him, wrapped a towel around his waist, and reached for his boxers. His satellite phone buzzed with a message from Jenna.

`I can take a short break now.`

He finished dressing and met her at the back door. "We need to talk—in private."

They walked in silence to the Land Cruiser and climbed inside, where it was much warmer.

"Thanks so much for what you did last night. You saved—"

"What I did was save *your* ass. You came close to starting a riot."

"I had to do *something*." The anguish on Jenna's face was real. "If I hadn't, a twelve-year-old girl would have suffered until she died with her baby still inside her."

"I know *why* you did it." He'd heard the girl's cries, each one sending shivers down his spine. The screams of the injured and dying were nothing new to him, but the girl's cries had gotten beneath his skin. "*Why* you did it doesn't matter—not to those men. I spent the next twenty minutes talking them down. Some of them wanted to fetch the nearest Imam. You could have been dragged out by your headscarf and flogged. You put the other midwives, the students, the staff, including Farzad and his men, at risk."

Her face paled, but her chin went up. "What was I supposed to do—watch her suffer for endless hours and then die? Do you have any idea how painful that would have been? Oh, wait, you're a man, so you have no clue."

"You haven't had any babies—not that I know of, anyway. How can you have more personal insight into how painful it is than I do?"

"I'm a *midwife*! I hold their hands. I see the pain in their eyes every time they have a contraction. I see their despair when labor drags on."

Against his better judgment, Derek reached over, cupped her cheek. "You can't save everyone, Jenna."

She drew away from his touch. "Are we done?"

"Farzad knows. I told him I would talk to you so that he wouldn't have to."

Without another word, she opened the door, hopped to the ground, and disappeared inside the compound.

~

"THE HEAD IS OUT. The worst of your pain is over." Jenna put her hands atop Lailoma's, guiding her as she supported the baby's head while the other students watched. "Check to see that the cord isn't around its neck."

With no cord, all the baby needed was another push.

"Take a deep breath and push," Jenna said to the mother, a twenty-three-year-old who was about to give birth to her fourth baby.

The woman's mother-in-law held her hand.

"Push! Push!"

Jenna shifted Lailoma's hands as the baby began to turn. "The baby will rotate so that the shoulders can be born. It doesn't matter which direction it turns. Sometimes the shoulders can get stuck, and that's an emergency."

They had talked about shoulder dystocia in class, but Jenna could tell that it wasn't going to be a problem this time.

The mother let out a shriek as first one shoulder and then the next emerged. The baby slipped from its mother's body and into Lailoma's hands in a rush of amniotic fluid, flinging its little arms out as if in surprise and letting out a lusty wail.

"It's a boy!" Lailoma's face lit up with a smile. "You have another son."

Jenna let Lailoma take over, watching as she tucked the baby into a blanket and handed him to his mother. "It's important to give her the oxytocin injection as soon as you can. If the baby weren't breathing, you would need to treat him before giving the mother the injection. Those first few minutes are important for the baby's survival."

This little guy was already using his lungs to their full capacity, his healthy cries making everyone in the room smile.

Lailoma reached for the prepared syringe and injected the life-saving hormone into the mother's thigh then went about clamping and cutting the cord.

Jenna's phone buzzed, but she didn't have time to check it. She hadn't spoken to Derek since the day before yesterday in his Land Cruiser. He'd been so angry with her, as if she'd done something deliberately to endanger everyone.

Stop thinking about him.

"After the baby is safe and breathing and the afterbirth has been safely delivered, we will check the mother for birth injuries—vaginal tears, fistula, anything that might require treatment."

Everything had gone as it should this time—no hemorrhaging, no retained placenta, no vaginal tears—giving Jenna time to focus on lessons about newborn care. Here, midwives were often the first and only people to screen new babies for problems. A proper neonatal evaluation could save a child's life.

Under Jenna's supervision, Lailoma checked for hip dysplasia, listened to his heart and lungs, and put ilotycin ointment in his eyes. Then she gave him an injection of vitamin K and a bath, and placed him, diapered and swaddled, in his grandmother's waiting arms.

A toothless smile on her face, she carried the baby out to the waiting area so his father could see him—and whisper the name of God in his ear, a sweet tradition known as the *azan kawal.*

Jenna's sat phone buzzed again. She peeled off her gloves, drew the phone from her pocket, and read his first message.

`Do not come outside! A mullah is here to speak with Farzad about you.`

Shit.

Pulse racing, she scrolled to the second.

`Be ready to shelter in the safe room.`

"What is it, Miss Jenna?" Guli asked.

"My brother tells me a mullah has come to speak with

Farzad about me." The students stared at Jenna in stunned silence that was broken by the whoops and shouts of celebration that came from the waiting area. "He says I should be ready to shelter in the safe room."

At those words, the students flew into action, apart from Lailoma, who was still tending to the woman and her newborn. The girls took Jenna's hands, guiding her out of the hospital wing and toward the kitchen as if she didn't know the way.

It was like being carried away on a tide.

"Get her to the safe room."

"Come now. Hurry!"

"We will hide you there."

But this wasn't necessary, was it?

"He didn't say I had to hide now. He just said to be ready."

"If you're already down there, that is the best kind of ready," Chehrah said. "Then we can go about our work and not worry."

Jenna couldn't argue with that.

She was touched by their concern for her. This situation was *her* fault. If anything happened to them or Derek or Farzad or any of the men...

Then she remembered. "Someone needs to warn Marie and Delara."

Marie and Delara were in the OR with Zari and Parwana in the middle of another C-section—a woman with twins who had arrived with precariously high blood pressure.

"I'll go." Guli turned and hurried back to the hospital wing.

Even before she reached the kitchen, Jenna could hear the squeaking of the refrigerator's wheels as Mina and

Mahnaz admonished each other to move it quickly and quietly.

In a blink, Jenna found herself staring at the safe room doorway. She had everything down there that she might need—light, food, water, blankets—but the idea of sitting down there for hours alone was unnerving.

This is your *fault. Deal with it.*

She pushed on the panel, and the door popped open. She reached in and flicked on the light then turned back to the students. "Don't risk anything for me. If anyone is to suffer for this, it should be me."

She stepped inside and turned on the light, then locked the door behind her and walked down the stairs as the refrigerator was pushed back into place. She grabbed a blanket, wrapped it around her, and sat on a concrete bench.

There was nothing she could do but wait.

7

Derek was relieved when he got Jenna's message that she was in the safe room. He kept to the background, let Farzad do the talking. As an Afghan and a Muslim, Farzad could do far more to help Jenna at this moment than he. That's why one of the first jobs of a Green Beret—or a Cobra operative—was to cultivate local assets, allies who would knowingly or unknowingly aid the mission.

Farzad made the Mullah welcome in the barracks, the two making polite small talk over tea, dates, bread, and almonds before turning to the thorny subject of Jenna.

"I am told by a man from my village that a midwife here, a Westerner, violated the rules of modesty to speak in the hearing of unrelated men. I came to hear the truth of this. We cannot allow outsiders or Western women to corrupt our culture."

Farzad's men, who had not yet heard this news, reacted with outrage, the mood in the room turning ugly.

"Is this true?"

"She must be sent away!"

"No virtuous woman would do such a thing."

"She is an infidel," Hamzad said. "Why should any of you be surprised?"

"Quiet!" Farzad silenced his men. "Let our honored guest speak."

The Mullah went on for some time about how women should behave, quoting the Quran and various teachings on the subject, while Derek quietly sent a text message to the team in Mazar-e-Sharif to be on standby. His mind raced through different rescue scenarios, but none of them held a high probability of success. He was outnumbered more than twenty to one. He would need additional assets—a chopper, ground support.

What a mess that would make. Once bullets started flying, there was no way to make sure that only bad guys got shot. Innocent civilians would die, too—and all because of Jenna's damned idealism.

He got it. He really did. She hadn't been able to let that girl and her baby die needlessly, so she'd done something about it. But actions came with consequences.

The Mullah then told about several Afghan women who had spoken to men who were not relatives and who had been beaten or flogged for their immodesty. Not long ago, a woman had been shot by the Taliban in the neighboring Kunduz Province after someone had seen her talking to a man in front of her home.

Over my dead body.

Farzad listened to all the Mullah had to say, pondering his words, a pensive expression on his face. "I will tell you the truth of what happened here."

He told the Mullah the story—how a young wife had been in labor with a child that was too large for her to bear and how the Western midwife had told the girl's mother-in-law to say to the husband that his wife needed an operation or she and the baby would die. "The mother-in-law didn't repeat her message to the husband but instead chose her own words. The husband refused the surgery."

Then Farzad described how this midwife—he never said Jenna's name—had opened the door just a crack and spoken to the mother-in-law. "She spoke respectfully, calling her 'Grandmother,' but there were men in the room, and they heard her. They grew angry and confused by this. But the husband, hearing the truth from her, changed his mind and allowed the surgery. His son was born through that surgery, and both the baby boy and his mother survived."

Derek waited, along with every man in the barracks, for the Mullah's reaction.

The old man stroked his gray beard. "She did not let the men see her?"

"No, no. She opened the door just a crack so the mother-in-law could hear her. She said nothing in a flirtatious tone of voice, for her only concern was ensuring that the mother-in-law told her son the full truth so that she could save the life of the wife and baby. She does not understand our culture, but her brother, who is here with us and has lived in our country as a guest for a long time, has disciplined her."

Heads turned Derek's way, but he waited for an invitation to speak.

"Do you understand our words?" the Mullah asked.

"Yes, I do."

"What can you tell me about your sister?"

"She is a virtuous woman who cares for the lives of women and children. I was in the waiting room when my sister spoke through the crack in the door. If she had said anything flirtatious or disrespectful, I would have silenced her myself. She did something she shouldn't have done, but she did it to try to save the young mother and her baby because the grandmother hadn't been truthful."

The Mullah seemed to consider this. "If the mother-in-law's words had not been corrected, the husband would have lost his son and his wife. Surely, that is a reason for gratitude. And, yet, we cannot have Western women who come as aid workers casting aside our ways because their culture tells them they are free to do so."

Everyone seemed to agree on this point.

"We will not sacrifice our culture or religion for them," Hamzad blurted to the approval of the other men.

The Mullah went on. "The prohibition against women's speech in the Quran is against complacent speech—words spoken without a thought for consequences, speech intended to incite lust or bring about flirtation. It does not seem to me that this midwife was complacent in her speech. Rather, she behaved recklessly out of a desire to ensure that the husband knew the truth of his wife's situation. I cannot see a need to punish her more than her brother already has. If the mother-in-law had been more careful in passing on the message, this would likely not have happened at all."

"It is good to hear your wisdom in this matter." Farzad was clever with his words, flattering the Mullah. Derek would give him a brand new M4 for this. "I will consider it settled then."

"God is most merciful." Derek tried not to let his relief show. "I thank you for your understanding and wisdom. I will speak with my sister again to make certain she knows that you have been good to her today."

He didn't miss the look of disappointment on Hamzad's face.

The men finished their tea and went back to their posts. Derek stepped outside, too, waiting until the Mullah and his men had climbed into their vehicle and driven away before texting Jenna to tell her that the danger had passed —for now.

Jenna stepped outside, holding her headscarf in place as she hurried through the cold wind to Derek's Land Cruiser, which he had parked inside the compound near the back door. Derek had said he'd waited until everyone was busy with evening prayers to talk because he wasn't sure how Farzad's men would react to seeing her.

What had he meant by that?

He pushed the front passenger door open for her, and she climbed inside. The engine and heater were on, so the vehicle was deliciously warm.

One look told her he was still angry. "I have just a few minutes. What happened?"

"I spent almost an hour today trying to figure out how I was going to get us both out of here alive without killing a whole lot of people." There was a hard edge to his voice. "Thanks to Farzad, it all ended well."

Derek told her how someone had reported what she'd done to a mullah and how the mullah had come with a small entourage to find out if what he'd heard was true.

"The mood in that room was pretty hostile. For a while, I thought it would end with them trying to drag you outside to flog you. I put our team in Mazar-e-Sharif on standby just in case. It worked out in the end, but only because Farzad knew exactly what to say—and because this mullah wasn't an extremist."

Jenna's stomach rolled. "What did Farzad say?"

"He explained what had happened in detail. The Mullah

agreed that you'd done something wrong but for good reasons. He decided you didn't need to be punished."

Jenna wanted to roll her eyes. "Wasn't that merciful of him?"

"Actually, yes, it was—both merciful and wise."

Derek's rebuke left Jenna feeling like a selfish, stupid child. Thanks to her, he'd truly believed he might have to go into combat mode to keep her safe. "Please thank Farzad for me."

"I already did."

"I'm sorry to put you through this." She hadn't meant for this to happen. "What should I have done—let the girl and her baby die? What would *you* have done?"

"Hell, Jenna, I don't know. This isn't your country or your culture. Sometimes, it's better just to let things take their course."

"Oh, that's rich coming from you, the guy who fought in a war here. By that standard, you should just have let them flog me. There would be no fighting, no killing, no dying. This isn't your country or your culture, after all. Don't interfere. Just let things take their course."

His gaze bored into hers. "If you think I'd stand there and watch men beat you with rods until you were a bloody mess, you don't know me very well."

His description sent chills down Jenna's spine, but she held her ground. "If you can't stand by and do nothing, don't expect me to. My job is to save lives."

"My job is to *end* them if necessary—to protect *you*." He cupped her cheek with a callused palm, his gaze going soft, his face inches from hers. "I admire and respect you, Jenna, but things here are precarious. I will back you up to my last breath no matter what for as long as I'm here. But please don't do anything to push the boundaries, or I might not have any choice but to fight."

Jenna's pulse skipped, her gaze dropping to his lips. "I-I didn't ask you to come to Afghanistan."

"I know." He leaned closer, brushed his lips over hers, once, twice.

Jenna sucked in a breath, the contact sending jolts of pleasure through her. Then his mouth closed over hers, and he kissed her. It was a gentle kiss, but it scorched her to her core, his lips exploring hers with deliberate tenderness.

God, yes.

He stiffened, drew back. "We can't do this—not here."

Jenna knew what he said was true. If they were caught...

Afghans kissed their close relatives, but *not* like that.

He put both hands on the steering wheel and held on, his knuckles white. "You should get back inside."

She cleared her throat, clenched her trembling hands in her lap, her pulse thrumming, her lips still tingling. "You're leaving tomorrow, aren't you?"

"I don't know." He glanced over his shoulder as if to see whether anyone was watching. "Your father threatened to make trouble for us in the Senate Armed Services Committee if I don't bring you back. He wanted me to bring you home by force if you didn't come voluntarily."

"What?" Jenna gaped at Derek, stunned. "That's abduction. What did you say?"

"I told him that it was illegal and I wouldn't do it."

This was low, even for her father, and it *hurt*.

"I'm so sorry, Derek. My father is such an asshole. Please don't let him hold you or your company hostage over this."

Derek reached over, took her left hand. "It was the thought of you being Jimmy's sister that got me on the plane, not your father's threats. If I'd had a sister, I know Jimmy would have done anything for her. I don't want to leave here without you, Jenna, not because of any threat your father made against Cobra, but because I wouldn't be able to live with myself if something happened to Jimmy's little sister."

Jenna's heart melted. "My father made you feel guilty about James, didn't he?"

She could see the answer in Derek's eyes.

Oh, the bastard!

"My father is a manipulative jerk. It's not your fault James died, and it won't be your fault if anything happens to me."

Derek nodded. "But that doesn't mean I can just walk away."

Still reeling from their kiss and from what Derek had told her, Jenna found herself at a loss for words. "I should go back inside. We've got two laboring moms and our two recovering C-sections. I just wish..."

"What?"

"I wish there was somewhere we could talk that was more private, where I could take off this headscarf and just be myself."

Liar.

What she really wanted was to kiss him again—without risking their lives. But that wasn't going to happen.

"Hey, you don't like my big, armored Land Cruiser?" Derek grinned, gave her hand a squeeze, released it. "I'll see what I can do."

~

DURING HIS YEARS IN COMBAT, Derek had learned to fall asleep fast. He could sleep anywhere—in a foxhole, in a barracks surrounded by sweaty, snoring soldiers, lying on bare ground. But it was well past midnight, and he hadn't slept at all, his body alive with unspent sexual energy.

Jenna.

He'd been a damned idiot to kiss her—not that it had been much of a kiss. He'd gotten only a taste of her before his self-control had kicked in. But now he couldn't get her off his mind. Every time he closed his eyes, she filled his head—the auburn silk of her hair, her green eyes, the soft curve of her cheek, the minty taste of her lips, her sweet, floral scent.

He wanted to kiss her—hard. He wanted to peel off those layers one by one and taste everything beneath them. He wanted to get her on her back and—

She's Jimmy's little sister. She's your job. She is out of bounds.

Yeah, well, someone needed to remind his dick.

He'd broken a fistful of rules today, and now he was paying for it with lost sleep and frustration. Normally, he'd jack off and be done with it. But he couldn't do that here with a dozen other men in the room. He couldn't wank in the shower either, given that someone was always around. And his Land Cruiser? The damned thing had windows, and, thanks to him, there were cameras everywhere.

Live with it, dumbass. It's your own fault.

And what about the shit he'd said?

He'd seen in her eyes that his words had had an emotional impact on her, and he'd tried to tell himself that he'd only been doing his job, trying to get under her skin and bend her will so that it aligned with his mission. But the strange thing was that he'd meant everything he'd said. He hadn't been trying to manipulate her. It was as if his mouth had opened up, and what he truly felt had come out.

I will back you up to my last breath no matter what for as long as I'm here.

Yeah, he'd meant that. He wasn't afraid to die. Hell, he owed Jimmy his life.

It was the thought of you being Jimmy's sister that got me on the plane, not your father's threats.

He'd meant that, too. Nothing Senator Hamilton could have said would have made him budge if Jenna hadn't been Jimmy's sister.

I don't want to leave here without you, Jenna, not because of any threat your father made against Cobra, but because I wouldn't be able to live with myself if something happened to Jimmy's little sister.

He'd meant every word of that. When he'd arrived, he'd told her he would stay for a week. The week was up, but he couldn't leave her—not yet. There was still a chance that what she'd done would blow up in her face. Also, the package he'd asked Corbray to ship to Mazar-e-Sharif hadn't yet arrived.

Yeah, whatever. It was all a bunch of excuses. The truth was that he wanted to be close to her. What the hell was the matter with him?

Sure, he was attracted to her. He found a lot of women sexually attractive. But he'd never done this kind of shit on the job before.

Fuck.

Maybe it was natural for him to feel drawn to her. She *was* Jimmy's little sister. There was a strong family resemblance, and some of the things she did and said reminded Derek of Jimmy.

When did you ever want to get into Jimmy's pants?

Hell.

He levered himself upright, got up, and walked to the

bathroom to take a leak. On his way back, he spotted Dawar in the kitchen, sound asleep in front of the security monitors. He walked over, gave the kid a nudge.

Dawar jerked upright, saw Derek, and his eyes went wide. "Sorry. I didn't mean to fall asleep. Will you tell Farzad?"

"Not unless it happens again. Security cameras are worthless if no one pays attention to the monitor."

Rather than trying to sleep again, Derek laced up his boots, grabbed his parka, and walk through the cold and dark to his Land Cruiser. It was almost five in the afternoon in Washington, D.C. He might as well check in with Corbray. He had to ask about the package—and explain that he wouldn't be heading back to the U.S. any time soon.

"I was going to call you," Corbray said. "Hamilton fired us. We're off the case. You can pack up and head home."

"I can't. Not yet." He brought Corbray up to date on what Jenna had done and the Mullah's visit. "I'll stay until I'm certain this has blown over and cover the cost myself."

Corbray narrowed his eyes. "Is something else going on here?"

"Like what?" Derek played stupid, but he knew what Corbray was asking.

"Like you and Ms. Hamilton."

"Hell, no. She's the sister of a buddy who took bullets for me. I want to make sure she's truly safe. And let's keep this whole fired thing between us for now."

"Right."

8

Jenna hurried to her room, pulled off her headscarf, and brushed her hair. Not that Derek would see it, but still. When it gleamed, she brushed her teeth, put on a touch of mascara and some lip gloss to add color, and tied on her headscarf again.

She checked her reflection.

Oh, who was she fooling? No man would find her pretty dressed like this. She looked like a nun.

You don't have time for this.

Derek was probably already waiting. He had texted her and asked her to meet him during evening prayers because he had a surprise for her. He hadn't given her any hints, so her imagination had run wild.

Chocolate? Hand cream? A book or DVD from home?

No, that wasn't Derek. The surprise was probably her very own Kevlar vest.

Buzzing with anticipation, she grabbed her coat and hurried out the back door.

Derek stood there, bundled into his parka, hands in his

pockets, the last rays of the sun turning the stubble on his jaw to copper. "Hey."

"Are you growing a beard?"

He grinned—a smile that gave her belly flutters. "I need to blend in."

Jenna laughed. "I haven't seen many Afghans with red beards."

"You'd be surprised." He scratched his jaw. "This damned stuff itches. Come."

"Where are we going?"

"Nowhere."

That was mysterious. "Nowhere?"

They walked around to the back of the hospital toward the big shed that housed the emergency generator. He opened the door, held it for her.

"The generator shed?" She'd never been here.

She stepped inside to find an old wooden table with chairs sitting in the center of the available floor space, an elegant Afghan rug beneath them. The shed was heated, probably to keep the generator, which dominated the room, from freezing over.

He slipped out of his parka, revealing a firearm in a shoulder holster. "You said you wanted to find a place where we could talk and where you could be yourself. I told Farzad we wanted to spend a little time as a family where you could let your hair down, so to speak, and he asked an uncle to bring a rug and some furniture."

"Oh! That was so sweet of him—and you." Jenna stared up at Derek. "Does this mean I can take off my headscarf and tunic?"

"That's exactly what it means." He reached over and locked the door.

Jenna pulled off the headscarf and shook her hair free,

then unzipped her parka and unbuttoned her gray tunic, draping both over a chair. If she'd known this was going to happen, she'd have worn something nice—a blouse and a bra at least. Now, she stood, braless, in a black T-shirt and gray leggings.

It had been a long time since a man had seen her like this. "Wow. I feel naked."

His gaze moved slowly over her, stopping at her breasts. "You don't look naked."

Her nipples drew tight. "This is a great surprise. Thank you."

He looked at her like she was nuts. "This isn't the surprise."

He pulled out a chair for her, so she sat, her anticipation growing.

He removed his parka and sat across from her, a small box in his hand. "This rightfully belongs to you. I kept it because I didn't want your father to have it."

He handed her the box, watching while she opened it.

Jenna stared, stunned. "Oh!"

Tears blurred her vision, and her throat went tight.

James' dog tags sat on top of an old photograph of her, one that her brother must have carried with him when he'd been deployed.

"Jimmy couldn't stand your old man. When he was killed, I felt he would want me to take care of these and not let your father have them. For the rest of that deployment, I wore his tags together with my own. Now I can give them to you."

Jenna took the dog tags from the box, ran her fingers over her brother's name, pain lancing through her chest.

HAMILTON, JAMES R.

Then she picked up the photo, found herself smiling,

tears streaming down her cheeks. "I was twelve in this photo. James took me to the zoo when he was home on leave. I had just seen the giraffes."

"He called you Punk."

Jenna swallowed the lump in her throat. "I was almost eighteen when he died. My father didn't tell me. I got the news when a reporter called our home and asked for a comment. I was devastated. When I confronted my father, he said he didn't want the news to spoil my SAT scores."

"I'm sorry."

"That's how he works. He never told me that my mother died by suicide. I learned that from James when I was fifteen. I thought she'd died in a car crash."

"What an asshole."

"He blamed you for James' death."

"I'm not surprised."

"He learned all he could about you and told me that James had died for nothing, that he'd given his life to save a nobody." Jenna's gaze jerked to Derek's, blood rushing to her head. "I'm sorry. I shouldn't have told you that."

Derek didn't seem to feel insulted. "It's true. I am a nobody. I grew up in the foster system until I was old enough to join the army. I have no family, no ties."

"That sounds lonely. Where are your parents?"

"I don't think anyone knows who my father is, but my mother died of an overdose when I was a toddler." There were shadows in Derek's eyes, but he spoke as if none of it mattered. "Someone found me next to her corpse in an alley."

"I'm so, so sorry."

"Don't be. I don't remember it. What I do remember is foster parents who were drunk or a bit too eager to hit me with a belt. One of my foster fathers beat the shit out of me when I refused to suck his dick."

"God, Derek, that's awful."

"I ran away, but the cops found me and brought me back, and he beat me again. I told them what had happened, but the cops thought I was lying. So, yeah, your father was right about me."

"No, he wasn't. None of that was your fault. Did you have friends at least?"

"Jimmy was my first close friend—and the best friend I've ever had."

"Can you tell me what happened? How did my brother die?"

DEREK DIDN'T KNOW why he was telling Jenna all of this. He'd never shared the truth about his past with any woman. He especially didn't want to talk about the day Jimmy had died, but that was the one thing Jenna deserved to know.

"We'd been working in Kandahar for a while, moving back and forth behind enemy lines. We were patrolling an area in the Sulaiman Mountains, looking for some caves where AQ shitheads were supposedly hiding. I was ahead of Jimmy when I heard your brother shout, 'Sniper!' I don't know how he spotted him—the glint of sunlight on the sniper's scope maybe. He slammed me to the ground, knocking the breath from my lungs. Then ..."

Rat-at-at-at!

Derek thrust all emotion aside. "Then the sniper opened fire as we fell. Your brother ended up taking four or five rounds meant for me. They penetrated his helmet, blew his skull apart. He died instantly."

Derek could still smell the blood, feel Jimmy's weight on his back.

Something warm touched his hand.

Jenna.

She watched him through green eyes filled with tears—and worry. "I'm sorry. I shouldn't have asked. I shouldn't have made you relive that."

Derek twined his fingers through hers, her touch bringing him back. "You deserve to know the kind of man your brother was. He was a hard charger, a true warrior, a credit to the uniform."

Jenna's face twisted with grief, tears streaming down her cheeks. "I'm glad he didn't suffer. After I became a nurse, I... I wondered how bad it had been."

"I don't think he felt a thing." Derek rubbed a hand over his right cheek. "When I hit the ground, I struck my face on a rock and fractured my cheekbone. I came close to losing consciousness. When my head cleared, I saw blood on my arms and on the snow around me. For a moment, I thought I'd taken a round to the face. Then I realized Jimmy was on top of me, and he wasn't moving. Our guys took out the sniper."

"I didn't realize you were hurt, too."

"I had one hell of a black eye. It was the last thing your brother gave me." Derek had savored that pain, his fractured cheekbone a parting gift from a brother, a gift that had meant life. "I know it sounds crazy, but I was sad to see the bruise go."

"That doesn't sound crazy to me." Jenna wiped her tears away with her free hand. "I wish I'd gotten to know him as an adult. I was so much younger than he was."

"You know the army awarded him the Silver Star, right?"

"Oh, yes. In private, my father seethed because he

thought James had died for nothing. But on the campaign trail, he wore James' medal and bragged about his heroic son who'd died to save another soldier and earned a Silver Star. It made me sick."

Senator Hamilton was a hypocritical piece of shit.

Jenna looked down at the photo again. "Did you find them?"

"Who?"

"The bastards hiding in the caves, the sniper's buddies."

Derek nodded. "We found them, and we sent them to hell."

"Good." Jenna's face crumpled again.

"Hey." Derek released her hand, got to his feet, and went to sit in the chair beside hers. "Come here."

He drew her into his arms, her sweet floral scent filling his nostrils as her head came to rest against his chest. He stroked her hair, savoring the feminine feel of her.

"He adored you. He told me so many stories about his little Punk. How you'd broken your ankle in soccer tryouts and your father had forbidden you to play. How you'd thrown up in your father's lap when he'd forced you to eat escargot at some fancy restaurant. How you got sick of your dad telling you how to wear your hair and cut it yourself with a pair of kitchen scissors."

Jenna sniffed, laughed. "My father was so angry. It looked awful, but I loved it."

Derek wanted to comfort her somehow. "Jimmy was the closest thing I ever had to a real brother, but you and he shared a special bond. Now you share Afghanistan. He would be proud of you—I know he would."

Jenna looked up at him, her cheeks wet. "We share one other thing—*you*."

Derek told himself not to do it. She was Jimmy's little

sister, and she was crying. They were in rural Afghanistan, pretending to be brother and sister. He was on the job, for God's sake. Hell, she *was* the job.

But then she reached up and ran a hand over his cheek.

Aw, fuck it.

He shifted her in his arms, lowered his mouth to hers, and kissed her.

JENNA'S BODY came alive the moment Derek's lips touched hers, the sweet shock of it making her pulse go wild. He tasted her lips one at a time, teasing them with his tongue, nipping them with his teeth, sucking them into his mouth, paying attention to all the little details. The cleft in the center of her upper lip. The corners of her mouth. The curve of her lower lip.

Oh, she had always wanted to be kissed like this—slow, sensual, seductive.

She slid her arms around his neck, kissed him back. "*Derek.*"

A big hand fisted in her hair, angling her head to allow him better access, his tongue seeking hers. She met him stroke for stroke, the intensity of the kiss building until she could barely breathe. But it still wasn't enough.

Jenna pulled back, stood, and straddled him, bringing them face to face. She caught his cheeks between her hands, his stubble rough against her palms, his pupils dilated, his lips wet. Her gaze locked with his. "Kiss me."

This time, he crushed her against him with strong arms, that deliberate tenderness gone as he claimed her mouth with his, ravishing her in the best possible way. His strength was intoxicating, his body so much bigger than hers, his pecs hard against her breasts, the firearm he carried pressing into her ribs.

She wrested control away from him, biting down on his tongue, nipping his lips with hers, only to yield once again, savoring the sensation of being overpowered.

"God, Jenna." He slid the fingers of one hand into her hair, the other moving beneath her shirt to cup her right breast. Pleasure made her gasp as he squeezed, his thumb teasing her already tight nipple. "You fill my hand."

She pressed her breast deeper into his callused palm, arousal pooling in her belly, making her ache, driving her hips forward.

Beneath his jeans, he was rock hard.

God, she wanted his cock inside her. It had been six months since she'd had an orgasm, even longer since she'd been with a man.

She had an IUD, a precaution against sexual assault, but did she really want to have sex with James' best friend in a generator shed in Afghanistan?

Abso-freaking-lutely.

Craving release, she ground herself against the hard ridge of his erection, but the pressure only made her need for him sharper.

With a moan, he tugged up her T-shirt and lowered his mouth to one aching nipple and sucked.

"Oh!" Her head fell back, her hips pressing hard against his.

"Can you get off like this?" His voice was deep, rough.

"I-I don't know."

"How about I help?" He yanked down her zipper, slid a hand inside her panties to cup her, his fingers finding and teasing her clit. Oh, he knew what he was doing. Give the man an A for female sexual anatomy.

"You are so wet." He slid a finger inside her, gathering her moisture, using it to stroke her clit, playing with her. "How does that feel?"

"So... good." She moaned, her nails digging into his shoulders.

He found a rhythm, his hand working magic between her thighs until she hovered on the brink. She thrust against his hand, her body taking over, pleasure coiling tight inside her. She bit back a cry as orgasm washed through her, sweet and shimmering.

The light went out, darkness filling the space, cutting short her bliss.

They both froze, Jenna's heart slamming in her chest, the space silent apart from their rapid breathing. Derek moved her off his lap, pushed her behind him, hand moving to his firearm.

Click.

The roar of the generator as it kicked on made Jenna shriek. She covered her ears.

The power had gone out.

Great.

"We need to go!" Derek shouted, zipping her jeans.

Jenna reached for her tunic and headscarf, the fabric of her T-shirt rubbing against aching nipples, the last ripples of her climax still fluttering through her belly.

"I'll go out first!" He drew the pistol out of his shoulder holster.

She nodded to show him she'd understood, buttoning her tunic and tying her headscarf in place with trembling fingers. She took the box with James' dog tags and the photo and shoved it into her pocket.

When she was ready, he unlocked the door and stepped outside, weapon in hand.

She waited, hands covering her ears until the door opened again and he motioned her outside. She stepped out into the dark and closed the heavy steel door behind her, cold wind hitting her in the face, her ears ringing. "Sorry."

It was so quiet out here.

In the dark, she couldn't read his expression. "Sorry for what?"

"Well, I did ... but *you* didn't."

He leaned down close and whispered in her ear. "If you don't think I enjoyed watching you get off, you're wrong. You look sexy as fuck when you come."

Jenna's breath caught in her throat. "Really?"

No man had ever said anything like that to her before.

"Hell, yes." Derek caught her arm with his, and they walked together around the hospital building toward the back door, boots crunching in the snow.

"You're not sorry?"

"I should be, but I'm not. We need to be careful, Jenna. This isn't a game."

No, it wasn't. If they'd been caught...

Jenna wished she didn't have to say goodnight. But he couldn't come inside, and she needed to get back to work.

"Goodnight." She rose onto her toes and kissed his cheek as a sister should. "Thank you for the surprise. It means a lot to me to have something that belonged to James. And thanks for the... uh... family time, too, Mr. Magic Fingers."

With that, she turned and keyed herself inside, her heart singing.

9

Derek sat in the Land Cruiser, his body aching with sexual frustration while he tried to write the daily report for Cobra HQ. What the hell was he supposed to say?

Brought subject into generator shed, gave away my greatest tactical advantage without seeking gain, then kissed her, got her off, and left the shed with a hard-on.

Yeah, no.

If Derek had wanted a plan to ensure that he fucked up this job completely, that plan would look something like this past week. He hadn't managed to persuade Jenna into coming back to the U.S., but he had made out with her and given away his strongest leverage without using it to his advantage.

Jimmy's dog tags and the photo were supposed to be the breaking point, the moment when this softer approach turned into hardball, pushing Jenna's emotions to the edge. But Derek had handed her the dog tags and the photo without saying the things he'd planned to say.

Your brother wouldn't want you to die here, too. He would

want to know that his Punk was far away from danger. Please come back with me, Jenna—for Jimmy's sake.

No, he hadn't said it.

Instead, he'd told her things he'd never told anyone, whining about his childhood, explaining to her how Jimmy had died. Then he'd tried to comfort her, kissed her mouth and her breasts, and given her a hand job. Would it make any difference if he explained in his report that her breasts were amazing?

He didn't think so.

Operatives did *not* get sexually involved with people under their protection. Derek had helped write the damned rule book. If any other Cobra operative had done this sort of shit, Derek would fire him—or her—on the spot.

The really fucked-up part of this was that Derek knew he wasn't finished.

He wanted her. He wanted Jenna.

The need for her burned through him, leaving him horny and grouchy and strangely off-balance. He could still taste her, smell her, feel the satin of those lush breasts in his hands, see the expression of bliss on her face when she'd come.

What the *hell* was wrong with him?

He'd never been the kind of man who got turned inside out by women. He'd always been able to control his emotions and to separate his mind from his body when his body became a liability from physical pain, hunger, thirst, exhaustion, or sheer horniness. He'd taken pride in his ability to get people to do what he needed them to do through whatever means necessary—charm, fear, threats, violence. Hell, during his military years, he'd talked young Afghan men into betraying their AQ and Taliban relatives. What was so difficult about this job?

Jenna.

Somehow, she'd gotten under his skin. Maybe it was just the fact that she was Jimmy's little sister, or maybe—

The crunch of boots on snow brought his head around.

Farzad walked up to the window, his expression troubled.

Derek powered down the satellite connection on his iPad, slid the device into its locked drawer, and climbed out to see what Farzad needed.

"Two boys arrived at the gate. They say Daesh fighters attacked a village about twenty kilometers east of here, killing the men and raping the women and girls. Some of the women are pregnant and need help."

Daesh—the Arabic name for Islamic State and the name IS fighters hated most—were known to be in Afghanistan. That's where they'd gotten their start. Now that their so-called caliphate had fallen, fighters were fleeing wherever they could, stealing food and money, killing and raping fellow Muslims and non-Muslims alike. For all of their talk of Islam, IS was nothing more than a band of murdering thugs.

"How did the boys get away?"

"They said their mothers hid them. They walked all this way. We are feeding them now."

"Did they bring the injured women here?"

"They say the women are too afraid to come because they feel shame. They want us to send midwives to the village."

Derek's first impulse was to tell Farzad that hell would freeze over before he would allow Jenna to leave this compound, but he bit his tongue. He wasn't in charge here. "What do you think?"

"It would be dangerous to go to the village. Daesh might

return, or we might be ambushed on the road. We would have to send some men to protect the women. But we can't send many, or we'll leave the hospital vulnerable. For all we know, those sons of pigs could be headed our way next."

"I agree." Derek was glad Farzad saw it his way. "It would be far too dangerous to send the midwives to the village, and it would be foolish to divide our numbers and leave the hospital more open to attack."

"Can you speak to your sister, ask her what she and the others wish to do?"

Wait. *What?*

A part of Derek wanted to tell Farzad that he wouldn't let Jenna go no matter what she wanted to do. But then he'd be just like her father, denying her the freedom to make her own choices. And yet if she went, she'd be putting herself and whoever went with her in grave danger.

Hamzad strode up, spoke to Farzad. "It is the right thing to do. These are our people, our women, Afghan women. I volunteer to go. I am not afraid of Daesh."

Farzad turned back to Derek. "Please tell your sister."

"I'll ask her."

He knew what she would say.

~

"I'll go." Jenna had experience in treating sexual assault victims. "Marie, you should stay. Delara, you, too, in case Marie needs you in the OR."

Delara looked both relieved and guilty. "You shouldn't deal with all of it alone. You don't know how many victims there are or how serious their injuries are."

"I'll be fine." Jenna sent Derek a text message to meet her by the back door in ten minutes and started filling a mobile medical kit with supplies. "I'll need a vial of ceftriaxone and syringes."

Ceftriaxone could prevent a rape victim from contracting gonorrhea and other bacterial STIs. But if they were going to give these women the same quality of care they'd get in the U.S., they would also need to bring HepB vaccines, a week's supply of prophylactic medication for HIV, as well as vaginal suture kits, pain medication, sedatives, and Ovral to prevent pregnancy. She ought to take a Doppler, too, as well as other OB supplies just in case one of the pregnant women in the village delivered while Jenna was there.

She put the medical supplies near the back door then made a quick dash to her room to gather a bag of essential supplies for herself—soap, her hairbrush, toothbrush and toothpaste, a change of clothes. She grabbed her parka, her gaze landing on the box with James' dog tags and the photo inside.

She lifted the dog tags out of the box and slipped the ball chain over her head, tucking it inside her T-shirt. "You're coming with me, big brother."

Outside, Derek was waiting for her, his lips a grim line. He spoke in English. "This is dangerous, Jenna."

She'd known he wouldn't want her to go. "I'm just doing my job."

"If we run into anything that hints at trouble, I turn this vehicle around. Got it?"

"Got it."

He picked up her duffel and loaded it with the boxes of supplies in the back of his Land Cruiser, switching to Dari. "You will ride with me. Hamzad and a few of the men will be just ahead of us, making sure the way is safe."

She climbed into the back seat, and buckled in, while

Derek made a call on his satellite phone. Then he held out a dark, heavy bundle of ... something.

"Put this on over your T-shirt."

A Kevlar vest.

Good God.

She peeled off her clothes down to her T-shirt, strapped into the body armor, and put on her tunic and parka again.

Derek got into the driver's seat and started the engine. The dashboard lit up with a display screen. "Cobra, this is Tower. The drone is five mikes out. Roger. Out."

Who was he talking to? "What drone?"

Derek pushed a button, and an eerie green image filled the screen. He glanced over his shoulder and found her staring. "We launched a drone from Mazar-e-Sharif when I learned where we'd be going. I want to make sure those IS assholes aren't lying in wait along the way."

"Wow." Rather than comforting her, this news drove home the danger they faced, making her pulse quicken. They were heading into an area where IS fighters were hiding with only an armored Land Cruiser, the hospital's old Humvee, and a handful of men to protect them.

If they were ambushed...

Had she made the right decision? Was she doing the right thing by putting all of them in danger? If she'd refused to come, they would all stay safe—or relatively safe—right here, rather than heading off into the unknown.

And what about the girls and women who were hurt?

Jenna couldn't turn her back on them.

They left the hospital, the Land Cruiser grinding its way over rutted dirt roads, headlights illuminating a rugged, snowy landscape, the tail lights of Hamzad's vehicle red in the distance. Derek communicated with someone via the mic in his helmet. It was all military-speak, none of it making a bit of sense to her.

It will be okay. Everything will be okay.

~

DEREK FOUND himself in a scene that was all too familiar. All of the adult males and older boys of the village lay dead in the snow, the eerie silence interrupted by the occasional wail of grief or child's crying.

If there was a hell, this was it.

Hamzad looked around, fury naked on his face. "When The Lion hears of this..."

Derek knew that Kazi would scour the countryside looking for the Daesh fighters who'd done this. He might be a petty tyrant with delusions of grandeur, but he was also a useful ally against terrorists. If he found these fighters, he would see them hanged.

"Let's move the bodies so their loved ones can wash them," Hamzad called to the other men. "We can prepare graves in the morning."

While Hamzad and the others moved the bodies of the dead, Derek followed Jenna to the homes of the women who needed help. He stayed outside, on watch, still in touch with the team in Mazar-e-Sharif. They monitored the visual feed from the drone, ready to give Derek advanced warning should anything move their way.

After close to forty minutes, Jenna stepped outside, clearly upset.

"A pregnant mother and her two daughters," she said. "The younger is only ten. They're in shock. I examined them, did what I could for them medically, and made them tea. I thought it might soothe them."

"It might."

"What are these women going to do?" Jenna looked up at him, distress in her eyes. "The men are all gone. How will they live in this world?"

"I don't know."

Life for widows, especially those who had no grown sons, was rough.

"I need to get to the others."

Derek moved with Jenna back and forth from house to house, remaining outside each door. His breath formed crystals in the air as the night grew colder, clouds hiding a waning moon.

It was almost midnight when Jenna finished.

"I don't know what else we can do for them." Jenna looked exhausted. "They need trauma counseling, but there's no one to provide that for them. One woman is due to deliver in a month. I tried to persuade her to bring her children and come back with us, but she can't handle that now."

"You can't fix everything, Jenna."

"Why would anyone do this? These are simple people, farmers and shepherds. They have no money, nothing to steal. They don't want to be a part of any war. How can anyone just kill them? How can anyone rape pregnant women and little girls? These are their fellow Muslims."

"I don't know." Derek found himself wanting to hold her. "Some people have nothing inside them but hate. You need sleep."

While Hamzad and his men stayed in an abandoned home on the other end of the village, Derek stayed near Jenna as she settled in for the night with one of the pregnant victims and her children.

"I'll be out here."

"In the cold?"

"In the Land Cruiser. Do you have your phone?"

"Yes."

"Good." He took her hand, gave it a squeeze, aware that others might be watching. "You've done all you can. Try to rest."

She shook her head, looking defeated. "I've done nothing."

He wasn't going to argue with her. "Get inside where it's warmer."

Derek parked the Land Cruiser so that it blocked the gate to the home. If those Daesh fuckers wanted to get inside again, they'd have to go through him.

He checked in with the team in Mazar-e-Sharif. "Cobra, this is Tower. I'm going to get some shut-eye. Over."

"Tower, this is Cobra. Sweet dreams. Out."

Then Derek checked his weapons, unzipped a sub-zero sleeping bag, and tilted the seat back, using the open sleeping bag like a blanket. But sleep was slow in coming.

~

JENNA LAY AWAKE in the darkness, the day's horrors stuck in her mind. Bruised and swollen vulva. Teeth marks on budding breasts. Vaginal lacerations.

The youngest victim had been only seven.

From the other side of the room came the sound of quiet weeping.

Jenna's heart broke.

~

Jenna stood in the back of the cemetery with Derek, tears in her eyes, the cold pinching her cheeks and biting through the soles of her shoes. Hamzad and his men joined with men from neighboring villages to say the funeral prayers for those who'd been murdered, the victims' grandmothers, mothers, wives, sisters, and daughters standing in the back in burqas and sobbing in their grief.

Life in this tiny village would never be the same.

The women of the village had woken early this morning, made breakfast for themselves, their guests, and their children, looking dazed by terror and grief. Then, while Hamzad and his men had dug thirty-six shallow graves through the snow, the women had washed the bodies of their loved ones, weeping over them and wrapping them in whatever cloth they had on hand that could act as a shroud.

By late afternoon, relatives from neighboring villages had begun to arrive, and Jenna had been relieved to see the survivors embraced by loved ones, who'd made food and cared for them. They'd spoken of the slaughter, but no one had said a word about the violence the women had suffered. Rape was a taboo subject here.

Hamzad had insisted they stay for the funerals out of respect.

Derek hadn't been happy. "The longer we stay out here, the more dangerous it is."

He stood beside her now, his gaze never resting, tension rolling off him, earpiece still in his ear.

In the cemetery, the bodies were lifted and placed by male relatives on their right sides in the graves so that their faces were turned toward Mecca. Then dirt was thrown in to cover them, first in ceremonial handfuls and then by the shovelful.

When at last the burials had ended, Derek started back toward the Land Cruiser. "Let's go."

As before, Hamzad and his men led the way, Derek following at a distance.

Exhausted, Jenna fought to stay awake, the motion of the Land Cruiser lulling her to sleep. She jerked awake when the vehicle came to a sudden stop.

"Hang on!" Derek shouted.

He threw the Land Cruiser into reverse, slammed on the gas, and drove backward—fast.

"What's happening?"

"The drone spotted a reception committee waiting for us up ahead—several large vehicles blocking the road."

A reception committee?

Her heart gave a hard knock. "Is it Daesh?"

"Let's not find out."

"What about Hamzad and the men?"

"I'm not here to protect Hamzad."

"Are we going back to the village?" Jenna wanted to know his plan.

"No—and no more questions."

Jenna looked back over her shoulder, searching for someplace Derek might be able to hide the vehicle. If they kept going backward, they would end up in the village. What was to stop whoever was blocking the road from finding them there?

Then she saw it—tire tracks through the snow.

There was a road there, heading off to the east.

"Cobra, this is Tower. Good copy, out." Derek shot past the junction, slammed on the brakes, then threw the Land Cruiser into gear again. He turned left, leading them off to the east.

"What if they follow us?" The words were out before she remembered that he didn't want her asking questions.

He met her gaze in the rearview mirror. "They already are."

10

Derek should never have agreed to bring Jenna out here. He'd known it was too damned dangerous. IS and Taliban fighters were roaming the area. Militias, too. It had gone against every instinct he had, and he'd accepted her decision anyway.

You've gone soft.

He drove as safely and as quickly as he could, guided by the operatives watching the drone feed. If he slid off the road into a ditch, they would be fucked and beyond help. It would take a helicopter an hour to get airborne and most of an hour to reach them.

"Jenna, you've got your sat phone, right?"

"Yes."

"Keep that on your body somewhere—inside your bra or something."

"I-I'm not wearing a bra."

Right. He knew that.

Shit.

"If it looks like we're going to be taken, hide it in your

underwear or socks. Don't leave it in your pocket. As long as it's on you, Cobra can find you."

"Won't you be with me?"

McManus spoke in Derek's ear again, his Scottish accent thick. "Tower, this is Cobra. There's a hill to your left that's high enough to conceal the vehicle. If you can, pull off the road *now*. How copy, over?"

"Cobra, this is Tower. Good copy, over." He veered to the left, hoping the snow wasn't deep.

And there they sat for two long minutes.

He looked over his shoulder, saw the fear on Jenna's face, and reached back to take her hand. He couldn't promise her that everything would turn out okay. "If we're taken, they'll separate us. I'm doing everything I can to make sure they don't catch up with us, but if they do, I want you to be prepared to be rescued."

McManus spoke again. "Tower, this is Cobra. Enemy QRF has passed the intersection and is continuin' south toward the village, over."

"Cobra, this is Tower. Copy that. Out." It was the break Derek had hoped for.

He released her hand, turned around, and drove back toward the main road, doing the best he could to stay in his tire tracks.

"What are you doing?"

He had enough to deal with listening to McManus in his earpiece. "Cobra, this is Tower. I'm backtracking to the main road. Warn me if they turn around, over."

"Tower, this is Cobra. Wilco. Out."

It was a gamble, but he couldn't be sure he had enough fuel to head into the countryside of Afghanistan without a clear route home. If they got a flat tire or ran out of fuel out here, they'd be stuck and vulnerable until Cobra could mount a rescue. Also, he'd seen the tire tracks. They'd looked fresh. He couldn't be sure that they hadn't been left by the Daesh fighters who had attacked the village.

This was their best bet. With any luck, they would be well on their way to Mazar-e-Sharif before their pursuers realized they hadn't gone back to the village. If they were *really* lucky, the bastards would spot their tracks on the side road and waste time searching for them there.

Derek turned onto the main road and headed north again, pushing the speed as much as he safely could.

"Tower, this is Cobra. One of the vehicles is turnin' around," McManus said. "It's Hamzad, over."

"Cobra, this is Tower. Copy that." Derek would bet that Hamzad was involved in this. He'd pushed them to go to the village. "What are the others doing, over?"

"Tower, this is Cobra. Enemy QRF is continuin' toward the village, over."

A few minutes later, McManus told Derek that Hamzad had stopped at the side road. "He's spotted your tracks, and he's takin' the bait, over."

Derek wasn't at all surprised when the other vehicles turned around a moment later and met Hamzad there before heading off to pursue the Land Cruiser's tracks.

The bastard had sold them out—that much was clear—but to whom? IS? The Taliban? One of the militias? And who was their target—Derek or Jenna?

He would rather not find out—not out here.

Derek pushed the Land Cruiser to go faster. He had close to three-quarters of a tank of gas now, plus another tankful in cans. That would be enough to get them to Mazar-e-Sharif.

Jenna didn't know it yet, but he wasn't taking her back to the hospital.

~

JENNA HAD to resist the urge to look over her shoulder. She told herself that Derek was in touch with his men, that they had a drone overhead, that he would warn her if their situation went from bad to worse. But knowing all of that didn't make her any less afraid.

She tried to listen to every word he said, not that it all made sense to her.

"Cobra, this is Tower. Enemy QRF five klicks behind us and heading our way. Acknowledged. Out."

Who were the QRF? What was a "klick"? Who was this enemy?

It had to be IS. They had attacked the village. They were known to be out here. Maybe they'd heard that Westerners were in the village and had come for them.

You don't know that.

"Cobra, this is Tower. Enemy QRF no longer in pursuit. Acknowledged. Out."

Thank God for that!

"Cobra, this is Tower. ETA to Mazar is forty-seven mikes. Out."

Mazar?

Blood rushed to Jenna's head together with the abrupt realization that they ought to have turned off the highway by now. They weren't going back to the hospital.

He was taking her to Mazar-e-Sharif.

Why hadn't he told her?

Your father wanted me to bring you home by force if you didn't come voluntarily.

No. No, Derek wouldn't do that. He'd told her father that he wouldn't abduct her.

Or did he only tell you that to win your trust?

James had once tried to explain what he did as a Green Beret.

"We go into enemy territory and learn what we can for the troops that follow. We make friends there, get people to trust us, and hope they will help us."

"What if no one wants to help you?"

"We do whatever we can to make *them want to help us."*

Jenna had later come to understand that their work included getting inside people's heads and using what they knew to manipulate people or even entire villages.

Was Derek manipulating her now?

Come to think of it, she hadn't seen the roadblock herself. She hadn't seen anyone following them. She didn't know for certain there was a drone. She hadn't heard the people talking to Derek. Could all of this be some kind of elaborate show to scare her and get her to agree to leave the country?

You're crazy.

But even as she dismissed the thought, doubt settled inside her.

Your father threatened to make trouble for us in the Senate Armed Services Committee if I don't bring you back.

"Why are we going to Mazar instead of the hospital? Why didn't you tell me?"

"I'm taking you where I know you'll be safe." Derek met her gaze in the rearview mirror. "I didn't tell you because I didn't want to waste time debating in a survival situation."

His words were sharp, his tone of voice making it clear that the discussion was over—and reminding her for a moment of her father.

Jenna felt an old familiar rage rise inside her. No one had the right to make decisions for her no matter what the situation. Shouldn't he have at least asked her what she thought?

By the time they reached Mazar-e-Sharif, Jenna was fuming. She said nothing as Derek drove them to a compound on the outskirts of the city surrounded by a high concrete wall and razor wire. A gray, steel gate opened to let them inside, where men stood guard with military rifles at the ready.

He parked in a secured underground garage beside a dozen other Land Cruisers like this one and other vehicles —pickup trucks, Jeeps, dirt bikes, ATVs, and some battered Toyota Corollas clearly meant to blend in on the streets.

"Bring your bag. I'll have someone come down for the rest of it." He pulled off his helmet and put it on the seat and then climbed out and grabbed a duffel from the back of the vehicle.

She jumped to the ground, went around to the back to get her bag. Now that the danger was over, Jenna didn't see the need to hold back. "You should have asked me before bringing me here. If this is all some elaborate ploy to get me out of Afghanistan, I'm going to be furious."

He glared down at her as if she were nuts. "You think I made all this up?"

"I didn't see the roadblock."

"You were asleep!"

"What about the QRF guys who were following us? They conveniently disappeared."

Derek shook his head, his blue eyes going cold. "You don't trust me."

Gear slung over his shoulder, he turned away, walked over to an elevator, and punched in a password. "The guys who were following us didn't come here because they went to *your* hospital."

Stunned, Jenna could only stare.

~

DEREK WASN'T USED to emotions he couldn't control. Right now, he wanted to punch something.

Did she hurt your feelings? Poor baby.

Any relief Derek had felt at reaching Cobra HQ with Jenna in one piece had vanished in the wake of her suspicions. She had all but accused him of lying to her and faking their entire escape. What the hell?

You should have explained the situation earlier. You know her history.

Yeah, okay, so her father had lied to her and manipulated her all of her life, but Derek wasn't her old man. She ought to trust him. He glanced back to find Jenna standing where he'd left her, staring at him through wide eyes.

"You coming, or would you rather try your luck on the streets?"

She hurried into the elevator. "What do you mean they went to the hospital?"

The elevator door opened, and they walked in.

"I mean exactly what I said. They turned off the highway and drove to the hospital. I expect that's where they thought we would go."

"Maybe it was someone from the hospital. Maybe—"

"Do any of the staff drive around in a convoy of armored Humvees with fixed machine guns?"

"Of course, not! They had machine guns?"

Rather than getting her settled in quarters, he led her to the operations room, where McManus and Cross were analyzing the drone footage on a bank of flat-screen monitors. McManus had served as an intel specialist with the SAS—Britain's Secret Air Service—while Cross was a former Navy SEAL coms specialist. Together, they made one hell of an intelligence team.

The two looked up, their gazes moving from Derek to Jenna, who technically wasn't allowed to be in here.

McManus covered his surprise, got to his feet. "I'm Quinn McManus, ma'am. Glad you're here wi' us and safe."

"Thank you."

Cross stood, held out a hand. "Alex Cross. Glad to see you safe, Ms. Hamilton. You, too, Tower, for what it's worth."

"Thanks." Derek set his duffel bag on the floor. "I'd like Ms. Hamilton to see the drone footage. Start with the roadblock."

"Yes, sir."

McManus gestured to his chair. "Sit here, lass."

"Thank you." Jenna set her bag down and sat, still wearing her headscarf.

McManus scrolled through the footage, pointed to the screen. "This is your Land Cruiser. This is the vehicle driven by that Hamzad character. See these? There are six vehicles clustered together, blockin' the road."

Jenna studied the screen. "Those are the QRFs? Who are they?"

"That means 'quick reaction force.' Bide just a wee, and I'll show you."

"'Bide a wee' means 'wait a minute,'" Cross told Jenna. "I've told McManus that he ought to learn English, but..."

"Shut your gob, you feckin' bawbag," McManus shot back. "Pardon, ma'am."

Jenna clearly had no idea what any of that meant. "That's fine."

McManus moved slowly through the footage. "Hamzad reaches the roadblock just after we warned Tower to start haulin' ass backward. Hamzad speaks wi' this fellow, who just got out of one of the vehicles, and it's more than two minutes before he realizes you're no longer behind him. When he sees you're no' comin', he sprints back to his vehicle, as does the man he was talkin' to. They all turn and drive south to find you."

Derek reached over and blew up one of the images to get a clear look at the face of Hamzad's contact. "Who is this fucker?"

"I'm glad you asked." Cross brought up a mug shot on another screen. "That's Alimjan Qassim, a Uyghur fighter. He spent eighteen months in Guantanamo before being released. Word is that he's leading one of Kazi's secret militias, doing the dirty work Kazi wants to be able to deny."

What the fuck?

Kazi was involved in this?

"How do we know they were after us? I met with Governor Kazi. He welcomed me and gave me his blessing to work here."

"I'll show you." McManus forwarded the drone footage again. "This is your vehicle. Here, you can see Qassim and his goons turnin' 'round when they get word from Hamzad about the tracks you left. Here's Hamzad. See? They were huntin' for you, and this Hamzad fellow was helpin'."

Derek blew up the image so Jenna could see Hamzad's face. "I was warned that he worked as Kazi's eyes and ears at the hospital."

"Maybe he saw or heard somethin' Kazi didn't like." McManus moved through the footage, showing Jenna when Qassim had realized his prey was gone. "He got back on the highway here, but he turned off toward the hospital. We followed him. He stopped just down the road and waited. Hamzad walked out of the compound at one point to talk wi' him, maybe to tell him you weren't there. Then Qassim drove off toward Mazar."

"Any questions, Ms. Hamilton? Or maybe you think all of this is part of my elaborate abduction scheme, too." Derek gestured toward the screens.

Jenna's face flushed scarlet. "No. Thank you. I'm sorry I doubted you."

Her apology did nothing to blunt his dark mood.

"You think we faked this?" Cross snorted, a big grin on his face. "Tower here is good, but he's not that good."

But McManus glared at Derek. "The lass has had a hard time of it. She's pure done in. Surely you can see that."

"Thank you all for working so hard to keep me safe." With that, Jenna picked up her duffel and walked out of the room.

"Does she know where she's goin'?" McManus asked.

Hell.

"Have someone from internal security meet me at the guest suite." Derek went after her. "Jenna!"

She stopped and turned toward him, distress mingled with exhaustion on her face.

"The barracks are this way." He led her down the hallway and to the east wing of the building. "I would never lie to you."

Why had he said that? He shouldn't have to defend himself.

"I really am sorry. You told me my father had paid you to take me out of Afghanistan by force and that he'd threatened your business, and I... I was afraid, and I guess I wasn't thinking clearly. I didn't mean to hurt you."

That's what you get for sharing your mission parameters.

Still, the regret in her voice eased some of his anger.

"Like you said, you didn't see any of it." He stopped outside the suite of rooms set aside for guests—Pentagon officials, members of Congress, foreign dignitaries. "You should be comfortable here until we can figure out what happened today. It's my expert opinion that you shouldn't return to the hospital until we know for certain whether Qassim and his men were after you."

She nodded, her expression troubled. "I'm letting them down. I've left them understaffed. They must be worried about me."

"I'll get in touch with Farzad and tell him what happened." The man needed to know about Qassim—and Hamzad.

Grant, head of Internal Security, strode toward them. "Hey, Tower. Welcome, Ms. Hamilton. I've got your keycard here. It's encoded to allow you access to authorized areas of the building—your suite, the mess hall, the gym, the laundry, the media room."

Jenna took the card from him. "Thank you."

"The bed is unmade," Grant told Derek. "We weren't expecting anyone."

"I'll handle it."

"I hope you'll be comfortable here, ma'am." Grant disappeared down the hall.

Jenna swiped her card, and the door opened with a buzz.

"You get settled. I'll be right back."

"Thanks."

When Derek returned, bedding in his arms, he found her sound asleep on the bare mattress, lashes dark against her cheeks, auburn hair fanned against the pillow, her headscarf clutched in one hand. He set the sheets and pillowcases on the nearby chest of drawers and covered her with the blanket. For a time, he stood there like an idiot, watching her sleep, an unfamiliar tenderness seeping in behind his sternum.

You're out of your mind, buddy.

Before he could do anything stupid, he left her room.

11

When Jenna woke the next morning, she had no idea where she was or what she was doing sleeping in her clothes on an unmade bed. Someone had put a blanket over her.

Derek.

Her heart plummeted as memories from yesterday crashed in on her. The terrifying flight from the village to Mazar-e-Sharif. The stupid things she'd said to Derek. The drone footage his men had shown her.

It's my expert opinion that you shouldn't return to the hospital until we know for certain whether Qassim and his men were after you.

Was this all fallout from her trying to save Behar's life?

She sat up, glanced first at her watch, and then around at the guest suite. Compared to her dorm room at the hospital it was luxurious—big, bright, and warm. There were windows set high on the walls so that no one could see inside or out, their glass thick and probably bulletproof. The queen-sized bed sat next to a nightstand. There was a chest of drawers, a desk, and a plush leather sofa. White concrete walls held framed photos of iconic events in U.S. history—President Lincoln at Gettysburg, General Pershing arriving in France in 1917, Marines raising the flag on Iwo Jima, firefighters climbing through the wreckage of the Twin Towers after 9/11.

She got out of bed and walked into the next room to find a white-tiled bathroom with a shower and a vanity. In the drawers, she found toiletries—small tubes of toothpaste, dental floss, disposable razors, men's shaving cream, shampoo, conditioner, body wash.

A shower.

She hadn't taken a shower since the morning before all of this started, the morning before she and Derek had kissed in the generator shed.

You did a lot more than kiss.

She didn't want to think about that now.

She found towels and washcloths in a cupboard under the sink and stripped out of her clothes, setting James' dog tags carefully on the counter. She put a razor, washcloth, and some toiletries on a shelf in the shower and turned on the water, delighted to feel it was hot. Then she stepped under the spray—and sighed with pleasure.

For a little while, she forgot she was far from the hospital at a paramilitary compound and that some jerk might be hunting for her.

When she dried off, she felt clean and much more like herself.

She hadn't brought a change of clothes, but the security guy who'd given her the keycard to her room had said there was a laundry room. Maybe she could borrow a T-shirt and jeans from someone until she was able to wash her things.

She wrapped herself in a towel, gathered her dirty clothes in her arms, and stepped out of the bathroom just as someone knocked. She tossed her clothes onto the bed and walked to the door. "Who is it?"

"It's Derek. I brought you some breakfast."

Jenna glanced at the pile of dirty clothes. She couldn't stand the idea of wearing them again. She opened the door and stepped back, holding tightly onto the towel.

Derek stood there dressed in a tan T-shirt and desert camo and carrying a tray that held orange juice, scrambled eggs, bacon, toast and...

She inhaled. "Oh, my God, is that real coffee?"

His gaze slid over her, as intimate as a caress. "You bet."

She hadn't had coffee since she'd left the U.S.

He carried the tray to the desk and set it down. "Did you get some sleep?"

"Yes. Thank you. You?"

"I'm good." He stepped back. "I'll let you dress and eat. I've scheduled a meeting for zero-eight-thirty."

"A meeting? Did you learn something new?"

"I went out to the hospital early this morning. I gave them the remaining medical supplies and told Farzad what had happened. The women boxed up your things. Everything is sitting here outside your door.

Boxed up her things? "But why—"

"You can't go back, Jenna. Farzad doesn't want you to come back."

Jenna's heart sank, the rejection painful. "Why not?"

"That's what the meeting's about. I'll meet you in the conference room then."

He left her alone.

She sat on her bed, the news like a punch to the gut. She'd set aside two years of her life to help train midwives so that Afghanistan could get on its feet again, but now...

Tears blurred her vision.

She hadn't even gotten to say goodbye.

~

DEREK DID his best to forget the sight of Jenna wearing only a towel and focus on the meeting. It wasn't easy, not with her sitting beside him looking good enough to eat. She wore a long-sleeved, dark blue V-neck tee that showed a hint of cleavage and jeans that hugged the curves of her luscious ass, her hair still damp, but uncovered and free. He could almost feel its silky strands on—

Get a damned grip!

He finished telling others what he'd learned this morning. "When Hamzad got back to the hospital, he wanted to know where Ms. Hamilton was. He didn't ask about me. He asked only about her. When he found out she hadn't returned, he told everyone that she and I are not brother and sister and that I'm a private military operative. Farzad warned me against either of us returning. He said that Hamzad had turned his men against her. He also said that if Qassim was looking for her, he couldn't protect her."

Jenna stared at him, clearly taken aback. "How could Hamzad know that? I swear I didn't tell anyone. I've never even spoken to him."

"Who in Afghanistan outside of this building knows who we are?"

Jenna's brow furrowed as she thought through this.

Cross answered for her. "Abdul Jawad Kazi."

Jenna looked from Cross to Derek. "Why would he send someone after me? He gave me his permission to work here."

"Kazi giveth, and Kazi taketh away," McManus said.

"Does this have to do with the night I shouted into the

waiting room? Or maybe he's angry because we pretended to be brother and sister."

Derek couldn't be sure. "I think we can assume that Kazi heard about that."

"It's no' like him to give a damn about such matters," McManus said.

Derek turned to Elizabeth Shields, a linguist and former CIA analyst. "Shields?"

"I have to agree with Quinn. Kazi doesn't care about moral issues. There's something bigger going on here. We've been trying to monitor his coms, but, as you know, that's become more difficult."

War had made Kazi a multi-millionaire. Whatever tech he couldn't get for free from the U.S. government, he bought from the Saudis or the Chinese.

Derek took another sip of coffee. "What we know for certain is that Qassim was searching for Jenna but made a point of staying out of sight. He didn't try to take her from the hospital. After the failed attempt this afternoon, he stopped down the road from the hospital where he couldn't be seen. What do we make of that?"

Levi Segal, a former counter-terrorism agent with Israeli Defense Forces and the head of their Middle East tactical team, spoke up. "He could be working for Kazi, as our sources claim, or he could be working for some unknown player on the side. Or maybe he's gone rogue. Regardless, the fact that he tried to acquire Ms. Hamilton while she was far from the hospital proves that he's keeping a low profile."

"My gut tells me Kazi is behind this," Shields said. "I don't think Qassim would risk his life by betraying his boss. You know what would happen to him if Kazi caught him moonlighting."

Kazi was merciless to those who betrayed him.

Shields' analysis made sense to Derek. "You think he's working for Kazi and that Kazi is trying to make sure that no one can tie him to whatever he has planned."

"I do."

Cross stood, walked to the coffee pot for a refill. "There is the possibility that Qassim and his men attacked that village, pretending to be IS fighters to lure Ms. Hamilton outside the compound walls."

Derek shook his head. "How could they know she'd be the one to volunteer? I think it's more likely that Hamzad took advantage of the situation created by IS fighters and told Qassim where she'd be. He pushed Farzad to agree to the trip and volunteered to go with us."

"So, Kazi ordered Qassim to abduct Jenna," McManus said. "I can believe that. But whatever for?"

Motive was the missing piece.

"What could Kazi want from me?" Jenna looked overwhelmed and confused. "This makes no sense."

For a moment, no one spoke.

Derek broke the silence. "Whatever his reasons, the prize has to be big for him to risk crossing swords with Cobra. If they had tried to take Ms. Hamilton from my vehicle, there would have been a firefight. He would have lost men, and I might have been killed or wounded. He must have known that and been ready to accept the consequences."

Cobra had been working in Afghanistan since the day its doors opened and had an amicable relationship with Kazi. Had that changed?

"Kazi is a snake," McManus said.

"It seems to me the most important thing is to get Ms. Hamilton out of the country," Segal said. "We can sort out Cobra's relationship with Kazi once she's beyond his reach.

Until then, she's vulnerable, and that means we're vulnerable as an organization."

Heads nodded—all except for Jenna's.

She looked lost, shell-shocked, miserable.

"I want a viable strategy for evacuating Ms. Hamilton by zero-eight-hundred tomorrow." Derek stood, ending the meeting.

The staff headed back to their desks.

Only Jenna remained. "I'm going back to the U.S., then?"

"I'm sorry, Jenna. I know it's not what you wanted." Derek walked over to her, sat on the edge of the conference table. "Before Kazi was named governor, he was a butcher. He killed our enemies, so the U.S. rewarded him and made him powerful. If he's willing to kill me to get to you, that's bad news."

Jenna got to her feet. "Thank you for saving my neck yesterday, but I don't want you or anyone else dying for my sake."

Derek stood, too. "None of this is your fault. Even if this is the result of what you did for that girl and her baby, it's not your fault. You came here with the best of intentions. You've saved lives. You've done more than most people."

She didn't look comforted by this. "Does Farzad think I'm evil now?"

Derek shook his head. "He cares about you, Jenna. He said he thought you were a brave woman. He wanted me to tell you goodbye and that they all wished you well."

Jenna's chin quivered, tears spilling down her cheeks. "I care about him, too."

Not knowing what to do, Derek drew her into his arms.

Cross stepped in. "Hey, boss, I ... Oh. Sorry."

Jenna drew away. "I'm going back to my room—if I can find the way."

Derek walked over to Cross, cleared his throat, fighting not to bite the guy's head off. "She's upset."

"I bet."

"What do you want?"

JENNA FOUND her way back to her room, sank onto her bed, and stared at the ceiling, tears running from the corners of her eyes and down her temples. She thought of Farzad, Marie and Delara, Lailoma and all of the other students. She would probably never see them again.

She'd come to feel at home there, despite the lukewarm showers and lack of coffee and the strangeness of wearing cover and not being able to speak to men. She'd been a part of something bigger than herself, part of an effort to save the lives of women and children and help Afghanistan recover from endless war.

Now, she would be heading back to the U.S. because of some freaking warlord. What did he want from her? What had she done to anger him? What would he do if he got a hold of her?

No one knew.

She wasn't afraid. Derek wouldn't let anything happen to her. She was surrounded by tons of concrete, steel, razor wire, and badass operatives. But it would at least be nice to know *why* this had happened.

What would she do now?

She could get a job almost anywhere. She'd sold her condo before she'd come over, putting the money into savings. She would have to find a job, buy a place, and start over. That's what she would have done eighteen months from now.

Stop feeling sorry for yourself.

It wasn't like her to brood or lie around, so she got up, made her bed, and unpacked her belongings. There, tucked carefully in one of the boxes, was the photo of her childhood self that Derek had given her, and beneath it was a note.

She opened it and recognized Marie's handwriting.

Dear Jenna,

We're all afraid for you and sad that you won't be coming back to us. The girls are heartbroken. I think you were their favorite teacher. I hope you and I can meet again one day, perhaps in Paris. Of all the midwives I've worked with during my almost two years here, you were the best. Your compassion and courage are an example to us all. Be well, and stay safe.

Marie

The tears started again, but this time they were bittersweet. She had learned so much from Marie and the people of Afghanistan—her students, Farzad, the women who came to the hospital and those she met in the villages. Working here had changed her, made her stronger, more resilient.

Before she'd come to Afghanistan, she'd thought a week with five births was a busy one. Here, she'd sometimes caught five babies in a single day. At home, she would never have gone a day without a shower or skipped wearing makeup. Here, she hadn't always had time for a shower, and she'd rarely put anything besides moisturizer on her skin. Even so, she'd never felt better about herself as a woman.

She put the precious letter together with the photo into

her bag where they would be safe, then finished unpacking. She had no idea how long she would be here, but she might as well make herself at home.

By lunchtime, she had everything squared away. She went in search of the mess hall. She still didn't know her way around, but she was starting to get it. Each room had a letter and number combination with the letter representing the room's purpose. So residential rooms had numbers that started with Rs, while the conference room's designation began with a C.

M-002.

M for mess hall?

She opened the door and stepped through—to find Derek naked in the shower.

Oh. My. God.

She knew she shouldn't look, but she couldn't help herself. Water sluiced over smooth skin and scars, his body all muscle from his pecs to an eight-pack to his powerful thighs, his nipples flat and brown. His perfect cock hung, thick and uncut, from a nest of light brown curls, his testicles heavy.

Stop looking at his junk, for God's sake!

"Do you need something?" He turned off the water, reached for a towel.

Heat rushed to her face—and her belly. "Sorry. I'm lust … *lost*. I thought the M was for 'Mess Hall.'"

"Men's Locker Room." He rubbed the towel over his chest and arms, making no effort to hide any part of himself from her.

"Got it. Shit. Okay. Sorry." She took a step backward.

"Jenna, it's okay." He was clearly fighting not to laugh. "I don't embarrass easily. I'm surprised you do, given your job."

"I work in women's healthcare, not penises. No, I ..." *Quit while you're behind.* "I'll see you later."

She hurried from the room, his voice following her out the door.

"The mess hall is down in the basement."

12

Derek dressed and went back to work, both amused at Jenna's reaction and uncomfortably horny. He couldn't get her off his mind—not when he had a private conference with Corbray, not when he read Pentagon intel reports on Qassim, not when he went to the shooting range for target practice specifically to get her out of his head.

How could any man forget an attractive woman checking him out with such blatant lust in her eyes? Yeah, she'd taken a good, hard look at him, her gaze fixing on his cock, and the expression on her face had been pure sexual hunger.

The fact that she'd gotten so flustered afterward was interesting, too. He would expect for a woman who worked in reproductive health care not to be fazed by dicks. But her face had flushed bright pink, and she'd said things she hadn't meant to say.

I'm lust...lost.

Yeah, she was lust all right—for him. He'd never gotten hung up on a woman like this. Sure, he'd been sexually attracted to a lot of women, but he didn't walk around thinking about them all fucking day.

I work in women's healthcare, not penises.

He'd almost lost it and started laughing at that point. She could have said men's healthcare or male reproductive healthcare or almost anything, but his dick had apparently been foremost on her mind. That was okay with him.

Maybe it was time to do something about this. They were adults, and they were hot for each other. Maybe the best thing for both of them would be to get it out of their systems by fucking each other's brains out.

She's Jimmy's little sister. You're her bodyguard. You're at a job site.

These were three excellent reasons to keep his dick in his pants. What kind of example would he set if he, one of Cobra's owners, broke the rules while on the job?

It's not like he could hide what was going on. He was in a building full of operatives and intel specialists. There were no secrets.

None of this was enough to keep him from shooting Jenna a text message that evening and offering to give her a tour of the place.

`I don't want you getting lost.`

No, it hadn't been necessary to add that last bit, but it had been fun.

`Where should I meet you?`

`I'll come to you.`

He went to her room, knocked.

She opened the door. "Hey."

For some reason he couldn't fathom, she had trouble meeting his gaze.

He tried not to grin. "You ready?"

He gave her the same tour he gave U.S. Senators, Pentagon officials, and presidents, sexual tension humming between them like a live wire. Somehow, he managed to stay on topic. "We have close to five hundred staff and operatives spread out over eight major operation centers around the world."

"Antarctica?"

He chuckled. "No."

He showed her the infirmary, the gym, the shooting range, the holding cells, and the weapons locker on the lower level. "This is all mission-critical gear. Our armorer makes sure it's ready to go at a moment's notice."

"Wow."

"You found the mess hall, I assume."

"Yes."

He showed her the barracks next, opening a vacant room so she could take a look.

"It looks like a prison cell."

"Nothing fancy—just a bed, a sink, and a toilet. Most operatives stay for just a week or so at a time."

She smiled up at him, finally making eye contact. "My room is much nicer."

"Wait till you see mine. I am the boss, you know." He led her to the elevator and up to the barracks. "Corbray and I use this room whenever one of us is here. He stays in D.C. most of the time to be close to Laura, his wife. He heads her protection detail."

"She was abducted by al-Qaeda, right?"

"Abducted, held prisoner for eighteen brutal months,

beaten, raped. They claimed she was dead. Corbray found her during a SEAL raid and brought her home. She barely knew who she was. She still gets the occasional death threat."

Laura Nilsson was one of the strongest people Derek knew.

"Poor woman! It's a wonder she didn't get pregnant."

Derek swiped his keycard but said nothing. It wasn't his story to tell.

He opened the door and stepped aside to let Jenna enter, biting back a grin at her surprise. "Home, sweet home."

"It looks like an office with a bed."

"That's pretty much what it is. I'm able to view all the security feeds and the monitors in the operations room, as well as communicate with all of our operations centers from here."

"So, you're able to work in your pajamas. That must be nice."

"I don't wear pajamas."

A hot blush stole into her cheeks, and she looked away. "I'm sorry about what happened earlier today."

"No, you're not." He wasn't going to let her off easy.

Her gaze jerked to his, outrage on her face. She opened her mouth to object, but he cut her off. He wouldn't play that game.

"People who are sorry don't stare. You're as attracted to me as I am to you. If the two of us weren't trying so hard to follow the damned rules, I'd be fucking you—"

He never finished because Jenna jumped into his arms—and kissed him.

~

THE FEEL of Derek's lips against Jenna's was like the answer to a prayer. If she'd had any fears that he might not take what she was offering, she forgot them when he crushed her against him, answering her kiss with his own, his little growl of approval an aphrodisiac. In a blink, she was high on him —the spicy scent of his skin, the hard feel of him, the heat of his lips on hers.

He scooped her into his arms, and carried her a few steps to his bed, the power of his body making her ovaries purr. He stretched out above her, his hips between her thighs, his gaze searching hers. "Are you sure?"

"*God, yes.*" She pulled her shirt over her head and dropped it on the floor to drive the point home, a shiver running through her when his gaze shifted to her bra.

Oh, how she wished she hadn't worn one today.

She started to unfasten the front clasp of her bra, but he caught her hands.

"Let me." She stretched her arms over her head, a gesture of surrender.

"God, Jenna." His brow furrowed, and he rocked back on his heels, his big hands cupping her breasts through lace. "I love your breasts."

He flicked her nipples with his thumbs, making them draw tight against the fabric, frissons of pleasure shooting through her, the fire in his gaze as arousing as his touch. Then he unfastened the clasp with a single quick motion, tugging off her bra and lowering his mouth to an aching nipple.

She moaned, arching to feed him more of her, every tug of his lips and flick of his tongue making her womb tighten and flooding her belly with liquid heat. She slid her fingers into his hair, his mouth moving from one nipple to the other and back again until she was all but writhing on the bed, months of suppressed sexual need unleashed.

Abruptly, he got to his feet, removed his holster and firearm, pulled his shirt over his head, and tossed it. Then he shucked his pants and, with them, his boots and socks, bending down to give her a glimpse of his amazing ass. And there it was—all of that beautiful male terrain she'd seen this morning.

This time, she let her gaze wander where it would—the bullet scar on his chest, the planes of his pecks, his broad shoulders, the bulges of his biceps, the ridges and valleys of his belly, the length of his impressive erection.

She needed to get out of her pants *right now*. She reached down with trembling hands to unzip her jeans, only too happy when Derek took over. He jerked them down her legs and tossed them onto the floor then stretched out beside her.

"God, you're beautiful." His gaze moved over her, the desire on his face making Jenna feel like the sexiest woman alive. He ran his hand from her breast to her inner thigh, teasing her with callused palms, tickling her with his fingertips, grazing her with his knuckles. "Your skin is so soft, like silk."

"Yours, too." She explored his chest, his light brown chest hair rasping against her palms, his nipples tightening beneath her fingers.

He kissed her then, slow and deep, his fingers finding her swollen clit, stroking her, driving her crazy. "I want to taste you."

"Help yourself." Did he think she was going to say no to oral sex?

He chuckled, a warm sound, then lowered his lips to her throat, nipping and licking his way down her body, kisses spreading fire over her skin. When he passed her navel, he grabbed a pillow and shoved it beneath her hips, raising her bottom off the bed.

She let her thighs fall open, exposing herself to him, holding nothing back.

He slid his hands down her inner thighs, his gaze fixed on her most private self, naked hunger on his face. "So sexy."

Jenna was barely able to breathe as he situated himself, his gaze meeting hers for a moment before he parted her lips—and sucked her clit into his mouth.

The breath left her lungs, her hips jerking at the sweet shock of it, her fingers curling in his hair. "Oh. My. *God.*"

It was bliss. It was torture. It was blowing her mind.

Jenna tried to relax, to savor it, but he was just too good at this, pleasure rising too fast for her to stay on top of it. She couldn't think, couldn't say a single coherent word, panting and moaning as Derek pushed her closer and closer to the brink with his lips and tongue, taking all of her into his mouth, suckling her. He slid a finger inside her, stretching her, stroking her.

Heat drew tight in her belly—and exploded.

She came with a cry, climax washing through her, drenching her in bliss, leaving her breathless and limp. She felt him tug the pillow out from beneath her hips and opened her eyes to find him smiling down at her, his pupils dilated, a cocky grin on his wet lips.

"I like how you taste." He reached for something—a condom.

Her heart melted. With most men, she had to ask.

She trusted him. "If you've been tested, you don't need that. I was tested before I came here, and I've got an IUD."

"I was tested three months ago—and I haven't been with

a woman since." He dropped the condom and bent her knees back, opening her to him.

She took hold of his cock, stroked its hard length, then guided him inside her.

"I want you, Jenna." He entered her with a single, silky thrust, filling her, stretching her, making her moan. His eyes went shut, breath leaving his lungs in a long, slow exhale. "*Christ.*"

Then he began to move.

DEREK HAD FORGOTTEN what it felt like to have sex without a condom. Jenna felt so good—slick, tight, hot. His head was filled with her, her taste fresh on his tongue, her scent all over his skin. But if he wasn't careful, he was going to embarrass himself. He was *not* a minute man.

Keep telling yourself that.

He opened his eyes, looked down at her sweet face, willing his body to relax, taking it slow and easy. He wanted to make her come again. He wanted to watch her face when climax hit her. He wanted to see her lose control.

But right now, he was the one on the brink.

She reached down to stroke herself, the sight of her fingers on her clit sending a shockwave of lust through him.

Holy hell.

He loved a woman who knew her own body and took what she needed. That didn't mean he didn't want to help.

"Let me." He canted his hips so that his pubic bone touched hers then ground himself against her in slow circles, his cock buried deep inside her.

"Oh!" Her response was immediate, her moan erotic, her

eyes drifting shut, her hands sliding up his arms to rest on his biceps.

Holding himself above her like this, he couldn't suckle her, those beautiful breasts with their dark nipples swaying just beyond the reach of his mouth. But he could see everything—his cock sliding in and out of her, the pink flush that stole over her skin, her swollen breasts with their puckered nipples, the carnal delight on her face.

She caught on quickly, moving with him, her hips matching his motions.

He fought the instinct to thrust, letting her take everything she needed, his body a tool for her sexual pleasure. Her breathing had gone ragged, every exhale a whimper now, her nails biting into his skin like ten tiny razors, the pain sweet.

"Oh, God, Derek!" Her eyes flew open, bliss lighting up her beautiful face, their gazes locking as she came.

Derek rode through it with her, keeping up the rhythm, his heart thudding in his chest, some emotion he couldn't name swelling behind his sternum.

He gave her a minute to recover, holding himself still inside her.

Her eyes drifted shut for a moment, then she looked up at him once more, a satisfied smile on her lips. "You're too far away. Come here."

She drew him down against her, kissing him hard on the mouth, running her hands over his back, locking her legs around his waist.

Derek let himself go. He started slow, need for her driving him until he was pounding into her, his self-control in tatters. His balls grew tight—and he shattered.

"*Jenna.*"

Orgasm hit him with the force of a backdraft, scorching through him, leaving him to float like ashes in the wind.

For a moment, they lay there together, out of breath, hearts beating in tandem.

Derek's awareness returned piece by piece—the soft feel of Jenna's breasts against his chest, the caress of her fingertips along his spine, the musky scent of sex. Only when his erection began to fade did he withdraw from her.

He lay down beside her, drew her into his arms, his body replete, his mind blank. She snuggled against him, her head pillowed on his shoulder, the fingers of one hand tracing idly through his chest hair.

"I've never come like that before. I've always had to take care of myself if I wanted to climax through vaginal penetration."

Derek grinned at her clinical word choice. "So, the brain surgeon is good with a scalpel but clueless with his dick."

Didn't it just figure?

Jenna laughed. "He wasn't all that good with people, either—just brains."

"Then I'm glad he's out of your life." Derek was surprised to realize he truly meant that. "You deserve better."

That was the last coherent thought Derek had before he drifted to sleep, Jenna warm and soft beside him.

Buzz. Buzz. Buzz.

He opened his eyes, Jenna sound asleep in his arms, and saw the light on his main viewing screen flashing.

Shit!

It was time for his evening strategy session with Corbray.

He climbed out of bed buck naked, leaving Jenna to sleep, and logged in, Corbray's face filling the screen. He tried to block the camera's view. "Can I call you back in ten?"

Jenna sat up, sleepy and confused, the sheet falling to her waist. "What … oh!"

She yanked the sheet up to her chin with the little shriek.

Corbray glared at him, his expression telling Derek that he'd seen it all. "Call me when you're alone—and, bro, put on some damned pants. *¡Madre de Dios!*"

13

Derek walked back to the bed, sat beside Jenna. "Sorry about that. That's Javier Corbray, my business partner."

"I figured." She let the sheet fall, reached out to rest her hand on his thigh. "Did I get you into trouble?"

"No, I did that myself." He shouldn't have answered.

Corbray had looked *pissed.*

"Please don't say you're sorry." There was a vulnerability on her face that tugged at him. "What we did meant something to me."

Derek knew he ought to feel guilty. He'd broken Cobra's rules, not only by having sex on the job but having sex with a client who also happened to be Jimmy's little sister. But all Derek could feel was a bone-deep sense of contentment.

You are so fucked.

"I'm not sorry." He brushed a strand of hair off her cheek, knowing he had to be honest now or risk hurting her later. "I enjoyed it, too."

Enjoy it? Hell, it had been the best first-time sex he'd ever had.

"Jenna, I don't do relationships. You need to understand that upfront. I don't want to mislead you or hurt you or make you think there's a future for us, because there isn't. I care about you. I always will. You're smart and beautiful, and you're incredible in bed. But I can't promise you—"

"Don't worry." She smiled. "I wasn't about to propose or anything."

He chuckled. "I need to call Corbray back. I'll walk you back to your room first."

He reached for his clothes and dressed, then strapped into his holster. He might look like he was ready to get back to work, but he smelled like Jenna.

She dressed quickly. "Will I see you again tonight?"

It was on the tip of his tongue to tell her that this couldn't happen again, that their having sex had been a one-off, but he didn't want to. "I'll be working late. We have a lot to do before the meeting tomorrow morning. I'll check on you afterward."

When she had finished dressing, he looked out into the corridor.

"Is the coast clear?"

"Yeah. Come." He led her to the elevator and down one floor, careful to watch what he said and fighting the urge to kiss her or at least hold her hand.

There were cameras in the elevators.

"Supper is served from eighteen-hundred to nineteen-thirty. If you hurry, you won't miss it. Do you know the way back to your room from here?"

"Yes." The elevator doors opened, and she stepped out, an oh-so-sexy smile stealing over her lips. "Thanks for the tour. That was ... *amazing*."

The doors slid shut, and for a moment Derek stood there like an idiot, forgetting to push the button.

Get it together, man.

He went back upstairs to his suite, splashed his face with cold water to clear away the lingering sex coma, and then logged into the system.

Corbray answered on the first ring. "That better not have been who I think it was, or you and I are going to have difficulties."

"Drop it."

"Nah, man, I can't. Jenna Hamilton is a *client*, for God's sake. We do not fuck our clients. That's in the rule book you helped write. If you break the rules, how can you expect to enforce them?"

"We were discreet."

"Discreet. Right." Corbray snorted. "You're in a compound with a bunch of intel experts and analysts. Do you think they don't know? You need to keep your head in the game, *cabrón*. What happens when you toss Ms. Hamilton aside like you always do with women when you've had enough? What happens if you break her heart and she runs to her daddy?"

Now Derek was angry.

Is Corbray hitting a little too close to home?

"She would never run to her father." And Derek didn't want to hurt her.

She wasn't like the others. She wasn't just the best first-time sex he'd ever had. There was something about her, something more than sex...

Are you listening to yourself?

Maybe Corbray was right. He needed to get his head back in the game.

He changed the subject. "If you've read the report from our meeting this morning, then you know we believe Kazi is behind this."

"If that's true, it's a big problem for us—and for her."

They'd built their primary base in Afghanistan in Mazar-e-Sharif because of their relationship with Kazi. They had millions of dollars of vehicles, computers, small arms, and other gear here. If Kazi had turned on them, they were in trouble.

"Our priority is getting Jenna ... Ms. Hamilton... out of the province and the country. We've got a strategy meeting tomorrow at oh-eight-hundred."

"I've called in some muscle to help. You're going to need more boots on the ground. And, Tower, make no mistake, if we lose Ms. Hamilton, we lose the company, and we're out of business for good."

No way in *hell* was Derek going to lose Jenna.

Corbray moved on, going through their current operations one by one. "Our security detail has cleared the embassy in Venezuela, so the diplomatic team will be arriving tomorrow."

The operatives in Jakarta had noticed an uptick in the number of former IS fighters trying to recruit in Indonesia and had reported it to the Pentagon. A U.S.-owned hotel in Kenya had requested security personnel and training in the wake of another terrorist attack in Nairobi.

Then Corbray dropped a bomb. "Holly is pregnant."

"What?"

"You know what that means, right—baby in the belly, bun in the oven?"

"I know what it means."

Corbray chuckled. "I was on the phone with Andris when Holly told him. She was in a complete panic, telling him she wanted an epidural. He told her she'd have to wait until she was having the baby for that."

Derek was happy for them. "No more deployments for her for a while."

"She's on light duty stateside, effective immediately. We need to select someone to fill in for her."

"Yeah. Right." That was going to be tough. "What else do you have for me?"

~

Jenna stood in the elevator on her way down to the mess hall, reliving the past couple of hours in her mind. The tug of Derek's mouth on her nipples. The rasp of his beard on her skin as he'd kissed his way down her body. The bliss of him going down on her, pounding into her. The rush of having all that man and muscle focused solely on her.

Don't forget the greatest orgasm ever.

No, she wouldn't forget that. How could she? Her body was still singing, the wetness between her thighs a sweet reminder of what they'd done.

Jenna was amazed that a man who'd spent his entire adult life at war could be so tender, so thorough, so damned good in bed. He was a fantasy come to life.

Lord, have mercy.

She knew her time with him was going to end sooner rather than later. She'd heard every word he'd said afterward. She knew that Derek wasn't the kind of guy who planned on settling down, and she had no idea where she'd be tomorrow. Once Cobra got her out of Afghanistan, she would probably never see him again.

That's a depressing thought.

It was the truth, and she needed to accept it.

The elevator stopped, and the doors opened.

She now knew her way around—mostly—and found

her way to the mess hall. It looked like most people had already come and gone, trays stacked neatly on top of trash bins, a few people sitting at the tables.

Jenna got a tray, silverware, and a plate and went through the line, asking for the spaghetti and then visiting the salad bar. She sat by herself near the door and had just spread her paper napkin on her lap when a woman she recognized from this morning's meeting walked up to her, tray in hand.

"Do you mind if I join you?"

"Please."

"I'm Elizabeth Shields. I was at the meeting this morning." Elizabeth didn't look like Jenna's idea of a CIA analyst, with her long, strawberry blond hair, pretty face, and blue eyes. Then again, what did Jenna know about the CIA?

"I remember."

Elizabeth picked up her fork. "So, you're a midwife. What's that like?"

Jenna described the work she did from well-woman checkups to prenatal care to STI screenings and contraception to attending births. Elizabeth listened and seemed fascinated by it, asking lots of questions, which Jenna answered as best she could. Before long, it felt like she and Elizabeth had known each other for years.

Then the conversation drifted from Jenna's work to her brother's time with the Green Berets and then to Derek. But it wasn't Jenna's place to tell Elizabeth how her brother had died saving Derek's life. That was Derek's story to tell.

Elizabeth leaned in. "Do you think he's handsome?"

Jenna stared at her. "Derek?"

"Who else? Come on. You can tell me. It's just us girls here."

"I … uh … Sure."

"Oh, come on. You've got a thing for him, and he's attracted to you, too."

Heat rushed into Jenna's cheeks.

Quinn McManus, the tall, redheaded Scotsman, walked up to them on his way to the food line. "Be careful when you're talkin' wi' Lilibet. She's a human intelligence expert. She'll have you sharin' your deepest secrets and thinkin' it was your idea."

Elizabeth glared at him. "We're just enjoying some female bonding time."

"Are you now?" With that, McManus turned and walked away, a grin on his rugged face. "Wi' you, it's hard to tell."

Jenna looked straight into Elizabeth's eyes. "Was this all a fishing expedition to get information about Derek?"

Elizabeth popped a cherry tomato into her mouth, chewed. "Oh, honey, we all know you two have a thing for each other. I've worked with Derek for a few years now, and I've never seen him look at any woman the way he looks at you. As for you, you're an open book. Every emotion you feel is right there on your face."

Jenna didn't like that. She didn't want to be anyone's open book, and she sure as hell didn't want to cause trouble for Derek.

She willed herself to laugh. "I guess your CIA radar is broken. Derek and I are just friends. Talking about my brother brought back a lot of memories for both of us. That's all it is."

Elizabeth gave Jenna a contrite smile. "Sorry. I don't mean to be nosy or make you uncomfortable. It's none of my business. We're the only women in this building, and I guess I miss having someone to talk to."

Jenna could understand that. "A lot of women would

envy you. You're surrounded by tall, ripped guys all day every day."

Oh, yes, Jenna had noticed. How could she not?

Quinn McManus with his red hair and beard and his Scottish swagger. Malik Jones with his short dark hair, expressive face, and coppery skin. Dylan Cruz with his mixed Afro-Latin features and faint Spanish accent. Connor O'Neal with his dark hair, poet's face, and blue eyes.

"True—they're hot." Elizabeth's gaze drifted to Quinn. "But I can't hook up with any of them, not if I want this job. They won't come near me."

Was that a rebuke of Derek for having sex with Jenna?

Jenna changed the subject. "How did you get into human intelligence?"

"I studied criminal justice and applied to the agency after graduation. I got accepted and went through aptitude testing. They decided I had the skill set for languages and human intelligence." Elizabeth glanced at her watch. "Shoot. I've got to go. I've got a meeting in five minutes. It was fun talking. Maybe we can have lunch tomorrow. I'm usually here right around noon."

Jenna didn't have anything else to do. "Sure."

Elizabeth flashed a bright smile. "See you then."

~

DEREK MADE his way toward Jenna's room, knowing with every step that he shouldn't be doing this. Corbray was right. He had no business getting it on with Jenna or any other woman right now. He had a job to do, and it didn't include doing her. It wasn't the easiest thing to remember with her scent still on his skin.

You just need to check on her.

Right. That was fair.

There wasn't much to do here—nothing that might interest Jenna, at any rate. He'd left her alone all evening, working late with his team, analyzing the options and looking for the best way to get Jenna safely out of Afghanistan and back to the U.S. There were so many unknowns.

Why did Kazi want her? How many men and resources was he willing to commit to acquiring her? Did Kazi know where Jenna was at this moment? What was Cobra's standing with Kazi? And although the intel wonks said there was a ninety-eight percent probability that Qassim had been acting on Kazi's orders, that still left a two-percent chance that he'd gone rogue or was working for someone else.

All of this had left Derek feeling uneasy—and far more protective of Jenna than he usually was where a client was concerned. This was no longer just another job. It had become personal. He wanted to beat the *fuck* out of Qassim—and Kazi.

He knocked on her door. "It's Derek."

Nothing.

He knocked again. "Jenna?"

"Coming!" She opened the door wearing a white bathrobe, her feet bare. "I just got out of the shower."

Stay where you are. Don't go into her room.

"I don't want to keep you. I just wanted to make sure you were okay. I wasn't around much this evening, and I know there's not a lot to do here."

"You're working on my behalf. I know that." She ran a hand through her hair, teasing out tangles. "I hung out with Elizabeth. We went to the gym and then watched 'Afghan Star'—that's their version of 'American Idol.'"

Derek knew what it was.

Tell her goodnight. Go.

"Can I come in?"

Way to go, buddy.

"I wish you would."

Yeah, you're a fucking idiot.

He stepped inside, shut the door behind him, locked it. "I've spent every minute since I left your side reminding myself of all the reasons I shouldn't come here. I'm working. You're Jimmy's little sister. You're my client. Soon, you'll be on a plane back to the U.S. I don't do relationships. I'm always overseas. That's my life."

"I know." She untied her robe, let it fall open. "The way I see it, all we have is right now. We might as well make the most of it."

The sight of her sent of a ragged bolt of lust shearing through him—those perfect breasts, the curve of her hips, the thatch of dark curls between her thighs. He had tasted all of it, and he wanted more, rules be damned.

He backed her up against the wall and kissed her—hard. She kissed him back, her urgency matching his.

She tugged down his zipper, took his half-hard cock in hand, her touch bringing him to fullness. "*Now.*"

He jerked her off her feet, wrapped her legs around his waist, and pushed himself inside her, thrusting hard.

It was like coming home.

She arched against the wall, shifting her hips so that his cock rubbed her clit with each thrust. "*Oh, yes.*"

He buried his face against the side of her throat, inhaling her scent, his hips thrusting hard, her inner muscles gripping his cock like a fist, her sweet whimpers urging him on.

Harder, faster.

Jenna. Jenna.

He wanted her, needed her, needed all of her.

Sharp nails digging into his back. The hot, slick feel of her. Her legs a vice around his waist. Her panting cries.

Oh, she felt so fucking good.

He fought to hold on, to last long enough to please her, but his control had frayed to a single thread, his balls already drawing tight.

She cried out, coming apart in his arms.

He was right behind her, moaning out his pleasure against her soft skin, losing himself inside her.

For a moment, they stayed as they were, both breathing hard, Derek's heart thrumming in his chest.

He raised his head, looked into her beautiful eyes.

She smiled. "Do you know how delicious it is to be held like this?"

"What do you mean?"

"When I'm in your arms, I feel feminine, protected."

So, she liked muscle. Good to know.

"I'd just like to point out that you *are* feminine, and you're in a security compound, so you *are* protected."

"Doing it up against a wall like this was on my sexual bucket list."

"I'm happy to help you cross it off." He withdrew from her and scooped her into his arms and carried her to the bed, knowing now that she would like that, too. "Maybe I should take a look at that bucket list—while we have some time."

14

Jenna could get used to this.

Derek carried her to the bed, sank to the mattress with her still in his arms, the two of them laughing and rolling together in the sheets.

Jenna came to rest on top of him and straddled his hips. "God, I love your body. You're like a Greek statue, except you're real. I just want to play with you."

He grinned, tucked an arm behind his head. "I won't stop you."

Jenna indulged herself. While he watched, she ran her hands over his pecs and abs, squeezed his biceps. "Your arm is bigger than both of mine together."

"Testosterone. It makes men big, strong, and stupid."

She laughed. "Women have testosterone, too, just not as much."

"Listen to you—the midwife. The next thing you'll tell me is that men have estrogen."

"They do, and their estrogen levels increase as they grow older."

He frowned. "That explains a few things."

Then Jenna had to ask. "Where did you get this scar?"

The scar was L-shaped and sat near his left hip bone.

"I did a HALO jump and got blown into a damned fence post."

"It's a good thing you weren't impaled." She kissed the big bullet scar on the right side of his chest. It was darker than the other scars, proof it was newer than the others. "This must have come close to killing you."

"I took a round trying to protect Laura and spent some time in ICU. They told me my heart stopped on the operating table. Obviously, they got it going again."

Thank God.

"What about this one?" She ran her fingertip along a thin white line below his ribs on the right side of his belly.

"Knife. Some Talib tried to gut me in a village outside of Jalalabad. He ended up dead. I got a dozen stitches."

"And this one?" She touched a finger to a gouge in his right shoulder.

"Bullet graze. Hurt like a son of a bitch." He took her hand, brought her fingers to his right cheek. "Do you feel that?"

Beneath his skin, there was a little indentation.

"That's where I broke my cheekbone. That came from Jimmy."

Jenna's throat went tight.

Derek ran a big hand up the bare skin of her arm. "I'm sorry. Did that make you sad? All the happiness just faded from your face."

"Yes, it made me sad, but not in the way you think. The brutality of war—it's written all over your body."

"A hazard of the job."

He might be able to brush it off, but she couldn't. "I hate knowing that you're in danger all the time, risking your life.

I mean, I know that's what you're doing for me—and I am grateful—but I wish your job were safer."

"We analyze the risks, and we do our best to manage them."

She stretched out on top of him, rested her head against his chest, his heart beating steadily beneath her ear, one strong arm coming to encircle her. "Have you ever thought of doing something else—something less dangerous?"

"Not really. I enlisted straight out of high school. I had no interest in college and no way to pay for it. I'm not sure I'd be good at anything else. I think being a loner made it easy for me to excel in special operations. I never had anyone to worry about, no one waiting at home for me to call, no one telling me not to go or holding me back."

She wanted to tell him that there could be more in his life than work and war, but she didn't want to come across as cloying. She tried to keep it light. "Well, if you're ever in Timbuktu or Hong Kong and you want to call someone to gossip or talk about whatever, feel free to call me."

"Thanks. I'll remember that." He kissed the top of her head. "What about you? What inspired you to be a midwife?"

"At first, I just wanted to be an RN. My father didn't like the idea. He thought it was beneath me."

"Which only made you want it more."

She smiled. "Exactly. While I was in school, I was drawn to labor and delivery. I loved the idea of helping women give birth safely and welcoming new life into the world. So, I got my master's degree in nursing and became a CNM—certified nurse midwife."

"You must like babies."

"There's nothing like holding a newborn—the little

sounds they make, their smells, their tiny fingers and fingernails."

"Do you want kids of your own?"

"One day—with the right man." For a second, she let herself imagine that Derek was the father. Her uterus contracted, clearly in favor of this idea.

He stroked her hair. "What a funny pair we make. You bring life into the world, and I take it out."

"I guess so."

She drifted off after that, waking briefly when he drew up the blankets. She snuggled deeper into him. "You're so warm."

He stroked her hair, kissed her again.

It was six in the morning when he left her, kissing her on the cheek. "Sleep, angel. I'll see you in a little while."

She was asleep again before he closed the door.

~

"MS. HAMILTON, this is Malik Jones, Connor O'Neal, and Dylan Cruz. Corbray sent them to bolster our operation here. Jones served as an Army Ranger. O'Neal joined us after a decade in Delta Force. Cruz comes from eight years serving as a SEAL."

Jenna shook each man's hand. "Thank you so much."

"That's what we're here for," O'Neal said.

"Did you have a good flight?" Derek asked.

Jones grinned. "Is there such a thing as a good flight?"

"Stop whining, man." Cruz slapped him on the back. "Get your black ass some coffee before the meeting starts. I'll need some, too."

Jones grinned. "How about you get your skinny Puerto Rican ass out of my way?"

Jenna looked startled by their words.

Derek knew how it must sound to someone who didn't know them. "Don't worry. They're best buds. They give each other shit *all* the time."

He opened the conference room door for Jenna and followed her inside, taking his seat at the head of the table and offering Jenna a place to his left. The staff was already there. He waited until Cruz and Jones had poured themselves cups of coffee and taken their seats to start the meeting. "Let's get down to business."

"Ms. Hamilton was the target of a failed abduction attempt by Abdul Jawad Kazi, former warlord, now governor of this province."

"And all-around asshole," Jones added.

Derek went on. "It is our job to get her safely out of the country and back to the U.S. We will not fail, am I understood?"

Jenna's gaze was fixed on the table, hands clenched in her lap. She was afraid—and not without reason.

Derek *hated* Kazi for this.

He turned to Segal. "Let's hear it."

"We've got three options. We can drive Ms. Hamilton north to Tajikistan and fly her from Dushanbe to Istanbul and home. We can fly her out on a chartered flight from the airport here. We can fly her via helicopter to Kabul and then fly her out of Afghanistan from there. Each option comes with its own set of risks."

Jenna's face had gone pale.

Derek held up a hand to stop Segal from continuing. "Ms. Hamilton, do you have any questions before we start, anything you'd like to say?"

"No. It's all just a little ... overwhelming."

"I bet." Derek had to stop himself from taking her hand.

Segal went through the risk assessment of each option. "Option A. We drive Ms. Hamilton across the border. The risks are obvious. There's one highway, and we could be ambushed anywhere along the road by Kazi's men, this Qassim bastard, Taliban fighters, or displaced insurgents from Daesh."

Derek shook his head. "I think we can assume that Kazi keeps this place under surveillance. Any vehicle leaving the compound is likely to be followed, and he'll have a pretty good idea where we're going."

Heads nodded.

"We've already had one close call on the road," Cross said. "Let's avoid another."

"It's a bloody long drive to Dushanbe," McManus said. "A lot can go wrong."

"I agree." Shields looked up from her iPad. "The probability of success is lowest."

Segal moved to Option B. "This is our preferred extraction method. We control the plane. We control the timing. We just need to get Ms. Hamilton to the airport. The safest way to do that might be to land our MH Little Bird on the roof and fly her there. The only drawback is that Kazi controls the airport. Option C bypasses that potential hazard by getting Ms. Hamilton to the airport in Kabul. The risk with this option is being shot down by random insurgents. We assess that risk to be small, but it is there."

"How far do you think he'd be willing to go to abduct her?" O'Neal asked. "A confrontation with Cobra would have serious repercussions for his relationship with Washington. He must know that."

Derek had spent no small amount of time thinking about this. "We don't know how far he'll go. He was willing to risk a firefight with me just a few days ago, but I'm only one guy. By working with Qassim and his militia, Kazi gains plausible deniability. He can claim that Qassim acted alone and that he knew nothing about it."

"Do you have any idea why he might want you, Ms. Hamilton?" Cruz asked.

Jenna told them about the night she'd shouted into the waiting room and had been overheard by men. "That's the only thing I've done since I got here to cause trouble."

"You rabble-rouser," McManus teased.

Shields held up her pen. "I have a theory. Maybe Kazi found out that you're the daughter of a U.S. senator who sits on the Armed Services Committee. Maybe he thinks he'll gain political leverage or financial reward by holding you hostage. Afghan presidential elections are coming up, and he has boundless ambition."

"That would be a dangerous game for him to play." Derek wasn't sure how Kazi would have gotten his hands on that bit of intel. The Internet? It wasn't something Jenna shared with people. "The risk of it blowing up in his face is extreme."

"Maybe Qassim abducts her, and Kazi rescues her," McManus suggested. "In that case, he ends up lookin' like a bloody damned hero."

And Jenna would be nothing more than a pawn.

~

Jenna splashed cold water on her face. She didn't want Derek or anyone else to see she'd been crying. They were putting their lives on the line to keep her safe. The least she could do was hold it together.

She dried off, her reflection showing red, puffy eyes.

This isn't what you expected.

That was an understatement.

She walked back to her bed, stretched out on her back, looked up at the ceiling.

Two weeks ago, she hadn't yet met Derek. Her days had been all about cold showers, hot tea, teaching, and catching lots of babies. Now, she was hiding from a warlord in a paramilitary compound under Derek's protection, waiting to be evacuated back to the U.S. It didn't seem real.

They had chosen Option B—evacuating her via helicopter to the airport and flying her out on a chartered jet to Istanbul. She had left the meeting when they had started going over the tactical details, too overwhelmed by all of it to want to hear more. It ought to have comforted her to see their professionalism, but when they'd gotten down to talking about weapons and who would do what, it had made her stomach knot.

What if Derek or someone else were shot and killed trying to protect her?

She wouldn't be able to live with that.

Why was this happening? It made no sense. Why would a man as powerful and ruthless as Kazi want anything to do with her?

Elizabeth had said she thought it might have to do with Jenna's father being a senator and, perhaps, the upcoming Afghan elections. There was no way to know whether that was true, but it wouldn't surprise Jenna. Her father had been interfering with her life since the moment she'd been born. But this time, it wouldn't even be his fault.

She'd been strangely relieved when they told her she wouldn't be leaving right away. Though she wanted to be safe and far from Qassim and Kazi, she didn't want to say goodbye to Derek—not yet.

He was everything she'd ever wanted in a man—smart,

kind, compassionate, courageous, good looking, and incredible in bed. But he wasn't available, not really. His life was his work, and his work took him far from the U.S. for long stretches. Being in a relationship with him would mean going to bed alone most nights of her life and wondering whether he was safe.

He doesn't do relationships, remember?

At least he was upfront and honest.

Jenna closed her eyes, drew a deep breath, trying to still her anxiety.

You can't lie in bed all day.

No, she couldn't.

She sat up, wondering what to do with herself. She could go to the gym to burn off some stress, but she couldn't work out all day. What she needed was a job to keep her busy, some way to contribute without getting in anyone's way.

She got to her feet and walked into the bathroom to refresh her mascara. She was happy to see that her eyes weren't as red as they'd been a few moments ago.

BOOM!

Glass exploded around her, the ground shaking beneath her feet, toppling her to the floor. Her head struck the vanity, and for a moment, she laid there, dazed.

A car alarm. Ringing in her ears. Shouts. Splitting pain in her skull.

She opened her eyes, the world spinning around her, and saw blood—*her* blood. She'd hit her head.

Head wounds bleed. Concussion.

She told herself to get up so that she could get a washcloth to apply direct pressure, but then her eyes closed again and she drifted.

"Jenna!" Derek shouted to someone. "Jenna is injured and unconscious. I'm taking her to the infirmary."

"I'm not ... unconscious. Hit my head ... on the counter."

He scooped her into his arms. "I've got you, angel."

Motion. Lights. Voices.

Jenna found herself lying on a gurney beneath bright exam lights, Derek beside her, her blood on his shirt, his fingers twined with hers. "What ... happened?"

A dark-haired man she didn't know leaned over her, studying her through green eyes, pressing something to her temple. "I'm Sean Sullivan. I'm a medic. It looks like you got a nasty cut on your temple, and some cuts from broken glass, too. I'm going to fix you up. Can you tell me your name?"

"Jenna Marie Hamilton." God, her head hurt.

"How old are you, Jenna?"

"Thirty."

Derek grinned. "Just a baby."

"Do you know who that ugly guy is?" The medic pointed to Derek.

"He's not ugly. He's Derek." It took her a moment to realize he was joking.

"Can you tell me what happened?"

"There was a loud boom. Glass went everywhere. The building shook, and I fell and hit my head." She met Derek's gaze. "What was it?"

His expression went dark. "Someone set off a car bomb across the street."

A car bomb?

Jenna thought she might throw up.

15

Derek stood in the operations room while Cross and McManus fast-forwarded through hours of security cam footage, rage like too much caffeine in his blood. He would find the son of a bitch responsible for this—and end him.

It had been a close call. Whoever had built the explosive device had fucked up, directing the blast downward. It had left a crater in the road and damaged the front gate, but it hadn't broken through the compound's concrete walls.

Then again, Derek couldn't be sure that Cobra had been their target. Their side of the street was blocked off with concrete Jersey barriers and razor wire. No one could park there. Did the driver park there because it was the closest he could get to Cobra—and Jenna—or was this act of terrorism completely random?

Derek had already gotten a call from Kazi's security secretary asking whether anyone had been injured or Cobra needed help. Derek had thanked him for the offer and reassured him that no serious damage had been done. "Just a few broken mirrors and some shrapnel damage to the front gate."

That wasn't the truth, of course. Jenna and the two men who'd been on duty inside the gate had minor injuries, but Derek didn't want to share information that might make Cobra seem vulnerable, especially not if Kazi was behind this.

"There!" McManus stopped the film. "Och, you bastard."

Derek leaned in. "I want to see the fucker's face."

Cross blew up the image. "He's just a kid. I don't recognize him."

Neither did Derek. It wasn't Qassim or Hamzad or any number of terrorists on the U.S. government's list of most-wanted assholes whose faces adorned the walls. "I want this image sent to Corbray and run through every database we have."

"Yes, sir."

Elizabeth looked up from her computer. "Afghan media is saying that the Taliban took credit for the blast. Fifteen people were injured, two of them seriously. There's no word yet on the intended target."

"That's obvious, isn't it?" McManus asked. "They sure as hell weren't tryin' to blow up the rug shop, now were they?"

"Shields, keep monitoring the media. Cross, McManus, see what you can get on that vehicle and its driver. Call me if anything pops." Derek started toward the door.

"How is she?" Elizabeth asked.

Derek did his best to keep his reply neutral. "She's got a concussion, and she needed some stitches. She'll be fine."

He went to Grant's office. "Pull up our evac plans. I want every member of the staff briefed on procedures in case we end up having to evacuate. I'd also like a report on our response efficiency today. Get it into my hands by sixteen-hundred hours."

"I'm on it."

Derek went back to his quarters, stripped off his bloody shirt, staring down at it. He'd had Jimmy's blood on his clothes and body once, and now he had Jenna's. "Goddamn it!"

It was his job to keep Jenna safe, and she'd been hurt *inside* the Cobra facility.

Not good enough.

He threw the shirt into his laundry pile, jerked another off the shelf in his closet, and pulled it over his head. Then he went back to the infirmary, where he found her sleeping. "How is she?"

Doc Sullivan looked down at Jenna. "She'll be fine. I gave her some anti-nausea meds and an analgesic for the headache. None of the other lacerations needed stitches. What she needs most right now is rest. She can go back to her room whenever it's safe again, but she shouldn't be alone for the next twenty-four hours."

"Thanks, man." Derek walked over to stand beside her.

She had changed into scrubs, her bloody clothes folded and tucked beneath the gurney. A dressing covered the wound on her temple, and she looked like she might end up with a black eye. A dozen little nicks and cuts covered her face, arms, and hands.

She said she'd been standing in front of the mirror when the bomb went off. The blast wave had shaken the building, breaking a few mirrors but doing no permanent damage.

It could have been much worse. If the fucker who'd made that IED had known what he was doing, he could have taken out all the shops across the street as well as the compound's perimeter wall and the front gate.

Jenna's eyes fluttered open, and she smiled. "Hey."

"How do you feel?" Aware that Sullivan was standing there, he did his best to act like his interest was professional.

"I've got a nasty headache." She held a hand gingerly to her temple. "This hurts."

"I bet."

"You've had much worse."

"I was a soldier." He'd willingly signed on for the risks. "Doc here tells me you can head back up to your room, but I wanted to check with you to find out whether you want to stay there or somewhere else. The janitorial crew has cleaned it up, but we'll have to order a new mirror."

"I told the boss here that you can't be alone for the next twenty-four hours."

Jenna knew head-injury protocols. "Right. Thank you so much, Sean. I guess I might as well go lie down in my own bed and leave you in peace."

Derek helped her to her feet. "I'll walk you up."

JENNA SPENT the rest of the day drifting in and out, Derek in a chair beside her bed. Once or twice, she jerked awake, the explosion echoing through her dreams, only to have Derek right there, comforting her, assuring her that she was safe.

He'd brought a laptop into her room and communicated with his team via text messages and emails, and she knew he must have a thousand other concerns on his mind and lots of things he ought to be doing.

She didn't want to burden him or take him from his work. "If you need to go, you should go. I'm fine, really. Maybe Elizabeth can check on me to make you happy."

"Shields is busy."

"So are you."

He shrugged that off. "Our people know how to do their jobs. Corbray is on his way. He left D.C. as soon as he got word of the bomb. He's going to take over management of operations when he arrives tomorrow."

She rubbed her forehead, her headache like a migraine. "What will you do?"

"Watch over you." He studied her, concern on every feature of his face. "Do you need something stronger for that headache?"

There was a lot of evidence that giving too much pain medication after a concussion set a person up for rebound headaches, but this was getting old fast. "Yes, please. This is pretty bad."

"I'll get Doc up here. You just rest—and quit worrying about the rest of us. We've got this."

"Derek, someone set off a car bomb right outside this building, and I might be to blame for that. Someone could have been killed. They could have done millions of dollars of damage to your company. How can I not worry?"

His brow furrowed. "Hey, this is *not* your fault. Even if the explosion is somehow tied to Kazi's reasons for wanting to get his hands on you, it is *not* your fault."

He enunciated every syllable of those last words.

Jenna knew intellectually that he was right, but in her heart...

Derek reached over, ran a knuckle over her cheek. "Sleep."

She didn't have much choice.

Sean came to check on her ten minutes later, doing a quick assessment. "Everything looks good. Here are some oxycodone and more anti-nausea meds. I'd like you to sleep tonight if you can."

"Thanks."

Elizabeth came up with a supper tray, giving Derek a break. "I brought all comfort food—nothing healthy. Chicken tenders. Mac and cheese. Chocolate cake. I also brought a few books in case you get bored."

She set a stack of romance novels down on the desk.

"Thank you." Jenna wasn't all that hungry, but she did finish the chocolate cake, the oxycodone making her headache better but leaving her loopy.

She and Elizabeth talked for a while, just small talk—Afghan cuisine, ex-boyfriends, favorite movies. Then Jenna had to ask. "Do you know who did it—who set off the car bomb?"

Elizabeth seemed to hesitate. "Haven't you asked Tower?"

"He doesn't want to worry me, but it worries me more not to know anything."

"Kazi released a statement to the media this afternoon saying that the Taliban claimed credit for the bomb."

"But you don't believe that, do you?"

"I'm not sure I'm supposed to talk with you about this."

"Why not when it involves me?"

"Kazi can say whatever he wants, and the media will report it, so, no, I don't. I've worked in intelligence too long to believe in coincidences. One of Kazi's goons tries to abduct you, and then a bomb goes off across the street. That's too much of—"

Derek stepped in.

Elizabeth stood, picked up Jenna's tray. "I hope you feel better soon."

"Thanks for everything."

"My pleasure." Elizabeth disappeared out the door.

Derek sat on the bed, took Jenna's hand. "I overheard

what Shields was telling you. I asked the staff not to talk about this in front of you right now. I want you to rest."

"Don't be hard on her. I asked her to tell me what she thought."

"I don't want you to worry about this."

"How can I not worry about it? Every time I close my eyes, I hear that *boom*. What if they come back with a bigger vehicle and more explosives?"

"That's not going to happen. The street is barricaded now. No vehicles can get through." His brow bent as if he were weighing what to say next. "For what it's worth, I agree with Shields. It's too much of a coincidence. I think they were trying to compromise our security and force us into moving you."

Jenna's stomach twisted.

Derek cupped her cheek, leaned close. "They failed, Jenna. You are safe here."

"What about the rest of you? Are you safe?"

His lips curved in a lopsided grin. "Are you seriously worried about me? Angel, I am hard to kill."

That didn't make her feel any better.

~

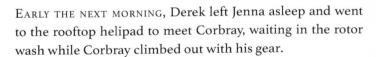

EARLY THE NEXT MORNING, Derek left Jenna asleep and went to the rooftop helipad to meet Corbray, waiting in the rotor wash while Corbray climbed out with his gear.

"Hey, brother."

"Hey, man. How was the flight?"

"It was eighteen fucking hours too long."

"I hear that." Derek had made that same flight a little more than two weeks ago. "There's breakfast and hot coffee downstairs."

"Hell, yeah. Give me some of that."

They ate a quick breakfast of eggs, sausage, toast, and coffee. Corbray went from table to table, talking with the staff one by one, then he and Derek headed to their private meeting room. There, they went over everything that had happened since Derek's arrival—except for the kissing and shagging, which Derek left out—and discussed the conclusions of their intel team.

"I think Shields is right," Corbray said. "Kazi discovered that Ms. Hamilton was related to Senator Hamilton, probably from the Internet, and sent his goons after her, hoping to force Hamilton into supporting his bid for the presidency. Or maybe he just wants money. That dawg loves cash more than he loves anything, including his kids."

Derek didn't doubt it. "I think I should meet with him, let him know what's going on, tell him our sources have linked him to Qassim, and see how he reacts."

"What if he reacts by putting a bullet in your brain?"

"He would have to be out of his mind to kill me. He knows what this organization can do. If he hears that we're onto his connection with Qassim, maybe he'll back off."

"I'll contact his people, set something up. In the meantime, how's Ms. Hamilton doing?"

"She's good." Derek wiped the smile off his face.

"You have it bad, *cabrón*. I say her name, and your eyes light up."

Derek glared at him. "My eyes do nothing."

Corbray got an idiot grin on his face. "If you say so."

Derek changed the subject. "The sooner we get her out of here, the better. I don't want to give him another crack at her. If the driver of that vehicle had crashed into our gates and detonated the IED there, it would have taken out the gates, maybe even brought down the perimeter wall, and left us open to attack."

Corbray nodded. "We need all boots on deck to finalize her extraction. I want to meet her. If she's special enough to turn you inside out—"

"I am *not* inside out."

Corbray chuckled. "Keep telling yourself that."

"Fuck you."

"Nah, man, you're not my type."

They met Doc Sullivan after that to see what he had to say about Jenna's condition and ability to travel.

"She's going to be recovering for at least a month, with headaches and brain fog, so if you can give her another few days, that would be ideal."

With that information, they went to work, Derek popping upstairs for a moment to check on her. He found her in her bathrobe brushing her hair, just the sight of her making his heart beat faster. Hell, maybe Corbray was right.

"How do you feel?"

She set her hairbrush down and stepped into his arms. "The headache is better, but my brain feels like it's full of cotton. I look like the Bride of Frankenstein."

"You've got a nasty bruise around your eye, but you look damned good."

She laughed. "That's your gonads talking."

He inhaled her scent, the feel of her precious. "You should listen to them."

"I'm too busy listening to my own. They want you to get inside my pants."

Didn't he wish? "Tell them to hold that thought. Javier Corbray, my business partner, wants to meet you when you feel up to it."

"Just let me get dressed and get some breakfast."

"Why don't we meet you there?"

Ten minutes later, she walked into the mess hall, wearing faded jeans and a soft lavender top that seemed to accentuate her curves.

That's your gonads again.

They both stood, Corbray extending his hand, a shit-eating grin on his face. "Ms. Hamilton, I'm so glad I finally get to meet you. I'm Javier Corbray, co-owner of Cobra."

Jenna gave him that beautiful smile of hers. "It's good to meet you, too. Derek has been taking good care of me."

Corbray grinned. "That's what I hear."

Derek wanted to punch him.

16

Jenna could tell something had changed. There was a tension in the air and more people in the building than before, all of them closed-mouthed and in a hurry. Derek spent the day with Javier and their team behind closed doors with little time for anything else. Even Elizabeth was quiet.

It left Jenna with butterflies in her stomach.

She knew they must be working hard on their plan to get her out of the country, so she tried to occupy herself by reading one of the books that Elizabeth had brought for her. But her heart wasn't in it. She needed to *do* something, to contribute in some way, rather than feeling helpless and afraid.

She made her way down to the infirmary to see if she could help Sean, only to find the door locked and the lights out. Apparently, the infirmary wasn't staffed unless someone needed medical help.

From there, she made her way to the mess hall. It, too, was closed, the salad bar and steam tray empty, self-serve cookies, rolls, and fresh fruit sitting near the coffee pots. From the back, she heard the banging of pots and pans.

She followed the sound—and the scent of roasting meat. "Hello?"

A burly older man in a white chef's uniform stepped out of the back room. "Can I get you something, Ms. Hamilton? We'll be open for lunch in two hours."

"Can I help? I'm tired of doing nothing."

He seemed to hesitate. "Let me clear it with Doc."

A moment later he reappeared and handed her an apron and a hairnet. "He says it's okay as long as you don't do anything strenuous. Everyone calls me Cookie."

"Thank you, Cookie." She put on the apron and the hairnet, careful not to disturb the bandage on her temple, then followed him into the kitchen, where she saw a few other staff at work—and a half-dozen frozen turkeys sitting in water in large steel sinks. "Wow! Was there a sale on turkeys somewhere?"

"Thanksgiving is only three days away."

Thanksgiving.

In the chaos of the past few days, Jenna had utterly forgotten about the holiday. Industrial-sized cans of cranberry sauce sat on the counter beside bags of potatoes and sweet potatoes and cans of pumpkin pie filling. "What can I do to help?"

She soon found herself wearing rubber gloves and up to her elbows in hot, sudsy water, scrubbing out the big pans used to roast the beef that one of Cookie's helpers was slicing for sandwiches. The monotonous work and the conversations around her were soothing and gave her something to do besides worry.

"You think she's gonna say yes?" said a man with a strong Brooklyn accent.

"I sorta gave her a hint when I started saving up for the ring. She seemed to like the idea then."

"That's not how you do it, man. You gotta surprise her, go down on one knee."

"I'd rather know before I ask whether she's interested. Besides, women find it romantic even if they're not surprised. Isn't that right, Ms. Hamilton?"

Startled to be brought into the conversation, Jenna looked up. "I don't know. No guy has ever asked me to marry him."

"That *right there* is proof that's something's wrong with this world," said the one with the Brooklyn accent.

Jenna smiled at the compliment, the two men drifting back to their conversation and leaving her with her thoughts.

What would she have done if Trenton had asked her to marry him?

If she'd had any sense, she would have said no. He was too in love with his job and his status to have room in his life for a wife and kids. And, yet, here she was, half in love with a man who, like Trenton, had chosen his career over everything else. But unlike Trenton, Derek's career took him far from the U.S.—and it might one day get him killed.

Not that Derek was in love with her or would ask her to marry him. He'd made it clear that he had no interest in a wife or family. Whatever they had together now was all she was going to get. She needed to accept that, or she'd end up getting hurt.

What if it's too late?

Then that was her fault.

She finished scrubbing, helped unload the industrial dishwasher and stack clean plates, before joining the kitchen staff for a quick lunch. They were full of questions about her work in Afghanistan, conversation helping to pass the time.

They cleared off their plates, and Jenna helped wipe down the tables. Soon, other staff filed in, but few sat. Most grabbed a tray, tossed on a sandwich, some fruit, and coffee, and disappeared back upstairs.

Something was going on.

Then Elizabeth hurried in. "Hey, Jenna."

"Has something happened?" Jenna's headache was starting up again.

"Sorry, but I'm in a hurry, and I can't stop to talk." Elizabeth grabbed a tray, piled three sandwiches, three bananas, a small carton of milk, a soda, and a cup of coffee onto it, and carried it out of the mess hall toward the elevator.

Jenna sent a quick text to Derek to make sure everything was okay.

She waited, but he didn't reply.

~

DEREK SAT in the front passenger seat of the armored Land Rover, taking mental note of the guards and security cameras. He'd come with a minimal security team—just Jones, O'Neal, and Cruz. This was a casual visit, after all. Arriving with the cavalry might give Kazi the idea that Cobra was intimidated.

Derek wasn't intimidated. He was angry as hell.

They'd gotten an ID on the kid who'd driven the car bomb. He was Qassim's oldest son, Perooz. It left no doubt in Derek's mind that the car bomb had been either a test of Cobra's strength or an attempt to force them to relocate Jenna. Neither one was acceptable.

"Park here. O'Neal, stay with the car. Jones, Cruz, you

come with me. Leave the hardware here." Derek adjusted his tie—they were all dressed in business suits with body armor beneath—and climbed out.

Kazi's uniformed security met them at the bottom of the front staircase and escorted the three of them inside, where guards scanned them for weapons. The scanner didn't pick up the wire that was stitched into his suit jacket.

If the situation went tits up, O'Neal and everyone in the Ops room would know immediately and move into action.

After the security check, Derek left Cruz and Jones at the entrance and followed one of the guards to Kazi's reception room, his shoes clicking on polished marble, the sound echoing thanks to the large domed ceiling.

Kazi sat on a gilded chair on an ornate Afghan rug, wearing a black suit, his beard short, his hair neat and trimmed. Years of violence seemed not to have left their mark on him, his demeanor like that of a benevolent prince welcoming peasants into his home. "Welcome, Mr. Tower. Won't you join me for some tea?"

It would have been unforgivably rude to refuse or to speak of business matters without first making conversation, so Derek thanked him for the tea, the conversation all small talk and bullshit. It would be another cold winter in Balkh Province. The Patriots might make it to the Super Bowl again. How wonderful that the winner of *Afghan Star* this year had been a woman.

"We are making progress, Mr. Tower." Kazi set his tea aside. "Why did you seek an audience with me?"

An audience.

The bastard thought he was a king.

"We know who planted the car bomb outside our headquarters."

Kazi's pupils dilated for a split second before he pasted a

look of concern on his face. "Yes, a terrible thing. One of the victims in that blast has perished, I am afraid. You say you know who is behind this atrocity?"

Derek handed Kazi the file folder with the drone images of Qassim from the abduction attempt on Jenna and of Perooz as he climbed out of the car. "The first images were taken during an unsuccessful attempt to abduct or harm a client of ours while she was out helping survivors of a Daesh raid on a village north of Bawrchi. One of the guards from the hospital, a man named Hamzad, appears to be working with Alimjan Qassim, a Uyghur fighter, who has been causing havoc in the rural part of your province with his militia."

Kazi studied the images of Qassim, a deliberate and fixed neutrality on his face. "You Americans and your drones."

He looked at the next image.

"The young man in the second photo is Qassim's oldest son, Perooz. He parked the car and disappeared around the corner ten minutes before it exploded outside our walls. We assess that he was working for his father. Perhaps Qassim meant to test our strength, or perhaps he hoped to force us to move our client. Either way, he failed and managed only to hurt and kill his own people."

A muscle twitched in Kazi's jaw. "May I keep these? I will pass them on to my intelligence unit and demand to know why I have not heard of this man."

"Of course. We are always happy to share what we learn with you."

When it serves our goals.

"I can assure you, Mr. Tower, that we will not rest until the guilty are punished." He slipped the photos back inside the folder and handed it to the silent guard behind him. "How is your client? How is Miss Hamilton?"

Derek had put Kazi off-balance, and Kazi was trying to do the same to him.

But Derek didn't bat an eye. "She's safe. She hopes to return to her work when this crisis is behind her."

That wasn't true, but it served Cobra's aims to make Kazi believe it was true.

Kazi gave a forced smile. "She is a brave woman."

He stood, clearly impatient to be done with Derek. "Is there anything else?"

"No, that's it." Derek stood, too. He shook Kazi's hand and found his palm damp. "I know how important it is to you to be aware of everything that takes place in this province. I knew you'd want these photographs."

"Yes. Thank you." Kazi didn't look at all grateful. "See our guest out, please."

Derek turned to go, then stopped. "Oh, there was one other thing. It slipped my mind. It's ridiculous, of course, but you'll want to be aware of it."

"Go ahead."

"Word on the street here is that Qassim secretly works for you."

~

JENNA COULDN'T BELIEVE IT. "You went to see Governor Kazi?"

That had taken balls of steel—or maybe Derek was nuts.

"It was a tactical decision." Derek sat on her sofa, wearing an expensive dark gray suit, as if he'd just come from a meeting on Wall Street. "We needed to send a message, and there was no better way to do it. After that, I had a debriefing with the staff."

"It sounds like a busy day." Jenna sat beside him. "After you didn't reply to my text, I couldn't stop worrying. I could tell something was going on. Everyone was closed-mouthed and serious. The mess hall was all but empty at lunch and dinner."

"I'm sorry. I didn't have that cell phone with me. If I was taken, I didn't want Kazi having access to you." Derek loosened his tie. "No one was trying to keep you in the dark, but none of us are used to having clients in the building. Usually, when we extract someone, we take them from wherever they are directly out of the country. We don't bring them here. There are limits to what we can share, even with you."

"I get it. You're a black-ops company."

"Private military company."

"Right." Jenna wasn't sure she understood the difference. "Do you think Kazi got the message?"

Derek nodded. "When I left, the son of a bitch was sweating. I'm certain he's behind all of this."

Chills skittered down Jenna's spine. "Why would Kazi want to come after me? This all seems so crazy—like something out of a bad dream."

"I suspect it has to do with money." Derek changed the subject, clearly not wanting to say more about it. "How are you feeling?"

"The headache is better, but I swear my brain has turned to mud."

Derek caught her chin and turned her face so that he could see her cheek and temple. "That's one hell of a black eye."

"Don't you know how to flatter a girl?"

Derek grinned. "Cookie tells me you went down to the kitchen and scrubbed some pans this morning. He said you did a good job."

"I was trying to be productive and not worry about you."

"I'd rather know you were resting."

"There's only so much resting a person can do in a day. I *am* a medical professional, you know. I can tell when I need to lie down."

Derek took her hand, his touch soothing. "The next couple of days are going to be busy. I won't be available most of the time. We're going to move quickly now to get you out of the country. I need to stay focused, keep my head in the game. I can't afford distractions."

Was he saying that *she* was a distraction?

Of course, she was. How could she not be? He was risking his life to protect hers. This was a private military compound, not a hotel. She'd known their time together was temporary.

She willed herself to smile. "Don't worry about me. I told Cookie I'd help with Thanksgiving dinner. I'll find some way to stay busy."

"Don't overdo it." He drew her close, kissed the top of her head. "Want to help me get out of this straight jacket?"

"I thought you didn't have time for—"

He looked into her eyes. "I have time now."

That was good enough for Jenna.

She stood, grabbed him by the tie, and drew him to his feet. Then she peeled off his jacket and unbuttoned his shirt, sliding her hands beneath the fabric of his undershirt to find... pockets?

"For body armor." Derek unbuttoned his cuffs, shed his shirt, then pulled the undershirt over his head and tossed it aside, offering himself to her. "Is that better?"

"Much better." She ran her hands over his chest with its smooth skin and slabs of muscle, need for him kindling to life inside her. "You have such an amazing body."

She leaned in, licked a flat brown nipple, and smiled when the muscles of his belly tensed. Then she unbuttoned the waistband of his trousers, pulled down his zipper, and helped herself, taking hold of his hard cock and stroking it, the feel of him such a turn-on. "I want to taste you."

She sank to her knees—and took him into her mouth.

Breath hissed between his teeth as she explored him. She looked up, saw that he was watching, so she gave him a show. Drawing back, then taking all of him again. Flicking the underside of the swollen head with her tongue. Circling it like the tip of an ice cream cone. Sucking on it like a lollipop. Stroking the shaft with her hand from the base to her lips and back again.

His gaze had gone dark now, the intensity on his face making her pulse skip.

She stroked him now, her hand and mouth moving in tandem from base to tip. She tried to follow his cues—the thrust he tried to suppress that told her to go faster, the shudder in his breathing, the way his fists clenched in her hair.

"*Stop.*" He drew himself away from her, his brow furrowed, his cock glistening. "I want to be inside you."

They both undressed her, clothes falling to the floor. Then Derek sat back on the sofa, his trousers still around his ankles and drew her onto his lap.

She held onto his shoulders for balance and straddled him, his hands gripping her hips, guiding her as she lowered herself onto him, taking every delicious inch of him inside her. Oh, he felt so good, his cock filling her, making her ache.

Slowly at first, she rode him, rocking her hips against him. When he didn't thrust, she knew he was holding back, reining himself in for her sake.

He cupped her breasts, played with them, licking one nipple and then the other, making her moan. Then he reached between their bodies with one hand to stroke her clit.

"*Derek.*" In no time, she found herself hovering on the iridescent edge of an orgasm, pleasure drawing tight in her belly.

He must have known she was close because he started to thrust, bucking into her, riding her from below, stroking her inside and out.

She shattered, climax burning through her like molten gold, making her cry out, his powerful thrusts carrying them both home.

She sagged against his chest, his cock still inside her, and for a moment, they stayed as they were, heartbeats slowly returning to normal. Then he kicked off his shoes, socks, and trousers, lifted her into his arms, and carried her to the bed.

She snuggled against him, her head pillowed on his chest. "I don't want you or anyone else getting hurt or killed trying to get me out of the country. I would rather turn myself over to Kazi."

"Shh." Derek stroked her hair, kissed her. "Everything is going to be okay."

And because she wanted desperately to believe that, she closed her eyes and let sleep take her.

17

Derek woke early Friday morning and met Corbray and the team in the ops room. Everyone knew their jobs, but they ran through their strategy in detail, a diagram of the airport on the big screen. There was no such thing as too much planning.

"I don't have to remind you that Kazi controls everything here—airport security, the police, Afghan security forces, private militias, merchants, random street vendors. Anyone and everyone could be on his payroll. In the past, we've relied on this fact to accomplish our missions. Today, it presents a threat."

Heads nodded.

There was one other thing Derek had to say.

"This is all new to Ms. Hamilton. The past couple of weeks have been hard on her, and I want to make sure that this doesn't add to what has already been a traumatic experience. Watch what you say around her. She's a midwife, trained to save lives, not watch people kill and die. She doesn't need to overhear your graphic war stories."

Cruz's gaze dropped to the table. "Sorry, man."

"Feckin' idiot," McManus grumbled.

Over Thanksgiving dinner yesterday, Cruz had told Jones about a time when his SEAL element had been ambushed, joking about the number of insurgents they had killed. It was trench warfare humor, the kind of thing operators talked about on their downtime, a way of processing what they'd seen and what they'd had to do to survive. But Jenna had overheard and had clearly been upset.

"Any questions?"

When no hands went up, Corbray turned off the screen. "Our mission priority is Ms. Hamilton's safety. Remember that a firefight would become an international incident that could potentially destabilize the province."

"Does Kazi know that?" O'Neal asked.

"I think he does. As angry as he was during my visit, he kept up an appearance of hospitality. He knows he can't afford to lose Washington's support." Derek glanced at his watch. "Let's make this happen."

"I'm packed up and ready to be bait." Shields drew Jenna's gray headscarf over her hair. "See you downstairs."

Shields would act as a decoy, heading to the airport with Jenna's bags and a convoy of three armored Land Cruisers to board a commercial flight to Kabul under Jenna's name. With any luck, she would draw Kazi's attention long enough for Jenna to board Cobra's private jet safely. By the time Kazi realized Shields was a Cobra operative and not Jenna, the plane would be airborne and on its way to Istanbul.

Leaving Corbray, McManus, and Cross in the operations room, Derek went to get Jenna. He found her sitting on her bed in jeans and a T-shirt, Kevlar vest in her hands, white burqa on the bed beside her. Her bags had been sent ahead with Team One and checked in by Shields. Jenna would catch up with them in D.C.

"Are you ready?"

She nodded, lines of worry on her face.

"I'll help you put that on." He took the vest, strapped her into it, saw that she was wearing Jimmy's dog tags.

The weight of what they were about to attempt came down on him hard. She was Jimmy's little sister. He couldn't fail her.

I'll do my best to get her safely home, buddy.

He drew her into his arms, held her. "I know this is scary, but we're going to do everything we can to keep you safe. This isn't our first rodeo."

"Just keep *yourself* safe, okay?"

That wasn't his job description, but he didn't say so. "I'll do my best."

Derek held her cold hand as they walked together to the elevator and rode it up to the top floor. "Time to put that on."

"I swore I'd never wear a burqa." Jenna pulled it over her head, white fabric concealing her from head to toe, the green of her eyes just visible through the front mesh. "I must look like Casper the Friendly Ghost."

Derek couldn't help but laugh. "Nah. Casper doesn't have feet."

The MH-6 Little Bird was waiting, rotors running, ready to get airborne, Cruz, Jones, and O'Neal standing nearby, automatic weapons in hand.

Derek shouted to be heard over the rotors. "Keep low, and I'll help you in."

"Okay." He couldn't see her face, but her voice sounded small and scared.

Cruz and Jones boarded first, Derek following with

Jenna, his arm around her shoulders. It was a big step for her, but she made it. Derek strapped her in and grabbed his loaded M4, which sat propped up against his seat. He buckled in and put on his earphones, motioning for her to do the same.

"This is how we'll communicate during the flight."

"Ladies and gentleman, welcome to Little Bird Airlines," said Fox, their pilot. "Please put your seats and trays in their upright positions as we prepare for take-off."

O'Neal grinned. "I hope the service on this flight is better than the last one."

Jones laughed. "Hell, you'd be lucky to get expired MREs from Fox."

"Have you ever flown in a helicopter before?" Derek asked Jenna.

She shook her head.

"It's fun." When the damned thing didn't crash.

The helicopter lifted off the pad, nosed into the wind, and gained altitude.

Cruz grinned. "And we're off."

~

JENNA LOOKED down on the maze of streets that was Mazar-e-Sharif, holding tightly to Derek's hand and trying to ignore the frantic butterflies in her stomach. There was the marketplace with its many stalls where merchants sold everything from tea to jeans to handwoven carpets. Over there was Sina Stadium, where locals attended soccer games and races. And there in the heart of the city stood the beautiful Blue Mosque with its twin minarets and two turquoise domes.

The sight put a lump in her throat.

She had taken a tour of the city when she'd first arrived and had been entranced by the new sights and sounds—the song calling Muslims to prayer, the scents of coriander, cardamom, and turmeric in the marketplace, bright colors everywhere. How exhilarated she'd felt, thrilled to be somewhere new and exciting and certain that her two years here would change her life.

That had turned out to be true, but not entirely in the way she'd hoped.

The helicopter headed out of the city toward the airport, the pilot speaking helicopter talk with someone on the ground.

"We'll be there in two minutes," Derek said. "We'll load into a Jeep and drive to the plane, which is waiting on the tarmac."

Jenna nodded. "Is Elizabeth okay?"

"She's fine. She's through security and about to board."

That was the part of this plan Jenna liked the least. What if someone shot or abducted Elizabeth because they believed she was Jenna? How would Jenna be able to live with that?

The helicopter descended as they neared the airport.

Derek pointed. "That's Cobra's hangar."

"You have a hangar?" Her head began to throb.

"We keep the jet and this Little Bird there. If we need heavier air support, we borrow from the U.S. military."

But Jenna barely heard him, wind buffeting the helicopter as the pilot carefully landed a hundred yards or so away from a small, white jet.

"Leave the rotors running until we're airborne," Derek said.

The pilot gave him a thumbs up. "You got it, boss."

Jenna did what Derek did, pulling off her earphones,

unbuckling the harness. The three men who'd come with them—Malik, Dylan, and Connor—were all business now. They jumped to the ground, bent low, spreading out, weapons raised.

It seemed unreal somehow, like something from an action movie.

Rifle in a sling on his chest, Derek climbed down and then helped Jenna out, her burqa making it hard for her to see, the fabric billowing around her in the rotor wash. With one hand protectively on her elbow and the other holding a weapon, he guided her to the Jeep. They piled in and set off for the waiting jet.

"Good morning, ma'am." The driver smiled at her from behind mirrored sunglasses. "I'm Gabriel Ortiz. I'll be your Uber driver today."

See? It's all going to plan. Everything is okay.

A minute later, they stopped and climbed out, Derek's men standing guard around the plane while Derek led Jenna up the mobile stairway and into the aircraft.

"Wow." The interior looked nothing like any airplane Jenna had seen.

Eight plush leather seats sat at comfortable distances from each other, a flat-screen TV at one end of the cabin, a bar at the other.

"Where should I sit?"

"Anywhere you want, angel." Derek held a finger to his earpiece, listening to Javier or someone in the ops room. "Cobra, this is Team Two actual. We're onboard. Out." He turned to the pilot. "Let's close the door and get underway."

"You got it."

Jenna pulled off the burqa and sat in one of the middle seats, then leaned back, closed her eyes, and drew a deep breath. It was almost over. In another few minutes, they would be airborne. This would all be behind her.

"Cobra, this is Team Two actual. Her flight is grounded, and they're boarding the airplane. Copy, out." Derek called to the pilot. "Get us in the air—*now*."

Jenna's eyes flew open. "Her flight is grounded? What will happen to—"

The pilot turned and shouted back to them. "Now *all* flights are grounded."

Derek repeated the news into his mic. "Cobra, this is Team Two. All flights grounded. We'll get her out on the bird and head to Kabul, over?" Derek unbuckled her seatbelt, shoved the burqa into her hands.

"Wh-what's happening?"

"They've probably discovered it's not you on that plane, so they've grounded all flights. We need to get you back to the Little Bird—now."

A surge of adrenaline brought Jenna to her feet, heart in her throat as she followed Derek toward the airplane's door. Questions raced through her mind, questions she didn't dare ask. If flights were grounded, how could they take off in the helicopter? Wouldn't they be safer in the airplane with the door shut than out on the tarmac in a Jeep? What had happened to Elizabeth?

Dylan ran up the mobile stairway, stopping when he saw them. "A whole lot of trouble is headed our way."

They ran down the stairs and toward the Jeep.

"Cobra, this is Team Two," Derek said. "Four vics and at least twenty fighters with small arms and an RPG coming our way, over."

"QRF coming in fast!" Malik shouted.

"Helo One, this is Team Two. We're not going to reach you. Get that bird in the air now, how copy, over?" Derek shouted into his mic, waiting just a moment before going on. "Cobra, this is Team Two. Retreating to the hangar and switching to armored Land Cruiser, over."

Jenna jumped into the Jeep ahead of Derek, and then she saw. "Oh, God!"

Four vehicles, each of them bristling with armed fighters, were speeding straight toward them.

DEREK'S MIND raced through their options as they sped toward the hangar. The Little Bird was lifting off, the pilot fighting for altitude to put himself beyond the range of automatic weapons fire and that RPG. The three armored Land Cruisers that had brought Shields to the airport sat outside the terminal, prevented from entering the grounds by armed airport security. The hangar, which wasn't bulletproof, had another armored Land Cruiser, but they had to reach it first.

Yeah, their options sucked.

Derek had to give the bastard credit. Kazi had moved fast and hard. But he wasn't going to get Jenna, not as long as Derek had breath left in his body.

She was terrified, her eyes wide, her auburn hair blowing in the wind.

He took her hand, held it. "When we get to the hangar, we're going to switch to the Land Cruiser. We'll have to move fast. That's all you need to think about now. I'll be right there with you. We all will."

She nodded. "Move fast."

"That's it."

Fast might not be fast enough. At seventy miles an hour, they were keeping ahead of the bastards. But the moment they stopped to switch vehicles, the men in those vehicles would catch up in a hurry.

Corbray's voice came over Derek's earpiece. "Team One, this is Cobra. Leave current position, head north down the highway to the end of the runway. Punch a hole in that perimeter fence to make an escape route and cover Team Two, how copy, over?"

"Cobra, this is Team Two. Good copy. Out."

"Almost there!" O'Neal shouted.

They entered the wide-open hangar door.

Ortiz slammed on the brakes, bringing them to a screeching stop.

"Everyone out!" Derek jumped down, then helped Jenna into the Land Cruiser. "Cruz, O'Neal, stay with the Jeep. Cover our rear. Let's catch them in a crossfire. Jones, you're on me."

Jones climbed into the front Land Cruiser's passenger seat, while Cruz jumped into the driver's seat of the Jeep, O'Neal riding shotgun.

"Let's move!"

"Team Two, this is Cobra. Enemy QRF almost at your position. How copy, over?" Corbray said.

"Cobra, this is Team Two. Acknowledged. Out."

Ortiz threw the engine into reverse and backed out of the hangar.

"Jenna, get down." Derek guided her to a sheltered position on the floor and piled extra Kevlar vests around her.

"I thought the vehicle was bulletproof."

"They are, but I won't take chances." Derek checked his M4. "Ortiz, they're probably going to aim for our tires and try to immobilize us."

He hoped to fuck these assholes wanted Jenna alive. In

fact, he was counting on it. No up-armored Land Cruiser could withstand a hit by an RPG.

Ortiz braked, shifted into drive, floored it, the vehicle's engine responding instantly. Thank God they weren't in a lumbering Humvee. Even so, changing to the Land Cruiser had cost them time. The bastards gained on them, Qassim in the lead vehicle. So far, they hadn't noticed Cruz and O'Neal, who were now in pursuit.

"Here they come!" Jones shouted.

Rat-at-at-at! Rat-at-at-at!

A burst of automatic weapons fire. The thud of bullets against armor.

Jenna screamed.

"Cobra, this is Team Two. Taking enemy fire, over."

"Team One, this is Cobra. Team Two is taking fire, over?" Corbray replied.

Jones leaned out his window, aimed his M4.

Rat-at-at-at! Rat-at-at-at!

One of the vehicles tried to pull in front of them, but the much-heavier Land Cruiser struck them hard, their momentum causing them to lose control and roll over.

"Woohoo!" Jones shouted.

"Bowling for terrorists." Ortiz grinned. "My new favorite sport."

Rat-at-at-at! Rat-at-at-at!

Jenna's body jerked, her hands over her ears.

The vehicle shuddered.

"We've lost a rear left tire!" Ortiz said.

If they had to, they could ride out small arms fire until the cavalry managed to punch through that fence and join the fight—*if* they managed to punch through.

"Fuck them!" Jones stood, fired three short bursts, taking out the driver of the lead vehicle and both of its front tires.

That was one enemy vehicle on its side and one crippled.

"Cobra, this is Team One. They have barricaded the main road. We are blocked from leaving the terminal, over?"

Son of a bitch!

The cavalry wasn't coming.

"Team Two this is Cobra, Helo One has returned to base. Reinforcements inbound. ETA ten mikes."

"Cobra, this is Team Two. Copy that. Out." Derek rolled down his window, leaned out, took aim at the nearest pursuing vehicle, and fired, and saw two men drop.

Rat-at-at-at!

Jones fired, too, one of the vehicles spinning out of control.

Rat-at-at-at!

"We lost the other rear tire!"

Derek looked for a way to hold out until that bird arrived. They could keep driving, but they would run out of runway soon. They could try punching their own hole in the perimeter fence and risk getting pinned down without cover. Or they could take cover and fight. They were outnumbered and, if the RPG came into play, outgunned, but Jones, Cruz, and Ortiz were skilled fighters, the three of them worth more than a dozen insurgents.

Then he saw it—a ten-foot-high wall of stacked jersey barriers ahead.

"Take cover behind that barrier!"

Rat-at-at-at!

Jones laid down suppressing fire as Ortiz maneuvered the Land Cruiser behind the wall of jersey barriers, giving them solid cover—but potentially leaving them trapped.

"Jenna, lock the doors, and stay down!" Derek didn't

want to make it easy for Qassim to grab her if they fell. "Don't come out for anyone or anything!"

She shook her head. "I won't lock you out!"

"*Do it!*" Derek threw open the door, strapped his helmet onto his head, and took up a position on the corner of the wall, while Jones climbed onto the Land Cruiser's hood and Ortiz took the other corner. "Cobra HQ this is Team Two, we have taken cover and are returning fire. Awaiting reinforcements. Out."

18

Jenna was trapped in a nightmare, barely able to breathe, pulse pounding in her ears as gunfire exploded around her. She squeezed her eyes shut and prayed.

God, please keep them safe! Keep them safe!

"Changing!" Derek shouted. "Ortiz, you've got one sneaking around your way!"

"I see him!"

Rat-at-at! Rat-at-at!

"Cruz is down!" That was Malik. "I can't see how bad it is, but he's not moving!"

Oh, God!

The two men were close friends. Was Dylan dead?

Her stomach rolled.

"Cobra HQ, this is Team Two. We have a man down. No details available. Still taking fire. Requesting medevac, over."

Please let him live! Keep them safe!

"Changing!" Malik shouted. "I've got two mags left!"

Were they running out of bullets? Is that what he meant?

"Conserve your ammo!" Derek shouted back.

Why was this happening?

She wasn't worth this. She wasn't worth the effort Qassim was making. She sure as hell wasn't worth other men's lives.

She could stop it. She could pick up a gun and shoot or step out of the Land Cruiser and give herself up to Qassim.

You'd probably get shot, and all of this would be for nothing.

Seconds dragged on like hours, the gunfire incessant, shouts mingling with the cries of injured men. Was one of them Dylan?

"Where the fuck is that bird?" Malik shouted to Derek.

"They're four mikes out!"

Four mikes?

Did that mean four minutes? Four minutes was an eternity.

We can survive that. God, help us to survive that long!

Malik cried out, fell back against the Land Cruiser's bullet-pocked windshield, blood hitting the glass with him.

"Cobra AQ, this is Team Two. We've taken multiple casualties and need evac *now*, over?" Derek shouted.

Rat-at-at-at! Rat-at-at-at! Rat-at-at-at!

Jenna didn't hesitate. She grabbed the big trauma kit she'd seen in the back and climbed out to find Malik already in shock, sweat beading on his brown skin, blood pouring from a gunshot wound to the right side of his chest just below his clavicle and from an exit wound in his back.

"Malik, stay awake! Help me get you down." She wrapped one of his arms around her shoulders and lowered him as carefully as she could to the asphalt.

"Jenna, get back in the vehicle!"

"Not without Malik!" She did her best to ignore the gunfire and focus on Malik, her training taking over. She pulled off his gloves, body armor, and shirt, then ripped into the medical kit and slipped into a pair of nitrile gloves. "How old are you?"

His teeth chattered. "Thirty-six."

Rat-at-at-at! Rat-at-at-at! Rat-at-at-at!

"I'm going to do my best to help you." She found an autoinjector of morphine, twisted off the top, and jammed it into his quadriceps, then searched for some way to seal his chest wound. She was about to use a plastic dressing when she saw an Asherman chest seal. "Are you allergic to latex?"

He shook his head, his breathing labored.

She ripped the adhesive strip off the back of the seal, wiped the blood off his chest as best she could, then lined up the vent over the bullet wound, and stuck the seal to his skin. She repeated the process for the exit wound on his back, air and blood burbling out of the vents—exactly what he needed.

Rat-at-at-at! Rat-at-at-at! Rat-at-at-at!

"I'm going to get an IV going so you'll be ready when the medics get here."

"Th-thanks." His body trembled. "You're one t-tough chick."

But she wasn't. She wasn't tough at all. She was shaking and scared to death.

Alcohol pads. Large-bore IV needles. Lactated Ringer's.

Thank God!

She searched for a vein, wiped his skin with an alcohol pad, then did her best to get the IV in place—not easy with bullets whizzing overhead. It took two sticks for her to get it right. "Sorry!"

He was all but unconscious now.

"Stay with me, Malik." She loosened the plastic tubing around the bag of fluids, hung the bag from the vehicle's antenna, then connected the tubing to his IV, and opened the fluids wide. But it wouldn't keep him alive for long. He needed to get to a hospital. He needed surgery—stat.

Rat-at-at-at! Rat-at-at-at! Rat-at-at-at!

Ortiz groaned and sank to the ground. "Fuck! I caught a ricochet in my goddamned thigh!"

Jenna started toward him, but he stopped her, tearing a small med kit out of his pack and treating himself. "I've got this! Stay with Malik!"

"Jenna, get back inside and lock the door!" Derek shouted. "Changing!"

Rat-at-at-at! Rat-at-at-at! Rat-at-at-at!

She picked up the trauma kit and ran toward the vehicle, then heard Derek grunt, his rifle falling to the ground.

Rat-at-at-at!

Another bullet strike. A dull thud.

Derek was thrown back and lay still.

"Derek!"

God, no!

She crawled over to Derek, saw blood seeping from the torn fabric of his shirt near his shoulder. "Derek!"

Please let him be alive!

She checked for a pulse and found one. He was breathing, his airway clear.

Thank God!

She tore open his shirt.

There was an entry wound on his left shoulder, but no exit wound.

Damn it!

That meant the bullet could have ricocheted inside him.

It could be anywhere—in bone, in his chest, in his abdomen. He could be hemorrhaging internally.

Get yourself together!

No blood in his mouth or coming from his ears.

That was a good sign.

She found a flattened lead ball embedded in the center of his body armor. It hadn't penetrated, but it had hit him hard.

But the gunfire had stopped, the silence sending chills down her spine.

Men shouted in a language she didn't understand.

Moans. Boots on asphalt. The distant thrum of a helicopter.

Hurry, Javier!

Derek moaned, drew in a breath, his eyes fluttering open, pain etched into his face. "Get ... into the vehicle."

"Stay quiet." She fought to keep her emotions out of it, tearing open a hemostatic dressing and fixing it over the bullet wound.

He tried to reach for his rifle.

"You've got a bullet still inside you, so take it easy." She jammed the autoinjector into his thigh, shoving another one into her bra just in case.

"No ... morphine."

"Too late."

He didn't seem to have a pneumothorax, so she focused on his bleeding. "This is going to hurt."

He grimaced as she pressed down hard on his shoulder.

The boots drew nearer.

"Stay still. They're coming."

Maybe if they thought he was already dead...

Her heart pounding so hard it hurt, she looked up just as

armed men came around both corners, weapons pointed at her and Ortiz, whose hands were red with blood.

She recognized Qassim from the drone photos and glared up at him, shouting at him in Dari, her fear momentarily gone. "You dog!"

He ignored her.

"What do you want me to do with them?" one of his men asked, pointing the barrel of his rifle directly at Derek's head.

"No!" Jenna cried out in a voice she barely recognized as her own, throwing herself over him, protecting him with her body. "Don't you touch him!"

"Bring him and the girl. Leave the rest to the vultures."

DEREK SLOWLY CAME out of his morphine haze, pain dragging him to awareness. His left hand was numb, but his arm hurt like hell. The pain in his chest was just as bad. The round that had hit his vest must have broken ribs or cracked his sternum.

God, it hurt to breathe.

He opened his eyes, found himself lying on his back in the rear of one of Qassim's Jeeps, his wrists and feet bound.

Okay, so he'd been in worse spots. But his men...

Jones, Cruz, O'Neal, Ortiz. Four good men wounded, maybe dying, maybe dead.

Goddamn.

They'd taken out his earpiece, so he had no idea what was going on. The bird had been on its way. Derek had called out medical. Were they still alive?

Derek had lost men before. He'd lost an entire team the

day Laura Nilsson had been abducted. That had been *his* fault, his responsibility. Was this his doing, too?

You can't change it now. Concentrate on getting through this.

He focused on his heartbeat, trying to assess his condition. It wasn't fast or thready, which told him that he hadn't lost too much blood.

Thank God for Jenna.

She had defied him and risked getting shot herself to care for him and for Jones. She'd slowed his bleeding and done her best to ease his pain. Then she'd thrown herself on top of him, trying to protect him. She'd even called Qassim a dog.

Don't you touch him!

Yeah, Jenna had her brother's strength.

She sat in the seat in front of him, arguing with Qassim, hidden under a burqa. "I'm a nurse! Let me care for him unless you want the death of an important U.S. citizen on your hands."

Jenna, be careful.

Qassim and his men laughed.

"Shut up, woman, or I'll cut out your tongue!"

Derek wanted to tell Jenna to keep quiet, to stay passive, but he didn't want to give away the fact that he was conscious. The weaker he seemed, the better the chance that Qassim would underestimate him. Not that he'd be any good in a fight just this minute, especially not trussed like a turkey.

"You wouldn't dare! I know you know who my father is. If you want money from him, you'd be wise not to touch me."

Then again, Jenna seemed to be holding her own against these fuckers.

"When we get to the camp, we're going to pass you

around, let all of the men enjoy you, and when we're done, we'll let the dogs have you. Isn't that right?"

Men's laughter and shouts of agreement.

"Be quiet, Perooz. No one is to harm her. Any man who touches her faces me."

So, the mouthy bastard was Qassim's son, the punk who'd left the car bomb.

Derek was going to enjoy killing him.

They turned off the highway and onto a rutted road, the jarring motion forcing Derek to grit his teeth to keep from groaning.

Son of a bitch!

"This bouncing might make him bleed to death. Please, let me help him."

"It might be better for him to die now." That was Qassim. "You we won't touch, but *he* killed more than a dozen of my men and passed information to The Lion."

"He was just doing his job, protecting *me*."

It put a hitch in Derek's chest to hear her fighting so hard for him. But if she was expecting forgiveness or mercy from Qassim, she was going to be disappointed. The folks around here were *still* angry at Genghis Khan, and he'd been dead for a while now.

"Cobra has more money than my father," Jenna said. "He's worth more to you than I am. You're a fool if you harm him or let him die."

Derek wasn't worried—not yet, anyway. By abducting him and Jenna, and attacking, injuring, and possibly killing Cobra operatives, Qassim had brought a metric shit ton of pain down on his head. He just didn't know it yet.

More ruts.

Pain lanced through Derek's shoulder and chest, drove the breath from his lungs.

Fuck!

"He's awake." Perooz peered at him over the back seat, grinning.

"Let me at least check to make sure he's not bleeding to death."

"Be quick," said Qassim. "If you try to escape, I will kill him."

The vehicle slowed, then stopped.

Jenna rose up and turned in her seat, and an arm emerged from her burqa, something gripped in her closed fist. "He is losing blood."

Their gazes met for just a moment through the mesh of her burqa, and Derek saw in those green eyes the fear and worry she was trying so hard to hide.

"They'll come," he whispered.

"I know." Without warning, she jabbed something into his thigh.

Morphine.

God, he loved her.

The drug rushed through him like warm honey, blunting his pain, making him high as a fucking kite.

It's not going to be like this when they get to where they're going. They're going to rough you up. They might even kill you if Cobra can't move in fast enough.

He knew it was true, but right now he didn't seem to care.

Perooz grabbed Jenna by her shoulders, shook her. "What did you do to him? What did you say?"

Bastard.

"I gave him pain medicine so that he won't suffer. I told him to sleep."

The last thing Derek saw as he drifted into unconsciousness was a distant flash of silver high in the blue sky above.

Jenna huddled inside her burqa, cold to the bone and hungry, the shackle on her ankle biting into her skin. They had taken her cell phone, searched her for weapons, and staked her like an animal in the corner of a house with dirt floors, the coal fire in the center of the room doing nothing to keep her warm.

But Derek was suffering much worse.

"What did you say to The Lion about me?" Qassim had been asking Derek questions for the past hour, beating him, Derek's suffering unbearable to her.

Still, Derek was a smart ass. "I told him you fuck little boys."

The dull thud of a fist striking flesh, another grunt of pain.

Tears streamed down Jenna's cheeks.

"You think you are a tough guy, I know. I think you are not so tough. That looks like a bad wound in your shoulder. How does it feel now?"

Derek cried out, a terrible, agonized sound, like a scream through gritted teeth.

What were they doing to him? Where was Cobra? Where was Javier?

If they didn't come soon, it might be too late. But without her phone, how would Javier find them to mount a rescue?

Jenna was used to the sound of suffering, the cries of women in labor. Their pain tugged at her heart, but this was different. Qassim was doing his best to *hurt* Derek, to break him. He might even kill him.

The cry ended.

"Go to hell!" Derek shouted.

Another blow. Another grunt.

"What did you tell The Lion?"

"Your best chance ... for ending today alive ... is to let Ms. Hamilton go."

He sounded like he was out of breath. Was he having trouble breathing?

She had asked to see him, offering to treat their wounded men in exchange for being able to care for Derek. But they had ignored her as if they hadn't even heard her, as if she were nothing and no one.

Another blow. A grunt.

"What did you tell The Lion? Speak—or I will geld you like a goat!"

"No!" Jenna jerked against the chain, her heart thudding sickeningly in her chest.

"I'll still be ... more of a man ... than you ... you son of a whore."

Another terrible cry—this one cut short.

"Leave him to bleed to death." Qassim stormed out of the room, ignoring her and stomping outside, his two men behind him.

There was blood on his hands—Derek's blood.

Had the bastard castrated Derek? Was Derek bleeding to death?

Feeling sick, her blood cold with panic, Jenna called to him, listening for any sound of life from the next room. "Derek?"

No answer.

"Derek!"

Still no answer.

Desperate to reach him, Jenna tried to pry the shackle open, then grabbed the wooden stake, rocking it back and forth with all her strength, trying to pull it out of the hard, dry earth. The stake came free without warning, and Jenna fell flat on her butt. It was a lot longer than she'd thought—and it was sharp on one end.

A weapon.

She picked it up together with the chain that was still shackled to her ankle and ran to the next room, the chain clinking softly.

"Derek!"

He sagged, shirtless and unconscious, from a tall wooden post, fresh blood streaming down his left arm, his pants down around his ankles, his body still intact.

Thank God!

Almost legless with relief, she ran to him. There was a terrible dark bruise in the center of his chest where the bullet had hit his body armor and fresh bruises on his ribs. His face was bruised, too, lacerations on his cheeks, his lip bleeding, the pressure bandage she'd put on his shoulder wound lying, bloody, in the dirt.

She dropped the stake, threw off her burqa. He was breathing, but his skin was cold and clammy, his pulse thready. "Derek, can you hear me?"

He raised his head. "Jenna? You shouldn't ... If he finds you ... he'll hurt you."

She looked for the knots that held his bonds then went to work untying them. "I can't sit there and do nothing while he tortures you."

"Yes, you can. If it means survival ... you can."

The knots were tight, but she kept at it until the one around his ankles and then the one around his wrists came free.

"I've got you." She eased him to the ground, grabbing the shirt they'd torn off him, and covering him with it for warmth. Then she tore the burqa, making strips and fashioning them into a bandage to stop his bleeding.

"You're a good ... field medic."

But bullet wounds were far beyond Jenna's experience. "I'm not a medic. I'm a midwife. Does anything here look like a vagina to you?"

She tore another strip off her burqa and dabbed at the blood on his lip, wishing she had clean hot water or ice packs or another morphine autoinjector.

"Hey." He reached up with his right hand, brushed a tear off her cheek. "You're going to get through this. Cobra will come—tonight, tomorrow."

"They took my phone, Derek. How will Javier be able to find us now?"

"They *will* find us. If Qassim kills me—"

"Don't say that!" Something inside her snapped, all the tension and terror coming together in a rush. "I couldn't take it if anything happened to you. Don't you understand? I love you, Derek. I can't do this without you."

What had she just said?

Except that it was true.

She loved him.

Well, damn.

He looked up at her, a startled expression on his bruised face. "Jenna, I—"

"You stupid whore!" Perooz stood in the doorway, rifle slung over his shoulder. "Father, come! The woman has untied him!"

"Easy, Jenna," Derek whispered, grasping the sharpened stake.

But Qassim was right behind his son. "Remove her. Kill him."

Adrenaline turned Jenna's blood to ice, but she stood. "If you want to kill him, you have to kill me first."

Perooz stormed over, grabbed Jenna by her arm, threw her aside—then stared down in shock at the stake that protruded from his abdomen.

Qassim let out a cry, raised his weapon, aimed it at Derek.

"No!" Jenna crawled toward Derek to cover his body with hers.

Something bounced across the dirt floor.

A grenade.

19

Derek saw the stun grenade and rolled Jenna beneath him, shielding her from hot shrapnel with his body. "Close your eyes! Cover your ears!"

BANG!

A loud blast. A flash of blinding light.

Jenna screamed.

Qassim screamed, too.

The heavy tread of military boots.

Derek opened his eyes to find Qassim staggering blindly, hands over his face, as a half-dozen Cobra operatives poured through the door. They threw Qassim to the ground, ignoring his shouts and curses as they handcuffed him.

"Nice of you guys to show up." Derek looked into Jenna's eyes. "Are you okay?"

"I will be now." She tried to smile, but he could see she was badly shaken. "I thought it was a real grenade. I thought..."

Corbray knelt beside them. "Dawg, you look like hell."

"He needs to get to a hospital."

"We'll take good care of him, Ms. Hamilton. How are you?"

"I'm okay—just a bit overwhelmed, I guess." There was a hitch to her voice, and Derek knew she was near tears.

"I bet." Corbray looked at Perooz, who lay lifeless beside him, his blood pooled in the dirt. "Looks like you two were taking care of business without us."

Derek gritted his teeth and struggled to lift his weight off Jenna.

"I got you." Corbray lent him a hand, leaning him back against the post. "You just take it easy, brother."

"How are the others?" Jenna asked. "Are they...?"

"Ortiz, Cruz, and O'Neal are out of surgery and stable. Jones is alive—but only because of you, Ms. Hamilton. It was touch and go for a while. He's in ICU at the U.S. military hospital in Kabul."

That was good news.

"Jenna is ... a good field medic," Derek managed to say.

But the adrenaline was fading, pain and cold and exhaustion taking hold.

Jenna drew him down, pillowed his head in her lap. "Rest. We need to keep him warm. He'll need IV fluids."

Corbray shed his coat, spread it over Derek, the warmth precious. "Hang on, buddy. Doc is on his way."

"Ms. Hamilton, Mr. Tower, you don't know how relieved I am to find you safe."

"Kazi." Rage had Derek fighting to stand. "You bastard!"

Corbray restrained him. "Hey, man, relax. This is a joint operation between Cobra and the governor's security forces."

Derek's gaze locked with Kazi's. "He's behind this. You know he is."

Corbray gave a little shake of his head, his gaze telling

Derek to shut up, that they would deal with Kazi later. "He's helping us out here."

Kazi turned to Qassim, drew his weapon. "You filthy son of a pig."

Corbray blocked the shot. "Not here! Not in front of Ms. Hamilton."

Kazi glared at Corbray but ordered his men to take Qassim outside.

"Wh-what's happening?" Jenna asked, eyes wide.

"I think Kazi is about to get rid of the evidence," Corbray said.

Qassim had begun to beg, his shrieks pathetic. "Please don't! They killed my son! I did what you told me to do! I only did—"

Bam! Bam! Bam!

Jenna gasped, jumped.

Derek took her hand. "It's okay, angel. It's okay."

But it wasn't okay. She'd been through hell.

"Oh, fuck." Derek's world started to break apart, turning to pixels.

"Derek?" Jenna lowered his head gently to her lap once more. "He's bleeding again. Hand me what's left of that burqa."

She pressed down hard on his shoulder, and he couldn't help but moan.

Then Doc Sullivan was there. "Hey, boss, Ms. Hamilton."

In a heartbeat, Jenna seemed to swallow her fear and went total nurse on them.

"He's got an entry wound in his left shoulder but no exit wound. I put hemostatic and pressure bandages on it, but Qassim aggravated the wound to cause him pain. I tore up my burqa and made a dressing with that. I think he has broken ribs from a bullet that struck his vest. He's had trouble breathing, but there's no pneumothorax. I gave him twenty mgs of morphine that wore off hours ago."

"Thanks for taking such good care of him. Let's get him comfortable."

A stick in Derek's thigh. A stretcher. A warm blanket.

And then Derek was floating, Jenna stroking his hair.

When he opened his eyes again, he was in a Chinook, an IV bag hanging above him, Jenna holding his hand, her worried gaze focused entirely on him.

She'd told him she loved him. Had she meant it, or had it been stress?

She smiled. "How do you feel?"

He didn't really register her question, his gaze on her face. "Beautiful."

Yeah, he was high as a kite.

He knew when they reached the U.S. military hospital in Kabul, when they took X-rays, when Jenna kissed him as they wheeled him into surgery.

"I'll be right here."

Then there was nothing.

~

JENNA SAT next to Derek's bed, watching his vitals, getting the nurse when his IV fluids ran low, changing the ice bag on his chest, doing her best to keep him comfortable. The staff had let her borrow a pair of scrubs, as her clothes were filthy with dirt and blood. They'd fed her, too, and brought in one of those chairs that opened into a bed so she could stay overnight.

It was almost midnight now. It had taken the surgeon a little more than three hours to remove the ball from his shoulder and repair the damage to bone and connective tissue. There was nothing they could do for his broken ribs or cracked sternum or the bruises and lacerations on his cheeks and lip. They would heal with time.

She had come so close to losing him, so close to watching him die.

She squeezed her eyes shut, tried not to remember. Malik hitting the windshield in a spray of blood. The sight of Derek falling back onto the asphalt. The sound of his cries when Qassim tortured him. Perooz falling to the dirt, impaled through the abdomen. The blast of the stun grenade.

Please don't! They killed my son! I did what you told me to do! I only did—

Bam! Bam! Bam!

Jenna had witnessed more violence, more brutality in the past two weeks than in the rest of her life combined. Through it all, Derek had been beside her, sheltering her, doing his best to keep her safe—and driving her crazy in bed.

She'd told him she loved him, and it was true. She had gotten involved with another man who was dedicated to his career.

Well done.

But she'd seen the shock on his face.

He'd told her upfront that he didn't do relationships. He'd warned her not to get tangled up in him. She'd gone and fallen for him anyway. Of course, there was a chance he wouldn't remember what she'd said. Then she wouldn't have to listen to him tell her that it wouldn't work, that whatever they'd had was over now.

Maybe if she pretended that nothing had happened, her feelings would fade. She'd studied some psychology and knew that people in survival situations sometimes forged special bonds—the product of hormones. Maybe what she thought was love was nothing more than stress-related brain chemistry.

Yeah, not a chance.

Nice try, though.

He moaned, his eyes fluttering open.

"Hey, there." She brushed a lock of hair off his forehead. "How do you feel?"

His lips curved in a drugged, sleepy smile. "Happy to see you."

"I'm not going anywhere." She picked up his water pitcher, guiding the plastic straw so it wouldn't jab him where his lip had split. "Drink."

He raised his head, did as she'd asked, then reached for her hand with his right hand, his fingers threading with hers. "How are the others?"

"I've been to see them all." She wouldn't go into detail. He didn't need to know that Cruz had almost bled out and had lost part of his colon, or that O'Neal would have to have his knee replaced and had come close to losing his leg. "They're all going to recover. They're moving Malik out of ICU tomorrow."

Derek squeezed her fingers. "How are you doing—and don't tell me you're fine. No one who has been through what you went through today is fine."

Jenna started to say that she was coping, but her throat went tight, tears filling her eyes. She wiped them away. "I'll be okay. I just need some time. I've never seen anything like..."

"I'm sorry, Jenna. I was supposed to keep you safe. I failed you."

"Don't say that! You did everything you could. You

almost died. If Cobra hadn't gotten there when they did, Qassim would have..."

In her mind, she saw Qassim raise his rifle, point it at Derek.

"You risked your life for mine, Jenna. You tried to reach me, to cover me with your own body. That's not how it's supposed to go with bodyguards."

"I couldn't let him kill you, Derek. I ..." She stopped herself from telling him she loved him a second time.

"Do you know who I saw today?" His gaze was soft, his swollen lips curling in a slight smile. "I saw Jimmy—in you. I saw his courage in you. What you did—for me, for Jones... You're one in a million, Jenna. Just like your brother."

Derek's words put a hitch in Jenna's chest, tears spilling down her cheeks.

But at that moment, the nurse walked in.

"You're awake!" She had a thermometer in one hand. "I'm here to check your vitals. How is your pain?"

Fighting to hold herself together, Jenna left the room on the pretext of refilling Derek's ice pack. She passed the little Christmas tree the nurses had put up in the hallway. Today had been Black Friday. Back home, people had been shopping, while Derek and his men...

Jenna left the ice pack on the counter, hurried into the bathroom, then locked the door and let her tears come.

THREE DAYS LATER, Derek was discharged, his left arm in a sling, an RX for pain meds in his hand. While Corbray stayed behind to oversee repairs of their compound in Mazar-e-Sharif and to deal with Kazi, Derek flew with Jenna, Cruz, O'Neal, Ortiz, and Jones on a special medical transport from Bagram Air Base to the U.S. military hospital in Landstuhl, Germany. From there, Cruz, Jones, and O'Neal would be admitted to the hospital, while Ortiz, Derek and Jenna stayed at Cobra's Frankfurt facility where Derek could heal up a bit before heading back to the States.

During the flight, Jenna watched over him and the others as if they were her patients, and it was clear that his men adored her. Jones told anyone who would listen how she had climbed out of an armored Land Cruiser with bullets flying to save his life.

Jenna deserved the glory.

She deserved more than that. She deserved a man who was good to her, a man who was worthy of her, a man who could give her the life she wanted—a happy home and her own babies to hold.

Derek wanted to be that man, but he didn't know how. He'd never been in a long-term relationship. Though he'd like to blame that on his job, the truth was more pathetic.

He'd never had a family. He'd never known that kind of life. Until he'd met Jimmy, he'd never even had a close friend. How could he give a classy, smart woman like Jenna the life she deserved when he didn't know what a normal life looked like?

Figure it out, or let her go.

It was that simple.

It wasn't simple at all.

She'd told him she loved him. The truth was that he loved her, too. He loved her down to his blood and bones. He hadn't said a damned thing about it since, afraid to set something in motion that she would come to regret. They hadn't spoken about the future at all—where she would go, what she would do, whether they would see each other once they got back to the U.S.

Fucking coward.

He watched her check Jones' dressings, a smile on her face. She was trying to hide it, but what she'd been through had left her struggling. He'd seen it before in young soldiers —the shock that followed that first battle and the brutality of combat.

She noticed him watching, and her smile brightened, putting a hitch in his chest. She stood, took off her nitrile gloves, and walked over to him, lowering her voice so that only he could hear. "How is my favorite patient?"

He caught her around her waist, breath hissing between his teeth at the pain in his chest. "Sit on my lap, and I'll show you how I am."

She laughed. "Those are big words for a man who can't move without wincing."

"Can I help it? I see you, and I want you."

"Sorry, but there is no Mile High Club on medical flights."

"Well, damn. You're no fun."

She sat beside him, leaned close. "Wait till we get to our room."

Corbray had taken care of everything. When they landed, Derek's gear and Jenna's luggage were transferred to the helicopter and flown with them to Cobra's Frankfurt complex, an enormous stone and glass building outside of the city.

He wanted to hold the door for her, but she held it for him, any movement with his arms or upper body excruciating.

"Wow." She looked around.

"Impressed?"

"This place looks like a fancy office building, not a bunker. But I guess we're no longer in a war zone."

He caught her hand, raised it to his lips. "You're safe here, Jenna. I promise."

They settled into the suite set aside for him or Corbray, no one batting an eye when Jenna stayed with him.

Jenna started to undress him. "Time for you to sleep."

"I *so* wish you were taking off my clothes for other reasons."

But, yeah, he was tired. Exhausted, really.

She gave him a glass of water and a pain pill. "Rest."

He dozed while Jenna took a shower, waking when his phone buzzed.

Corbray.

"We need to talk privately. I've got news—and you're not going to like it."

"Let's hear it."

Five minutes later, Derek ended the call, angry enough to put his fist through something. He was out of bed by the time Jenna stepped out of the bathroom, wrapped in her bathrobe. She took one look at him and stopped in her tracks.

"What is it? What's wrong?"

How was he going to tell her this?

He crossed the room, kissed her forehead. "I just got a call from Corbray. He had a long sit-down with Kazi. He also heard back from some contacts in Washington, people I had asked to do some digging."

"Tell me."

"Jenna, your father ..." *Shit.* This was harder than Derek had imagined. "He fired Cobra when it was clear I wouldn't be able to persuade you to come back."

"He *fired* you? All of this, everything you did for me—"

"Was my choice."

She stared at him, clearly astonished.

"After he fired us, your father contacted Kazi and bribed him to evict you from the province. We've got a record of the phone calls and the five hundred grand your father transferred to him."

"*What?*"

"Kazi still denies that Qassim worked for him. He says Qassim decided to abduct you and demand ransom, but Corbray and I don't buy it. We *know* Qassim worked for him. We think Kazi wanted to get more from your father and ordered Qassim to abduct you for ransom. He planned to tell your father bad guys had abducted you and then keep the ransom for himself, perhaps even claiming credit for rescuing you. Kazi only changed sides when it was clear that Cobra was going to come out on top."

The breath left Jenna's lungs in a gust, blood draining from her face. "My father was behind all of this? *He* started it?"

"He was the catalyst."

The hurt on Jenna's face broke Derek's heart.

"I'm so sorry." He ignored the pain in his chest and drew her close.

"He almost got you killed—and the others." She pulled back, clearly reeling. "How can you even stand to look at me? How can you touch—"

He cupped her cheek, looked into her eyes. "It's not your fault, Jenna. Nothing that bastard did is your fault."

When they got back to Washington, D.C., the first thing Derek was going to do was pay Senator Hamilton a visit.

20

"Oh!" Jenna stared in amazement and delight. "It's beautiful."

Frankfurt's Christmas Market at Römerberg was a sight to behold. Colored lights glittered everywhere, a three-story-high Christmas tree at one end of the square. Small cottages had been set up for vendors in neat rows. The scents made her mouth water—roasting nuts, grilled sausages, gingerbread, fresh pretzels, mulled wine, pastries, fresh-baked bread and more. There was even a merry-go-round.

They had decided to stay in Frankfurt for another ten days to give themselves both time to rest. Derek seemed to be in less pain, though his shoulder would take time to heal fully. Jenna had gotten her stitches out, and her headaches were becoming less frequent. Still, she was in no hurry to return home.

Derek kissed her temple, his left arm still in a sling. "That's the first time I've seen you smile in days."

"I smile when we're in bed, don't I?"

"Smile. Scream. Claw me. But that doesn't count."

It was true that Jenna hadn't felt like herself lately. The

news about her father had shaken her more than she would have imagined, and her entire life was up in the air. She had no home, no job, no idea where she would live. Worse, every time she closed her eyes, images from the day she'd been abducted filled her mind, following her into sleep.

Derek had been incredibly understanding about it all, especially considering that his injuries were a consequence of her father's deplorable actions. He'd listened to her while she'd raged about her father, woken her at night when she'd had nightmares, and held her when she hadn't been able to hold back her tears.

"You're grieving," he'd said last night. "Your father betrayed you, Jenna. If you weren't hurt, if you weren't upset, I'd think something was wrong."

His words had struck the source of her misery head-on.

What her father had done had left her feeling inescapably sad.

But she didn't want to think about that now, not standing in a Christmas wonderland with Derek still beside her.

They ate sausages in fresh-baked buns, then walked around to look at the vendors, their fingers twined. Jenna bought some gingerbread cookies for later, while Derek bought her a purple cashmere scarf.

He pressed a kiss to her nose. "To keep you warm."

She snuggled into it, brushed her cheeks against the softness. "Thank you."

The affection in his blue eyes gave her hope, lifted her spirits.

They stayed out until the night grew truly cold. Then Derek called for the car—a bulletproof limo—and they returned to the Cobra complex.

"How many of these does Cobra own?"

"Limos?"

"Limos, compounds, all of it."

Derek got a thoughtful frown on his face. "We have eight complexes—one in Uganda, one in Mazar-e-Sharif, one in Iraq, one in Israel, one in Australia, one in D.C., plus our main headquarters and a training facility in Denver, and this one—and probably twelve limos, plus Land Cruisers, a dozen or so helicopters, and a few jets."

"Wow. I guess it pays to be in the private military business."

He chuckled. "The pay is commensurate with the risk."

"I believe that."

When they got back to their room, they each ate a gingerbread cookie, Derek licking powdered sugar off her upper lip. Which led to kissing. And more kissing.

Jenna helped him undress, stripped off her clothes.

"I like where you're going with this, but you're on top again," he said.

"You say that like it's a bad thing."

"Hey, leave the scarf on."

Scarf wrapped around her neck, Jenna straddled him, took his hard cock inside her, the two of them moaning almost in unison. She ground herself against him while he cupped and teased her breasts, plucking and pinching her nipples, rubbing their aching tips with soft cashmere, abrading them with his callused palm.

It felt so good, *too* good. Panting, sweating, her body burning, melting inside, needing, needing more of him. Derek. Only Derek.

She came hard and fast, then rode him, his hips thrusting to meet her, the fingers of his right hand digging into her hip.

"Fuck, yes. *Jenna*." His head went back as he came, his eyes squeezed shut, breath rushing from his lungs.

God, she loved him. She hadn't said it again, had kept her feelings to herself. She didn't want to ruin what they had now by putting him on the spot.

He lay there for a moment, his body relaxed.

Then his eyes opened. "Damn, woman. Sex with you just keeps getting better."

Body languid, she kissed the big bruise on his chest, then snuggled against his right side, careful not to hurt him.

"When we get back to D.C., you're going to confront my father, aren't you?"

Derek was quiet for a moment as if he wasn't entirely sure what he could tell her. "Yes. Corbray is preparing a report for the Secretary of Defense, the Senate Armed Services Committee, and the Joint Chiefs."

"Wow." Still, she knew how this would end.

"He'll get away with it. You know that, don't you? He always does."

Nothing her father had done had ever stuck to him—not the campaign finance violations, not the allegations of sexual harassment, not his lies and many abuses of privilege and power.

"He won't get away with it, Jenna, not this time. His actions almost led to the deaths of four decorated US veterans—

"Five. You, too, remember?"

"Okay, five. And he cost Cobra at least a million in damages. We have more allies than he realizes—and he has more enemies. When the press gets a hold of this..."

Her father was in such deep shit.

"I want to go with you."

"I'm not sure that's a good idea. Some of what we have to discuss is potentially classified. It's likely to become confrontational."

"Good."

Jenna had things she wanted to say to her father, too.

DEREK SAT in the back of the limo wearing a suit, Jenna beside him in the designer outfit she'd bought for the occasion, looking like a million bucks, her beautiful hair hanging free. He could tell she was nervous. "It's going to be okay."

She nodded but said nothing, her fingers rubbing the bumpy surface of her brother's dog tags, which she still wore around her neck.

While Jenna had been off shopping, Derek and Corbray had met with the Joint Chiefs, the Secretary of Defense, and members of the Armed Services Committee behind closed doors, presenting their damning evidence, including their drone footage and phone and bank records, as well as a recording Corbray had made of Kazi's almost-confession.

No one had taken it well. Hamilton's allies had quickly distanced themselves from him as the tide turned. They'd proposed a congressional investigation but had granted Derek the favor of letting Jenna confront her father before announcing anything.

By the end of the day, Hamilton's empire of dirt would crumble.

They pulled up to the Dirksen Senate Office Building on Constitution, the driver stopping to let them out. Derek walked with Jenna up the stairs and through the front door. "Derek Tower, CEO of Cobra International Security, here to see Senator Hamilton. I am armed."

He surrendered his firearm and showed the man his ID then passed through the metal detector and signed in.

"Jenna Hamilton, daughter of Senator Hamilton." She gave them her ID and her handbag and passed through the metal detector.

"Is the senator expecting you?"

Jenna smiled. "I just got back from overseas. It's a surprise."

The security guard didn't look happy about surprises, but he let them through.

They rode the elevator to the top floor, Jenna growing visibly more nervous.

Derek wished he could make this easier for her. "You don't have to do this."

"I need him out of my life."

Okay, that made sense.

They reached the top floor and walked down a hallway crowded with lobbyists and sycophants to Hamilton's offices and stepped inside.

The administrative assistant looked up from her desk. "Can I help you?"

"I'm Jenna, Senator Hamilton's daughter, here to see my father."

"I'm sorry, but he's with someone right now."

"That's too bad." Jenna walked to the closed office door and let herself in, Derek following her inside.

"Jenna?" Hamilton stared at his daughter, his gaze shifting from Jenna to Derek, his expression turning wary.

So, the bastard hadn't known Jenna was back.

Kazi, as part of his penance, had promised not to warn Hamilton, and he'd apparently kept his word—about that, at least.

"We need to talk."

"As you can see, I'm in the middle of—"

"*Now.*"

"You know what, I'll go. We can finish this later." A man in a business suit got up from one of the plush leather chairs and hurried out the door, briefcase in hand.

Hamilton stood, his gaze meeting Derek's, his upper lip curling. "What are you doing here? I fired you. If you've come for money—"

Jenna cut him off. "I know what you did. Do you know what happened as a result of your actions?"

Hamilton's pupils dilated. *Fear.* "What are you going on about now? You just interrupted a very important—"

"You sent Derek to bring me home and told him to use force if necessary. When he wouldn't do that, you bribed Governor Kazi with five hundred thousand dollars to rescind my permission to work in Balkh Province."

The bastard's face flushed red. "Don't take that tone with me, little girl."

Derek's right fist clenched.

Oh, the fucker was treading on thin ice now.

Jenna wasn't cowed. "Do you know what happened next? Kazi sent one of his men to abduct me. He wanted—

"I told you it wasn't safe there, but you didn't listen. I told you to stay home, find a husband, and not waste your life—"

"I was safe and happy there until *you* started interfering! Kazi wanted ransom money from you. He thought he'd play both sides—the hero and the villain—and come away a few million richer. His men set off a car bomb outside of Cobra's compound. One person *died*, and I was injured. See this? Stitches."

"You should have stayed home."

"I was abducted, threatened with rape. I watched men die because of *you*."

Hamilton was getting flustered. "I don't even know this Kazi person."

"Liar! There are phone records and bank records. We know what you did, and so do the Joint Chiefs and half of Congress by now."

Hamilton had begun to sweat, beads of perspiration popping up on his forehead. He stepped around his desk, getting closer to Jenna. "You met with them?"

Derek moved closer, too.

"Five Cobra operatives were *shot* trying to protect me from Kazi's hired killers, including Derek. One of those men is still in the hospital."

"This is the first I've heard of any of this. You can't blame me. I had nothing to do with it. If you had stayed home like I told you to—"

"Shut up! Just shut up! You made James' life hell. You're the reason he went into the army. He wanted to get away from *you*. You made my life hell, too, interfering in every decision I've ever tried to make. You probably drove Mom to suicide!"

Hamilton drew back his hand as if to strike Jenna.

Derek caught his wrist in mid-air. "Touch her, and I will end you."

"That's a threat."

"You damned well better believe it is." Derek released him.

But Jenna wasn't finished. "As of today, you are out of my life. I disown you. You're not my father. You're just another corrupt politician who plays with other people's lives. I don't want to hear from you again for any reason."

"You won't get a dime of my estate."

"I don't want your money. I don't want anything from you."

Now it was Derek's turn. "We've handed all the evidence we collected over to Congressional investigators. They'll be in touch this afternoon. You'll be getting a bill from Cobra for damages later today as well."

"I'm not paying for anything Kazi did."

"Oh, I think you will." Derek took Jenna's hand in his, and the two left Hamilton's office, passing his stunned assistant, Hamilton's shouted threats following them down the hallway.

~

JENNA CLIMBED INTO THE LIMO, Derek sliding in beside her. She didn't want to cry. She didn't want to waste a single tear on her father, but her heart was in tatters. "He didn't even ask me how I was. I told him I'd been injured, abducted, and threatened with rape, and all he could think about was himself."

"I'm so sorry, angel." Derek wrapped his good arm around her and drew her against him. "It's okay to cry."

"You never cry." She'd never seen him in tears.

"I'm fucked up."

That made Jenna laugh. "You are *not* fucked up."

"How about we get our stuff and check in at the Four Seasons? You've had enough of living in private military compounds, haven't you?"

"I don't mind. Isn't the Four Seasons super expensive?"

"I can afford it. You've had a rough day. Let me do something to pamper you."

Jenna sniffed, not caring where they stayed. "Okay."

They went back to the Cobra building, packed their bags, and took the limo to the Four Seasons, Derek calling ahead on his cell phone to reserve a room. "Is the Royal Suite available?"

Royal suite?

Derek gave his credit card number over the phone. "Thanks."

She stared at him. "Are you nuts?"

He seemed to consider her question. "Fucked up, but not nuts."

"You've done enough for me, Derek. If not for you, I probably wouldn't be here."

"Let me spoil you—just a little."

If he was trying to distract her, it was working. The Royal Suite had twice the square footage of her old condo with high-end Art Deco décor, a huge sunken tub, and every luxury a hotel could offer. They ate room service in the dining room, stood for a time on the balcony overlooking the city lights, made love on the king-sized bed, soaked in the enormous tub.

"Am I hurting you?" Jenna leaned back, rested her head carefully against the right side of his chest.

"No." He kissed her temple. "How are you feeling?"

"There's going to be a media storm, isn't there?" It hadn't dawned on her until she'd caught a glimpse of her ex-father holding a press conference on CNN that reporters would probably show up on her doorstep.

"I imagine so. We can provide security."

"You've done enough for me—more than enough. You were fired, remember?"

"Yeah, but I don't follow orders well. I won't leave you alone with this."

His words put a lump in her throat. "I don't know where to go from here. I need to find a job somewhere, buy a home, get my stuff out of storage."

"Do you know where you want to live?"

"Not in D.C." She was done with this place.

"Why don't you stay with me for a while? I've got a place

in Denver not far from downtown. Until this shoulder heals, I won't be going overseas. You can take your time, figure out exactly what you want to do, get back on your feet. I can show you around Colorado."

"Are you serious? Won't I be invading your man space?"

He chuckled. "Invade all you want. There's a gym in the building. I think there's a big tub in my bathroom, too, but I can't remember."

"You can't remember?"

"I'm not home much."

She believed that. "Are you sure you don't mind?"

"I wouldn't have asked if I wasn't sure, Jenna. I ... care about you."

Jenna's heart lifted to hear those words. No, it wasn't *I love you*, but he'd just invited her to stay with him, giving them more time together. "Thank you. And, Derek, for the record, I care about you, too."

21

After arranging to have Jenna's belongings shipped to Derek's condo in Denver, they flew by private jet to Denver International Airport and took a limo through the city.

She craned her head. "Where are the mountains?"

He pointed to the west. "You'll see them from my balcony."

As they drew close to his building, Derek saw a group of reporters gathered on the sidewalk. *Shit.* He pushed the button to speak with their driver. "Let's go in through the garage."

"Yes, sir."

The reporters were there for Derek, not Jenna, but the moment they recognized Jenna, they would go after her, and his relationship with her—however one might label it—would become part of the press surrounding her father's downfall.

They drove around back and passed through a security checkpoint, the driver stopping near the elevators.

Derek thanked him. "Can you park and bring up our bags?"

"Yes, sir."

Derek would ordinarily handle that himself. But, although he was no longer wearing the sling, his shoulder and ribs made carrying anything difficult. He'd also rather focus on Jenna.

They rode the elevator to the eleventh floor.

Jenna glanced around the hallway outside his door. "This is chic."

"You like it?"

Derek would be a liar if he said he wasn't nervous. He'd brought women back to his place for sex, but he'd never had a woman move in with him, even temporarily. Some part of him was afraid that he was going too far, that crossing this threshold would only end with Jenna getting hurt. Even so, he couldn't find the strength to let her go.

He punched in his access code, opened the door, and moved aside to let her enter.

She stepped inside, looked up at the chandelier in the entryway. "Wow!"

Apart from the view of the mountains, he'd never thought much about the condo himself. It was just where he came to shower, sleep, and eat between jobs.

"Did you decorate this place? It's all so tasteful."

"Hell, no. I hired someone for that. If it had been left to me, it would probably look more like a gun locker or a gym."

He found himself smiling as she moved through the space, seeming to love what she saw. The kitchen with its aluminum appliances, marble countertops, and glass-walled, walk-in wine refrigerator. The living room, which had a fireplace and floor-to-ceiling windows that looked west toward the mountains. The master bedroom with its twin walk-in closets and enormous bathroom.

"You *do* have a huge tub—right in front of the windows. How could you forget that? Look how big this shower is! You could have four people in there."

He only wanted one—her.

He followed her to the second bedroom, which served as a storage area for gear.

"Your guns get their own bedroom. That's cute."

"Most of my firearms are locked up at the Cobra facility. This is for tactical gear, body armor, and personal firearms—concealed carry pieces, mostly."

"Concealed carry?" She looked him up and down. "Are you armed now?"

"Yes." He raised his shirt to show her the holster tucked into his trousers.

"Good to know."

The third bedroom was his home office and locked.

"This is where the state secrets are kept?"

There was something in there he wanted her to see. "I'll show you."

He entered the combination code, flicked on the light, and led her inside. He took the small album of photos off the shelf and handed it to her.

She looked up at him, curiosity on her face, then opened it. "Oh, God."

Derek and Jimmy smiled out from the photo, both wearing ACUs, a soccer ball in Jimmy's hand, a group of young Afghan boys around them. "He took a lot of photos. Sometimes he'd hand the camera to me. I wasn't very good."

Jenna sat, turned through the pages, smiling through her tears at the photos. Derek and Jimmy playing soccer with village boys. Jimmy sitting on the hood of a Humvee,

M4 in hand. Derek sitting shirtless in the shade at some forward operating base, cleaning sand out of his weapon, a long beard on his face.

"I miss him so much. I remember the moment the reporter told me he'd been killed in action. It was like losing my entire world. I felt so alone."

The despair in her voice opened up the pain inside Derek, his grief still sharp if he let himself think about it.

"It crushed me. It almost broke me." Derek had never admitted this to anyone, but then Jenna wasn't just anyone. He'd never felt more connected with another person, more intimate, more comfortable, than he did with Jenna. "I've spent a lot of days since then wishing that *I* had taken those rounds, not your brother."

Jenna set the photo album aside, stood, wrapped her arms around him. "My brother wouldn't want you to feel that way. You were his best friend. He loved you, Derek. I have to believe that he saved you so you could save me."

Some part of Derek wanted to reject that idea. He didn't believe in God. He didn't believe in fate. Even so, something about her words felt right. They slid inside him, took hold, warming the cold, desolate emptiness that was his soul.

He made love to Jenna after that, peeling off her clothes, spreading her out on his bed, and going down on her before driving himself home inside her. Then he held her, his head and heart full of her—her taste, her scent, the feel of her in his arms.

He didn't know if Jimmy could hear him, but he sent a thought winging skyward anyway.

I've got her, buddy. I'll watch over her.

Jenna woke the next morning to find Derek getting ready for work. She watched him button his white dress shirt and put on a gray silk tie.

When he saw she was awake, he walked over to her and planted a kiss on her forehead. "Did you sleep well?"

"Yes." No nightmares. "You've got physical therapy today, right?"

He scowled. "Don't remind me. Cobra is hosting its official holiday party tomorrow night. I completely forgot about it. I want to take you as my date and introduce you around."

"Ooh. A date." She sat up, holding the sheet to her bare breasts.

"It's a black-tie thing."

"I don't have anything to wear." Her belongings wouldn't be arriving until tomorrow, but she didn't own any fancy dresses anyway. "Is there a mall around here?"

"I don't want you going out unescorted, not with all the press surrounding your father. That's my official advice as your former bodyguard."

Jenna knew that a small cadre of reporters had been hanging out on the sidewalk out front, waiting to interview Derek. "I could call a cab."

He shook his head. "I'll have my personal shopper at Saks get in touch with you. She can bring the store to you."

"Your personal shopper? Saks Fifth Avenue?"

He pointed to his tie. "Do you think I go out and shop for this stuff myself? I'd be clueless. I can tell you how to accessorize for battle and know which body armor is chic this season, but I don't know jack about—" he flipped over the tie to look at the label "—Calvin Klein."

Jenna laughed but shook her head. "I think Saks might be out of my price range. I haven't been paid for six months, remember?"

She had financed her work in Afghanistan by herself, not the hospital, an NGO, or the Afghan government. Yes, she still had money in savings from the sale of her D.C. condo, but she needed that to buy a new place. And after six months in Afghanistan all of this—the luxury of Derek's condo, the limos, Saks—seemed frivolous, out of touch, even overwhelming.

It's reverse culture shock. That's all.

The midwife who'd worked at the hospital prior to Jenna had warned her this would happen.

"The personal shopper is free. Saks is on me."

She started to object, but he bent down and stopped her with a kiss.

"You might not have noticed, but I have a lot of money. Let me spend some of it on you." He kissed her again, grabbed his sports jacket, and gingerly slid his left arm into it. "I made coffee. There's a restaurant on the ground floor that makes incredible eggs Benedict. Just give them a buzz, and they'll charge it to me and deliver."

"Like room service."

"Just like room service. I think there's a menu by the phone in the kitchen."

"Have you eaten?"

He shook his head. "I'll grab something at the office."

This was what his life was like outside of war zones. He lived as if his home were a hotel. The revelation gave Jenna an idea.

She got out of bed, slipped into her robe, and walked him to the door. "Have a good day."

He raised a hand to her cheek, gave her a lopsided grin. "You, too."

She ordered breakfast, catching up on emails with her friends as she ate and sipped her coffee. Yes, she was back in the U.S. It was a long story. She had learned so much in Afghanistan—about herself, about the world. She was looking for a job now but wanted to focus on the Denver area. Yes, she would love to get together with them, too.

By the time she had showered and dressed, there was a message from Derek's personal shopper, Carolyn, on her phone. She returned the call, answering all of Carolyn's questions as best she could about her measurements, height, weight, and coloring. "I want a dress that will bring Derek to his knees."

Carolyn arrived in the early afternoon with a rack—a rack!—of dresses. Dresses with sequins. Velvet dresses. Silk dresses. Illusion dresses.

"You won the boyfriend lottery." Carolyn searched through the dresses for the ones she thought might suit Jenna.

Jenna stopped herself from telling Carolyn that she wasn't Derek's girlfriend. She could enjoy the fantasy for a while, couldn't she?

As long as you don't lose yourself in it, go ahead.

"But with that figure, those eyes, your hair... Let's just say that if I were your age, I would have tried to snap him up, too."

Jenna wasn't sure how to respond to this, so she let it go, trying on dress after dress until she came to a short, off-the-shoulder dress in dark blue velvet. "Oh!"

It fit her perfectly, making the most of her bustline, waist, and hips.

"He won't be able to take his eyes off of you."

Jenna studied her reflection, lifted her hair on top of her head. "I hope not."

"You'll need the right lingerie, of course—a bra that

accentuates your bust and maybe some matching panties. I took the liberty of bringing some."

Carolyn was right, but Jenna insisted on paying for the lingerie herself.

After Carolyn left, Jenna went ahead with her plan. She put together a menu, then looked in Derek's fridge and cupboards—only to find them bare, apart from coffee beans, some milk that was close to its expiration date, and mustard. He had pots and pans, but they looked brand new and unused, as if they were nothing more than props. But, apart from his office and the room where he kept his gear, the entire condo was like that—beautiful like something from a magazine but not homey.

She ordered groceries and wine online and let security know to expect a delivery. She wasn't a great cook or particularly domestic. She'd eaten a lot of carry-out during her life, too, but she could make a roast chicken as well as anyone.

It was time someone put this beautiful kitchen to use and gave Derek a home-cooked meal in his own home.

DEREK SHOT Jenna a text to let her know he was on his way home. He would see what she felt like having for dinner and maybe pick up some take-out from the sushi place downstairs. He drove home in his Range Rover, parked in the garage, and took the elevator up to his floor.

When he opened his door, he was hit in the face by the delicious scent of roasting meat. He stepped over a pair of Jenna's shoes, walked through the entryway—and found his immaculately clean kitchen a mess. There were dirty dishes in the sink, pots and pans on the stove, a dish towel in the middle of the floor.

Unaware that he was there, Jenna stood at one of the counters, slicing vegetables for a salad and wiggling her sweet ass in time to music playing in little pink earphones. He stood there for a moment, took in the scene, watched her, warmth stirring in his chest. The last time someone had cooked a meal in this kitchen was ...

Yeah, never.

"Hey."

She jumped, shrieked, and tugged out the earphones.

"Sorry. I didn't mean to sneak up on you." He walked over to her, wiped a smudge of flour off her cheek. "You've been busy. What's all this?"

She looked around, too. "I thought it was time you had a real meal and not MREs or take-out. Sorry about the mess. I meant to have it cleaned up and the table set before you got home."

Hell, he didn't care. "It smells delicious."

"How was PT?"

"Painful."

"I can massage your shoulder after dinner if you like."

"Will that help?"

"It might."

The food *was* delicious—roast chicken, buttered potatoes, a fresh salad, white wine, and a chocolate cake she'd made from scratch.

He shared news he knew she'd be happy to hear. "Malik was discharged today. He'll be on a flight home tomorrow."

He'd been the last of the five of them still in the hospital.

"I'm so glad to hear that." She looked up at him from beneath her lashes, tracing her fingertips along the stem of her wine glass in a way that immediately had Derek thinking of her stroking his cock. "I picked out my dress."

"Your dress? Oh. Right. Good."

"You don't get to see it till tomorrow night."

Now he was intrigued. "I can't wait."

They were in the middle of loading the dishwasher when Derek's cell rang.

"Turn on CNN," Corbray said. "Hamilton has just resigned. Word is investigators agreed to end their probe if he left office."

Shit. Typical.

"Thanks." Derek ended the call. "That was Javier. Your father just resigned."

"What?"

He turned on the TV, and there on the screen was Senator Hamilton.

"—has been my pleasure to serve the people of this great nation these past thirty-five years. Rumors that I conspired with foreign entities to the detriment of U.S. citizens, including my daughter, are blatantly false. I refuse to let politics and media lies ruin my legacy." Hamilton flashed a big smile. "I'm going to focus on my golf game instead."

Laughter. The clicking of cameras.

"Senator, is it true that you bribed an Afghan warlord—"

"The senator will not be taking questions," said some guy in a suit—probably an aide—into the microphone as Hamilton beat a hasty retreat. "Thank you very much."

"His *legacy*? What legacy is that?" Jenna picked up the remote and turned off the TV, her cheeks pink, rage on her pretty face. "He can never admit when he's wrong. He just lied to the American people, and most of them will never know that. Is Cobra going to issue a press release to refute what he just said?"

"We've already said all we're going to say to the public, but we are suing him for damages. He can't hide. The truth will come out." Derek took her hand. "Do you want to issue a statement?"

She let out a breath. "What would it say? 'Hey, everyone, my dad lied. He's a jerk.' I just want this to be behind me."

Derek could understand that. "Do you want to go for a drive and look at the Christmas lights? The City and County Building always puts on a pretty show."

She smiled. "I'd love that."

He drove her downtown, circled the capitol with its gold dome and then headed down Colfax past the City and County Building.

She craned her neck to see all of it. "That's beautiful. I love it! We should get a tree for your place."

Derek could refuse her nothing. They got a small Christmas tree and then bought lights and some ornaments at Target, Jenna putting everything from delicate glass balls to tinsel to kitschy plastic baubles to candy canes into the shopping cart.

"When I was a kid, our tree always had to look a certain way. Everything had to match and be placed just perfectly. This is going to be the craziest Christmas tree ever."

"I can get behind that." He tossed a plastic ornament that looked like a whiskey bottle and one that looked like a trout into the cart. "Let's do this."

They drove home, put up the little tree, and trimmed it, then sat back with the fireplace running and enjoyed the sight, the air scented with pine.

"Thanks, Derek. I needed this." She took off his shirt, sat on his left side, and went to work massaging his shoulder.

Derek sucked in a breath, her touch painful but mostly in a good way. "It's my first Christmas tree here."

She laughed. "Why am I not surprised?"

As she worked the stiffness out of his shoulder muscles,

he battled a tangle of emotions that threatened to make him say stupid things—things like "No one baked me a cake before," "I love you," and "Stay with me."

How a cold-hearted, selfish bastard like Hamilton had managed to raise a daughter as warm and loving as Jenna, Derek couldn't say. It must have been her mother's DNA. In a single day, Jenna had transformed his immaculate condo into a messy, festive, and sweetly scented home.

22

Jenna finished with her mascara then checked her reflection in the mirror, her pulse thrumming with excitement. She'd put her hair up in a twist, letting a few tendrils hang free at her nape and temples. It wasn't a professional up-do, but it was good enough. The cocktail dress clung to her curves, showing a tasteful amount of cleavage and leaving her shoulders bare, its velvet fabric shimmering.

She stepped out of the bathroom to find Derek partially dressed in an all-black tux, struggling with cuff links.

He looked up and stared, his expression slowly changing from surprise to sexual hunger. "Holy *fuck*. God, you look beautiful."

His cuff link fell to the carpet.

"Let me help you." She knelt and picked up the little thing then stood again to find his gaze fixed on her breasts.

"I'm not sure we should go to this party." He bent down, nuzzled her throat.

"What do you think we should do instead?" She popped

the cufflink through the fabric and twisted it so that it would stay.

"Fuck. We should fuck all night." He reached for her. "On the floor. On the bed. On the kitchen table. Everywhere."

His words sent a shiver of arousal through her.

She stepped away and picked up her clutch and heels, looking back at him over her shoulder as she walked out of the room. "Hurry, or we'll be late."

He bit his lower lip, his brow furrowed, his gaze on her ass now. "Damn."

She slipped into her heels—she hadn't worn heels since before she'd left for Afghanistan—and waited at the front door. He appeared, two black woolen dress coats draped over his arm, hers and his.

He helped her into hers. "I know what you're thinking."

"Let's hear it."

"You think that just because I have testicles, you can put on a sexy dress that shows off your breasts and sweet ass and turn me into a raging mess of pheromones." Then he whispered into her ear, his breath hot on her skin. "*You're right.*"

Another shiver.

Oh, she was right there with him.

But first, there was a party.

They rode the elevator down to the garage and walked hand in hand through the cold night air to Derek's vehicle. But if Jenna thought Derek was going to let her off the hook, she was mistaken. All the way to Cobra's offices, he kept at it.

"I'm going to go down on you until you scream. I'll rip those panties off and suck your clit. Then I'll get you on your hands and knees and fuck you hard from behind."

Warmth rushed into her cheeks. "Promises, promises."

"Or maybe I'll bang you up against the wall and mess up your dress."

Her inner muscles clenched.

"Maybe I'll tie you to my bed and fuck you so slowly that you lose your mind."

By the time they reached the office, she was horny as hell, aching and wet. They parked and walked to the elevator. As soon as the door closed, she was on him.

He caught her wrists, stopped her. "Surveillance."

"Oh, right."

"Can we have sex in a conference room?"

He laughed, seeming to find the idea hilarious. "God, no. Surveillance."

"Where then?"

He leaned down, a sexy grin on his face. "You have to wait—just like I do."

She gave a frustrated moan, took the hand he offered, and walked with him out of the elevator and into a long room or hallway crowded with people. The walls were made of burnished steel, the floors white marble, several tables of catered food set up on one side, a bar in the corner.

"Hey, Ms. Hamilton!" Dylan waved to her, looking nothing like the dusty operative in camo, his dark good looks set off by a white tux.

She hugged him. "I'm so happy to see you doing so well."

"Thanks." His gaze raked over her. "You look..."

Derek coughed.

"Lovely," Dylan said. "Hey, boss."

"Glad to have you stateside, Cruz."

Derek got them each a glass of champagne and guided her through the room, his hand on her lower back, introducing her to other staff, all of whom seemed to know who she was. Of course, they did.

Javier walked up to her, looking fabulous in black and white, Laura Nilsson, whom Jenna had seen on the TV news a thousand times, beside him. She was even prettier in person, with light blond hair, a slender figure, and lovely face.

"It's wonderful to meet you, Jenna. Javi has told me how incredibly brave you were. I'm so glad you're home safe now."

Jenna hadn't been brave—not compared to Laura, but she didn't say that. "Thank you. Javier, Derek, Malik, and everyone there in Mazar-e-Sharif were the brave ones."

"I've got to disagree," Javier said.

Derek gave Jenna's hands a squeeze, his gaze warm. "They're combat veterans, every one of them trained for that kind of work. You climbed out of a Land Cruiser under fire to save one of ours. No one here is going to forget that."

"You must be Jenna." The most beautiful woman Jenna had ever seen moved through the crowd toward them, her platinum blond hair in a stylish up-do, her perfect body in a beaded dress that hid almost nothing.

"Here comes trouble," Derek mumbled, smiling.

Javier introduced them. "Jenna, this is Holly Andris, Nick Andris' much better half. They both work for Cobra."

Jenna wondered what kind of work Holly did. "Nice to meet you."

Holly hugged her as if the two of them were old friends. "I've been dying to meet you. Thanks for saving Malik's life."

"I'm a midwife, so I have some experience—"

Holly's eyes went wide. "A midwife? That's right."

"Yes. I worked at a women's hospital in Afghanistan."

Javier explained. "Holly's pregnant—and a little nervous."

Jenna could understand that. "Is this your first? If you have questions, I'd be happy to answer them."

"Oh, you're a sweetheart!"

Jenna glanced back over her shoulder as Holly led her someplace where they could talk and found him watching her, a soft smile on his lips.

CORBRAY AND DEREK joined Andris in a corner.

"Congrats, man." Derek raised his champagne flute. "You're going to be a father. That's great."

That was a mind-blowing thought.

Derek had known Andris almost as long as he'd known Javier. He was one of the first hires Derek and Corbray had made. The man kicked ass—and he'd come as a package deal, bringing Holly with him.

"Thanks. Holly's pretty nervous about it."

"I can't blame her." If Derek knew that nine months from now he was going to have to shit a watermelon, he'd be pretty nervous, too. "Jenna is talking with her."

"Your Jenna is something else. I saw the drone footage. I saw what she did for Jones—and for you, too." Andris turned to Corbray. "I hear he's home."

"Safe and sound and damned glad to be alive."

Derek took hold of one of his lapels. "Hey, Corbray, remind me. Why do we force the staff to dress up like penguins every December?"

It was an old joke between them.

"Because we are a classy operation, bro."

"I think you're just living out some kind of James Bond fantasy."

Andris snorted, raising his tumbler of whiskey in a salute. “Right.”

Corbray rolled his eyes. “I know you two are probably more comfortable hanging out in week-old ACUs that reek of ball sweat, but I like not being in camo once in a while.”

“My balls don’t sweat,” Derek countered.

Andris laughed. “Dude, seriously? I have been with you in a tent in the middle of the desert. It wasn’t roses I was smelling.”

“It was your own armpits.”

Then Corbray brought them up to date on the lawsuit against Jenna’s father—and news from Afghanistan. Their attorneys were close to filing the case in civil court. Repairs on the compound in Mazar-e-Sharif were almost complete. The shot-up Land Cruiser was being sold off and replaced with a new armored Land Rover, which was faster, more maneuverable, and got much better gas mileage.

Then Corbray got down to the real news. “President Alghani has launched an investigation into the attack at the airport. Apparently, Kazi doesn’t have the authority to ground air traffic. Also, we may or may not have fed Alghani intel about Kazi’s ties to Qassim.”

“Kazi is up to his eyebrows in his own shit.” Derek searched the room for Jenna and saw her sitting at a table in the corner, a hand resting on Holly’s shoulder.

Corbray followed the direction of his gaze. “Jenna is one hell of a woman.”

Derek couldn’t disagree. “Yes, she is.”

“She’s smart. She’s brave. And, brother, she is crazy in love with you.”

Derek’s pulse skipped. “I know.”

Andris grinned. “You just scared the shit out of him.”

Derek glared at them. “I care about her, too.”

Corbray laughed. "Don't give me that 'care' bullshit. We're talking about *love* here. The Big L. The forever kind of thing."

Derek was tempted to tell both men to fuck off. "What's it to you?"

Corbray slapped him on the back. "You're hell in a fight, but you're not great with relationships. I'd like to see you happy. Try not to fuck this up."

The two men walked away, leaving Derek to stare after them.

Corbray's words stayed with him, running through his mind as he and Jenna drove home. Did Corbray truly believe Derek would intentionally blow things with Jenna? It was true that Derek had never gone the distance with a woman, but maybe he just hadn't met the right one.

That shit is for fairytales. You *are the problem.*

He had trouble getting close with women outside of sex, but it wasn't just women. He found the emotional messiness of being connected to other people difficult. The closer people got to him, the more he pushed them away. He considered Corbray and Andris friends, but he kept most people at arm's length, especially since Jimmy's death.

No attachment, no loss. Is that it?

"Derek? Are you okay?" Jenna asked, bringing him back to the present. "You seem a million miles away. Did you get bad news?"

"No. Sorry. What were you saying?"

"Oh, just that Holly is terrified of how painful birth is. I told her to expect the worst pain of her life and to keep her options open. If she knows up front that she wants an epidural, she should make sure her practitioner knows that and is supportive."

"Good advice."

"You are a million miles away." Jenna watched him, concern in her eyes.

Derek told her what Corbray had told him about Kazi. "I'd rather see the bastard get a bullet to the brain than come under investigation."

This wasn't what was on his mind, but what could he say—that he cared about her more than he'd cared about any woman and was terrified that he was going to hurt her?

He willed himself to focus on Jenna, only Jenna. "Don't think I've forgotten what I said earlier—about the going down on you, making you scream."

She ran her hand over his upper thigh. "You promised."

Derek's blood went hot, his mind shifting to a much more enjoyable train of thought. "Oh, angel, you just wait."

They parked, kissed on the way up in the elevator, Jenna arching against him. He punched in the entry code for his condo, getting it wrong the first time, lust making it damned hard to think.

They made it as far as the kitchen table.

He sat her on it, pushed her back, and tore off her pretty lace panties, tossing the tattered lace aside. Then he dropped to his knees, rested her feet on his shoulders, and got to work, sucking her clit, stroking her inside, making her scream.

But Derek wasn't done with her. When her climax had passed, he dragged her off the table, turned her around, and pounded into her from behind, reaching around to stroke her clit, carrying her over the edge once more before letting himself go.

"*Jenna.*" Her name felt like something sacred as he poured his soul into her.

They lay together in the darkness of his room after that,

the turmoil inside Derek pushed aside in the afterglow. "Remind me to give Carolyn a fat tip."

Jenna snuggled against him. "I'll say this for you, Derek Tower. You are a man who keeps his promises."

IT WAS early January before Jenna got serious about the job search. She made excuses for herself along the way. It was the holiday season. She was still dealing with the emotional fallout of what had happened in Afghanistan. She wasn't sure where she wanted to live. Blah. Blah.

It was all baloney.

She just didn't want to face saying goodbye to Derek.

"Do you mind if I stay through the end of January?" she'd asked. "The jobs I'm applying for don't close their searches until then, and I still need to find a place."

"Stay as long as you like," he'd said. But there had been something in his voice and the way he didn't meet her gaze.

Was he tired of her?

The thought put a knot in her chest, but she brushed it aside.

If he *was* tired of her, he was doing a good job of hiding it. He held her at night, made love to her like a sex god, did little thoughtful things, like picking up her dirty clothes from his bedroom floor without grumbling about the mess and making sure she had coffee when she woke up in the morning. The man had surprised her with a bulletproof BMW X5 Security Plus as a Christmas gift, for goodness sake.

No, it wasn't "I love you," but those were *not* the actions of a man who wanted her to go away.

Still, she could tell something was troubling him.

Though he'd never said a cross word to her, he seemed preoccupied. More than once, she'd found him lost in thought as if the weight of the world was on his shoulders.

Then again, he'd been tortured—stripped naked, threatened with castration, abused. If she was still haunted by what had happened that day, he must be hurting, too.

"Why don't you have nightmares?" she'd asked him one night when he'd woken her during a terrifying dream.

He'd kissed her temple. "I do sometimes, but I've been through this before. I'm trained for it. That wasn't the first time some asshole roughed me up."

The thought had sickened Jenna.

She pulled herself together and applied for two jobs in Denver—one with a large practice that included OB-GYNs and certified nurse midwives and one with a smaller practice that focused on reproductive healthcare for low-income women, migrants, and incarcerated women. To her surprise, both offered her a position before their job application deadlines.

Jenna gave Derek the news after dinner on a snowy evening in mid-January.

"Congratulations. What are the pros and cons of each?"

"The one at the bigger practice pays much better and would involve fewer nights on call. The one with Women's Health—the smaller practice—would mean a lot more nights and more deliveries, and I would have to learn Spanish."

"Anyone who can learn to speak Dari as well as you do can master Spanish." He drank the last of his red wine. "Which one appeals to you more?"

"To be honest, the job at Women's Health. The practice I worked at in D.C. served mostly wealthy women who wanted particular birth environments, like waterbirths with chanting and candles and a gong and a video crew."

Derek raised an eyebrow. "Seriously? A gong?"

His reaction made Jenna laugh. "Oh, yes. Well, only one with a gong."

He shook his head. "Okay."

"But the women in Afghanistan—all they wanted was for themselves and their babies to survive. It made all of the designer birth stuff seem..." Jenna searched for the right word, not wanting to be dismissive.

"Privileged?"

"Yes. That's it exactly." It helped that he understood. "I guess I want to be where I'm most needed. Does that make me a do-gooder?"

Derek reached over, took her hand in his. "If it were someone else, I might say yes. But I saw how hard you fought for that girl and her baby. You risked your life to treat the rape victims in that village. You saved Malik's life. You did your best to take care of me. Do-gooders want glory. They want to be recognized for what they've done. I don't see that in you at all. You truly want to help."

"Thanks. That means a lot to me."

"It sounds to me like you know which job you want."

"Yes." But now came the hard part. "The salary is pretty far below the median for a certified nurse midwife, so I need to find a condo I can afford, something not far from the clinic and Denver Women's Prison. Do you know a realtor?"

It *hurt* to ask.

Derek's gaze dropped to the table. "Yes. I can give you her number if you want."

It wasn't what she wanted at all, but she couldn't impose herself on him. It had been weeks since she'd told him she loved him. The most he'd done is told her he cared about her, which was nice. But it wasn't "I love you."

"Thanks." Jenna got up, carried their plates to the sink, afraid she was going to lose it and start crying.

He came up behind her, put his hands on the counter on both sides of her, pressed his lips against the back of her head. "Jenna, you don't have to move out."

She set the plates down. "I don't want to impose. I—"

"You're not imposing." He turned her to face him, his expression unlike anything she'd seen.

He looked ... afraid.

"Jenna, I ... I'm ...Ah, hell."

She rested her palms against his chest. "It's okay, Derek. I'm listening."

He drew a breath, blew it out, tension rolling off him. He hadn't seemed this nervous when bullets were flying. What was he trying to say?

"I wish this were easier." He looked into her eyes. "I'm emotionally fucked up. I have trouble getting close to people, and I'm not always easy to get along with. I have money but no education. Your dad was right when he said I'm a nobody. I am terrified of disappointing you or hurting you, but I'm more afraid of living without you. This place wasn't a home until you got here."

Jenna looked up at him, stunned. "Are ... are you asking me to stay with you?"

"I'm asking you to move in for good. I'm asking you to share my life. I'm trying to tell you ... *Damn*." He drew another breath. "I'm trying to tell you that I love you."

Jenna's heart skipped a beat. "You ... *what*?"

"I love you. I love you, Jenna. I love you with everything I am. Stay here—with me. I promise I'll do my damned best to be the man you deserve."

Jenna cupped his face between her palms, sure he'd never spoken those words to any other woman. "You don't have to change, Derek. We all have our rough edges. I love yours right where they are. My answer is *yes*."

The naked relief on his face made Jenna's heart swell.

He kissed her, spun her in a circle, the two of them laughing. "Champagne?"

"I'd love some." Jenna reached up to rub her thumb over James' dog tags, watching as Derek went into the wine refrigerator, chose a bottle, and uncorked it, so desperately in love with him that it hurt.

Thank you, James, for saving the life of the man I love. We're together now. Because of you, we're together.

EPILOGUE

Jenna held Holly's hands while the nurse anesthetist inserted the epidural catheter. "You're doing great. He's almost done. In a few minutes, you'll feel much less pain."

"Thank God!"

Nick watched the fetal heart monitor as another contraction started to build, his distress at his wife's suffering written all over his face. He stroked her shoulder. "Here comes another one. Hopefully, it will be the last one you feel."

Jenna had witnessed hundreds of husbands during labor, but few had been as caring or focused as Nick Andris.

Holly moaned, her eyes squeezed shut, her hands tightening around Jenna's as the contraction grew stronger.

"Open your eyes, Holly. Look at me. That's it. Just breathe."

The nurse anesthetist taped the epidural catheter in place. "Okay. You're all set. It will take a few minutes to kick in."

Holly was breathing hard, anguish on her face. "Why can't it kick in now?"

"The contraction is peaking," Nick said. "You're on the downhill side now. It's almost over. Just a few more seconds."

Holly's grip loosened, her breathing slowing as the pain ebbed. "This is *stupid* painful."

"Yes, it is, but you're doing great." Jenna had never seen the point of pretending as some midwives did. She'd met women who had grappled with PTSD due to the pain of childbirth, and she did her best to meet each woman's needs. If they wanted epidurals, that was fine with her. She never tried to talk them out of it, like some CNMs she'd known. She wasn't the one giving birth.

Nick helped Holly settle back against her pillows, kissed her forehead. "How does that feel?"

"Better. Thanks."

The next contraction came and went with little pain.

"Whoever invented the epidural deserves the Nobel Prize," said Holly.

Nick looked as relieved as his wife. He shook the anesthetist's hand. "Thanks."

"You're welcome." The anesthetist cleaned up and pushed his cart toward the door. "If you need me, I'll be around until seven a.m."

Holly had gone into labor just after midnight—six hours ago. It had been mild until her water had broken. After that, she'd gone from three to five centimeters in an hour, and the pain had been much worse.

Jenna rested her hand on Holly's thigh. "My advice, Holly, is that you rest now. When it comes time to push later, you'll need your strength—and let's face it, after tonight you won't be getting a lot of sleep. You, too, Nick."

Holly rubbed her swollen belly, looking gorgeous despite being in labor. "I can't wait to meet him—or her."

Jenna knew the sex of their baby, but they had wanted it to be a surprise. "I'm sure he or she is just as excited to meet you."

Jenna turned down the lights and sat in a rocking chair in the corner, while Nick watched over Holly, who quickly fell asleep.

Jenna watched the fetal heart monitor, checked Holly's vitals, cat-napping for short stretches in between.

Just after seven, there came a knock at the door, and an older woman stuck her head inside the room. She whispered, "Nika?"

"Hey, Mama."

Mama Andris—Nick's mother.

Jenna had heard about her—how she'd raised six children, immigrating to the US just before Nick was born and how she was the force to be reckoned with in the Andris family. No one messed with Mama Andris.

Jenna held out her hand. "I'm Jenna, Holly's midwife."

"Bless you, Jenna. How is our Holly?" Mama Andris asked, her accent strong.

Holly opened her eyes. "Hi, Mama."

"Oh, my sweet girl." Mama Andris hugged her. "How are you?"

"Much better since I got the epidural."

Mama Andris rested her hand against Holly's belly. "You are having a contraction now, I think, but you cannot feel this?"

"No pain at all."

"You don't know how I wish we had such things when you were born," Mama Andris said to her son. "Do you know how I suffered to bring you into this world?"

Jenna fought to hide a smile.

Nick let out a breath, shook his head, looking overwhelmed by the thought now that he'd had a glimpse of what labor entailed. "Sorry."

Twenty minutes later, Holly got a strange expression on her face. "Something feels different."

Jenna put on a pair of sterile gloves and checked Holly's cervix. "Guess what? You're fully dilated. It's time to have a baby."

Holly and Nick looked at each other, the anticipation and nervousness on their faces universal to first-time parents.

Jenna told Holly what to expect and how best to push effectively even though the epidural limited her sensation. "You'll need to listen to me. As long as the baby looks happy, we can keep going. If we have to, we can turn the epidural down so that—"

"No! No, no." Holly looked horrified by that thought. "I'll push. I promise."

With the support of her husband and mother-in-law, Holly was true to her word, working hard, bringing the baby's head farther down with each contraction.

"Good girl! Good!" Mama Andris said.

"Push, push, push!" Jenna coached. "Here's the top of your baby's head. Another few pushes like that, and you'll be crowning. Give me your hand."

Holly reached down between her legs, Jenna guiding her so that her fingers brushed the crown of her baby's head.

Holly's eyes went wide, and she smiled. "Oh, God! A baby."

"Nick, do you want to feel?"

He nodded, steeled himself as if he were about to jump

out of an airplane, and looked between his wife's thighs, his fingers joining hers. He laughed. "Wow."

Another push and another and another.

"The head is out. Reach down, Holly, and catch your baby." Jenna guided Holly's hands, supporting the baby's shoulders as it slipped into the world with an indignant cry.

"My baby!" Tears of happiness spilled down Holly's cheeks.

"Congratulations!" Jenna helped Holly lift the baby into her arms, rubbing it with a towel to stimulate it, leaving it to the nurse to wrap the baby in a warm blanket. "You did a great job, Holly. Good work, both of you."

Nick leaned in to look at his newborn, an ear-to-ear smile on his face. "It's a girl!"

Mama Andris crossed herself in the Orthodox way, her eyes bright. "She is beautiful, just like her mama."

It didn't matter how many babies Jenna had caught. Seeing the joy on parents' faces as they got acquainted with their healthy newborn never got old.

~

DEREK ARRIVED with flowers for Holly just after breakfast, jet-lagged and pumped up on caffeine. He found himself in the OB waiting room with Laura and Corbray—and a gaggle of Holly's friends from her journalism days. He knew most of them.

Kara McMillan, a freelance writer, and her husband, Reece Sheridan, the state's lieutenant governor. Marc Hunter, captain of Denver SWAT, and his wife Sophie, who still worked at the paper. Julian, head of Denver's vice unit, and his wife, Tessa Darcangelo, also a freelance journalist.

Natalie McBride, a romance author, and her husband Zach, now the U.S. Marshal for the Colorado Territory.

"Hey," Derek said. "I hear it's a girl."

"Aw, you brought flowers. Isn't he sweet?" Natalie said.

Derek had just gotten back from Afghanistan an hour ago. Cobra had been tasked with providing security for negotiations between Talib fighters and Afghan security forces. While there, Derek had also taken medical supplies to the Kazi Women's Hospital—a gift from Jenna. He'd had tea with Farzad, who had graciously accepted the supplies and sent his best wishes to Jenna. Hamzad, Derek had discovered, no longer worked there.

"After what he did, I sent him home," Farzad had explained. "Any man who works for me must be loyal to me and no one else—not even The Lion."

Derek had been happy to hear it.

Corbray motioned him over, and the two of them stepped off to one side.

"Any problems with Kazi?"

Derek shook his head. "He seemed a little less full of himself this time."

"I'll bet." Corbray glanced over at Laura, who sat talking with Natalie. "It's always hard for her when one of her friends has a baby. I told her she doesn't have to come, but you know Laura. She faces everything head on."

Derek respected her for that. "Have you two thought of having a baby?"

Corbray shook his head, but he didn't explain.

He didn't need to.

Some experiences changed a person forever.

"Here he comes!" Kara shot to her feet.

Everyone stood as Nick walked toward them, his gazed

fixed on the bundle in his arms, the expression on his face that of a man in love.

Jenna walked beside him, looking tired but happy in blue scrubs, her hair in a ponytail. "Time to meet your adoring fans, baby girl."

Nick walked to Derek and Corbray, held the baby so they could see her face.

Corbray shook his head. "You are in so much trouble, bro."

Derek had to agree. "Yeah. You're in for it."

Darcangelo looked down at the sleeping baby. "In about sixteen years, you're going to have your hands full."

"Oh, she's precious!" Tessa said.

Sophie took one glance and smiled. "She looks just like Holly!"

"She really does," Hunter said. "Are we sure there was even a father?"

Nick grinned. "*I'm* sure."

Everyone laughed.

From the color of the fuzz on her little head to her long lashes to her perfect Cupid's bow mouth, the baby looked just like her mother.

"What's her name?" Sophie asked.

"Katerina—after my mother." Andris let others take turns holding her.

"How was it?" Derek asked, curious.

Andris let out a breath, shook his head, clearly overwhelmed. "It was awful and wonderful and amazing. I hated seeing Holly in so much pain, but the epidural took care of that. Jenna was incredible."

"I was just doing my job." Jenna slipped into Derek's arms. "Welcome home."

Derek kissed her, glad to be back. "I missed you."

In the almost eight months they'd lived together, he'd grown more reluctant to leave Jenna, the days and weeks away from her harder than he had imagined. He'd only recently realized that *this* was how Corbray and the other married operatives felt about leaving home. But then, Derek had never truly had a home—until Jenna. It hadn't mattered to him where he was.

"I missed you, too."

McBride walked up, baby in his arms. "When are you and Jenna going to settle down and make one of these?"

Derek looked into Jenna's eyes. "All in good time."

"Don't pester the man," Sheridan said. "But if they're looking for someone to, say, perform a wedding ceremony, I know a guy."

That made everyone laugh.

Sheridan had officiated at Nick and Holly's wedding. Derek had been there and had thought it was nothing more than a costly and antiquated ritual. But now...

Now it didn't seem so absurd.

JENNA CHANGED out of her scrubs and collapsed onto the sofa, exhausted but happy. Holly's birth had been her fourth this week—a busy week for a midwife in the U.S. but an average day in Afghanistan.

Derek set his duffel down. "Want a drink?"

"God, yes."

"Pinot Grigio?"

"Perfect."

They settled outside on the balcony, Jenna leaning against Derek, his arm around her shoulders, the two of them watching the late August sun set behind the Rockies, a cool breeze blowing the heat of the day away. "I'm so glad you're home."

He'd been gone for two long weeks this time.

"So am I." He kissed her. "Farzad wanted me to say hello."

"How is he?"

"He's good. He fired Hamzad."

"He did?" That was good news.

"He said to thank you for the supplies, too."

It was the least Jenna could do. She'd left the hospital shorthanded, though they had replaced her six weeks later. Marie had finished her time there, and a new OB-GYN had taken her place. She and Jenna stayed in touch by email now.

Jenna sipped her wine, let herself relax. "It was wonderful seeing Holly and Nick so happy. Isn't that baby girl adorable?"

"She really does look just like Holly."

Jenna smiled. "She does."

"So, you want to go through that. You want to have a baby."

"I was thinking two, maybe three."

"Three." He repeated the word as if considering that. "And you want me to be the father."

She laughed, looked up at him. "Who else? You're the man I love."

He kissed her temple. "I might turn out to be a terrible father."

Aha. That's what this was about. "What makes you say that?"

"I never knew my dad, and the guys who fostered me were pretty much all assholes. I wouldn't trust any of them with a dog, much less a baby. I haven't exactly had good role models."

"I had a lousy father. My mother killed herself." Jenna sat up straight and turned to face Derek, knowing that this fear was real for him. "We are *not* our parents."

He didn't seem convinced.

"Look what you've done with the life you were given. You had such a rough start, but you prevailed. You've served your country as an elite operator. You're the wealthy CEO of a successful private military company. Most men in this country couldn't measure up to you if they tried. Any child would be proud to have you as their father."

He shook his head. "I wouldn't know what to do with a baby."

Jenna couldn't help but smile. She'd heard this from parents-to-be ever since becoming a midwife. The thought of caring for a tiny, helpless human being was overwhelming for most people. "Generally speaking, babies don't just drop into your lap. You get about nine months to prepare. There are books you can read, classes you can take. There's no such thing as a perfect parent. You can only do your best."

"And if your best sucks?"

Jenna didn't want him to feel pressured. "We're still young. We have time. This isn't something we have to worry about now."

"I'm all for it—on one condition."

What had he just said?

"You're for it? You're for us having a baby?"

He smiled, his gaze soft. "On one condition."

"What's that?" She hoped he wasn't about to say that he would never change a diaper. She found that kind of thing to be so disappointing in a man.

"We can have a baby—or two or three maybe—but only if you marry me first."

"Wh-what?" Was she dreaming?

No way had he just asked her to marry him.

"You'll have to marry me first."

Oh, yes, he had.

She hadn't seen this coming.

"I don't want to bring a child into the world unless we're official first. I grew up without a real family. I don't want that for my kids. If something happens to me—"

"God, don't say that." It was the fear that fueled her nightmares.

"It's a possibility in my line of work. You know that. If something happens to me, I want to know it's all legal and ironclad, that you and any kids we have are taken care of. So, you'll have to marry me first."

"Okay."

For a moment, there was silence.

"So, I guess I just proposed, and you said yes."

"I guess so."

They laughed, then kissed, happiness enfolding Jenna, palpable and warm, the last rays of the sun turning the sky pink.

"I'm so in love with you, Jenna." Derek ran his thumb over her cheek. "I didn't know it was possible to love someone so much. But can you promise me one thing?"

If she could, she would give him the world. "Anything."

"No gongs."

Jenna's head fell back, and she laughed, her heart soaring.

THANK YOU

Thanks for reading *Hard Target*. I hope you enjoyed this Cobra Elite story. Follow me on Facebook or on Twitter @Pamela_Clare. Join my romantic suspense reader's group on Facebook to be a part of a never-ending conversation with other Cobra fans and get inside information on the series and on life in Colorado's mountains. You can also sign up to my mailing list at my website to keep current with all my releases and to be a part of special newsletter giveaways.

ALSO BY PAMELA CLARE

Romantic Suspense:

Cobra Elite Series

Hard Target (Book 1)

I-Team Series

Extreme Exposure (Book 1)

Heaven Can't Wait (Book 1.5)

Hard Evidence (Book 2)

Unlawful Contact (Book 3)

Naked Edge (Book 4)

Breaking Point (Book 5)

Skin Deep: An I-Team After Hours Novella (Book 5.5)

First Strike: The Prequel to Striking Distance (Book 5.9)

Striking Distance (Book 6)

Soul Deep: An I-Team After Hours Novella (Book 6.5)

Seduction Game (Book 7)

Dead by Midnight: An I-Team Christmas (Book 7.5)

Deadly Intent (Book 8)

Contemporary Romance:

Colorado High Country Series

Barely Breathing (Book 1)

Slow Burn (Book 2)

Falling Hard (Book 3)

Tempting Fate (Book 4)

Close to Heaven (Book 5)

Holding On (Book 6)

Chasing Fire (Book 7)

Historical Romance:

Kenleigh-Blakewell Family Saga

Sweet Release (Book 1)

Carnal Gift (Book 2)

Ride the Fire (Book 3)

MacKinnon's Rangers series

Surrender (Book I)

Untamed (Book 2)

Defiant (Book 3)

Upon A Winter's Night: A MacKinnon's Rangers Christmas (Book 3.5)

ABOUT THE AUTHOR

USA Today best-selling author Pamela Clare began her writing career as a columnist and investigative reporter and eventually became the first woman editor-in-chief of two different newspapers. Along the way, she and her team won numerous state and national honors, including the National Journalism Award for Public Service. In 2011, Clare was awarded the Keeper of the Flame Lifetime Achievement Award for her body of work. A single mother with two sons, she writes historical romance and contemporary romantic suspense at the foot of the beautiful Rocky Mountains. Visit her website and join her mailing list to never miss a new release!

www.pamelaclare.com

57945205R00169

Made in the USA
Columbia, SC
15 May 2019